Chapter 1	1
Chapter 2	7
Chapter 3	13
Chapter 4	18
Chapter 5	27
Chapter 6	31
Chapter 7	38
Chapter 8	47
Chapter 9	54
Chapter 10	65
Chapter 11	73
Chapter 12	80
Chapter 13	88
Chapter 14	96
Chapter 15	103
Chapter 16	110
Chapter 17	117
Chapter 18	124
Chapter 19	131
Chapter 20	139

Chapter 21	147
Chapter 22	159
Chapter 23	166
Chapter 24	174
Chapter 25	181
Chapter 26	188
Chapter 27	194
Chapter 28	201
Chapter 29	209
Chapter 30	218
Chapter 31	226
Chapter 32	233
Chapter 33	241
Epilogue	248

Suzanne Boulet

November 2010-June 2011

Photography © Dani Prince

Chapter 1

Running in the forest was wonderful.

Even though he was running for his life, something about just being in amongst the trees and the foliage brought a sense of serenity. This was what life was about. People could admire their birds and their mammals, but trees were the only thing that he admired. Silent and tall, they were the true ultimate life-forms. And with his gummy powers activated, he truly felt like he was part of the Earth's most magnificent creation.

The trail was made of hard-packed earth; stomped upon by thousands, anything that tried to grow squashed mercilessly beneath their feet. It made him sad in a way, although he was thankful that such a clear, easy path existed. If it hadn't, he probably would have had a lot more trouble outrunning his pursuers. But as it were, he was so far ahead of them because he had an easy path through the forest, while he could easily make the going much more difficult for his enemy.

Speaking of which, the swearing of the Police following him had stopped a while ago. They had probably broken through his traps.

He turned around, calling upon nature once again. He could sense them under the ground, thick, strong tree roots and seeds, awaiting his call. He willed them to grow, to shoot from the ground and into the sunlight. Almost immediately, thick tree roots rose into tripping positions and thorny vines sprouted, gnarled in menacing patterns. They twisted and turned, turning into an almost wicked, but beautiful sculpture of deadly spines and precarious footfalls, making a natural trap. He only took a second to admire his handiwork, then took off again, certain of a lead against the Police.

He continued to run, gaps in the trees revealing his destination; a small clearing with what looked like an old wood house. Although, calling it a house would be an insult to houses. It was more of a triangular bunker, a shoddily-constructed thing made of rotting plywood. Two of its walls were simple triangles, the other a rectangle with a small door set in its middle. The back wall was practically non-existent; it was barely a few feet tall, and the roof sloped down to it. The whole thing was tiny...he could only guess that it could fit 3 or 4 people, and probably two or three would still end up sleeping on the floor.

But to him, it was safety.

A branch whipped him in the face, stinging for a second. He didn't have enough energy to focus on diverting the foliage away from his body. It was taking enough of a toll as it was, running and occasionally focusing his powers to create large traps. He didn't need to use any more of it to make his journey less painful.

His legs hurt, the thorn bushes and branches still managing to scratch him through his thick black jeans. The trees were thinning out now and he could glimpse the clearing he was running parallel to. A second later the trail bent, and he swatted aside a branch. And just like that, he was inside the clearing. He slowed down a little, trying to catch his breath.

That was his biggest mistake.

First, he saw the dart imbedded in his flesh, having pierced his grey sweater. The dart was a beautiful thing, with the best feathers for aerodynamics, and a long steel syringe designed for storing huge amounts of poison. A second later the pain blossomed, like the delay with light and sound, a sharp, stinging sensation. He could already feel his arm beginning to numb as he ripped out the dart from his shoulder. A slow, red stain started to spread, absorbed by the thick cotton. He only took one glance at the syringe as it dripped a clear looking fluid. It must have been poison of the paralyzing variety. He couldn't even feel his fingertips.

A group of five Police stepped out from the opposite end of the clearing, their weapons drawn and ready. He swore under his breath. It had been a trap all along. One group was as loud and obvious as possible, flushing him away from them and into the ambush like a wolf pack taking down a deer. And, being the idiot that he was, he had walked right into it. It was a classic trick, and he'd fallen for it.

The leader of the small group swaggered up to him, his sword flashing meanly in the sun. He was young for a Police officer, maybe only eighteen. Usually Police leaders were a lot older, having years upon years of training and experience in the field. But he couldn't really say that this Police officer looked fresh out of the training ground. His uniform was pretty beat up and the armour he wore had a few dents, some of the chainmail links already rusted. Police always got new armour when they graduated. But this guy's armour was full or wear and tear.

The Police pointed his sword at him, the end nearly pushing into his throat. Now that the sword was so close, he could see it in more detail. The hilt was carved into an elegant dragon's mouth, from which the blade seemed to be sprouting. It was finely crafted, so much so that even he, with no sword experience whatsoever, could tell that it was probably a blacksmith's proudest work.

"I am Lars. I now place you under arrest, Moss of the Flavours." Lars' pronounced, sounding strong and sure. The rest of his group started to come forward, one of them taking out handcuffs from their bag.

Moss cursed under his breath. He definitely couldn't take on all five, and his arm was already almost numb, and he could feel it moving closer to his sides, to his lungs...There was no time to lose.

He tried to move his numbed arm, reaching down towards his pocket. He kept a steady gaze into Lars' grey eyes, hoping that Lars would be so intent on keeping eye contact that he wouldn't notice...

Moss gulped as the sword flashed, this time the side pressed against his throat. Lars grinned. He had seen through Moss' attempt.

This close to his neck, Moss could make out what the writing on the blade said. Crudely carved into the beautiful metal was

'Monochrome'. Monochrome...the nickname used by Flavours to describe the Police. From the crudeness of it, and based on how insulting the nickname was, it was obvious that Lars didn't carve it himself.

"Nice try, Flavour." Lars' grin looked out of place, more like he had just won the school tournament instead of the grin of nearly killing someone. He looked a lot younger when he was smiling, and Moss wondered if he had overestimated his age. With that grin on his face, he looked two years younger. "But I have much better reflexes than any of you Flavours!"

Suddenly a pillar of flame exploded in front of him, singeing Moss' eyebrows. Moss stumbled away, as did Lars. It was Moss' chance to escape.

"Wrong!" Cried a sing-song voice, and Moss turned to see Pheonix standing on the front porch of the shack, a huge grin on her face. She had always had a thing for dramatic entrances. Her flaming red hair looked even brighter than normal in the sunlight, and the bandages on her right arm, along with her scratched up legs—that couldn't have been protected by her denim shorts—made her look like the veteran of many battles.

*Damn...*Moss thought, *She won the race.*

"Get her!" Lars called to his posse, and they all focused their attention on Pheonix. Expect for Lars. He slashed at Moss, who barely managed to stumble out of the way. Moss reached into his pocket with his good hand, grabbing a gummy and shoving it into his mouth. The flavour of lime tickled his tongue, and he could once again use the powers of the forest. He could sense the roots deep underground, a tangled mess caused by the trees surrounding the clearing. They were ready for his use.

A bow-woman aimed an arrow at Pheonix, and she leapt into action. With a flick of her hand, the wooden bow ignited, the bow woman dropping it with a shriek. Pheonix lunged forward and delivered a painful roundhouse kick to her face. The bow-woman went down, completely unconscious. Moss shuddered. That was the reason Pheonix wore such heavy boots; not for looks, but because she had a talent with kicking. And it was ridiculously easy for her to knock people unconscious when she kicked with them.

"One down!" Pheonix grinned at Moss, looking smug, "Better hurry up Moss, or I'll leave you in the dust!"

"Yeah, but you're not poisoned." Moss grumbled sourly.

Lars charged at him again, Moss barely managing to dodge by throwing himself to the side. He was already tired from all the running, and he could barely feel his arm. He almost didn't have time to call upon a root to stop Lars' next slash. Moss tried to wrap the root around the sword, but Lars was too fast, pulling his sword away and stepping away from the root that Moss had sent to tangle at his feet. Moss stood up shakily, his breathing ragged.

C'mon! This poison is way too efficient. I can barely stand on my own two feet!

Lars' eyes glinted and a slow smile played across his face, as if he knew that Moss was ready to topple over. It must have been pretty obvious. He could feel himself swaying a little.

What the heck is Pheonix doing?! Moss wondered, starting to panic, *Can't she see I'm having trouble here? C'mon! She's probably too caught up in her little fight!*

Lars charged again, and Moss raised a root with great difficulty. But this time he managed to tangle it around the sword. Moss grinned in triumph as Lars let go of his sword, using the root to pull the trapped sword far away from its user.

Not so tough without your sword, are—

Suddenly Lars jumped forward, surprising Moss. He jabbed his elbow into Moss' chest, all of the air whooshing from his lungs. He fell to the ground, Lars reaching over and pulling his sword back out of the root. Moss was seeing spots, black splotches that couldn't completely obscure the scene of his enemy ready to slash him.

Damn it, he's got me pinned! I need to get away...

Just as Moss finished the thought, Lars toppled over with a sharp cry. It looked almost like he had been hit by an invisible train. Something seemed to be pressing into his cheek.

What the—! No wait, it's her! Why does she have to be here? Darn it...

"You—!" Lars spluttered indignantly. Moss heard her laugh, sounding harsh and cruel.

On cue, as always, Imp materialized, her army booted foot pushing hard against Lars' face. Her mouth was twisted into a grin, her eyes feral and savage. She was wearing the same long-sleeve shirt she had been wearing the first time Moss met her: pink, with black striped sleeves.

"You owe me one, Moss." She winked slyly, her black hair shining in the light. The pink highlight on the left side of her face stood out like a sore thumb against her dark hair, "Now, if you'll excuse me, I have a twerp to deal with." She gestured down towards Lars, who was trying to roll around and break free of her grip, swearing under his breath when he couldn't shake her off.

"Why do you always have to show up?!" He growled, and Imp laughed again.

"You make it seem like *I'm* the one following *you*! Only in your wildest dreams, pretty boy!"

Lars growled, thrashing as he tried to reach for his sword.

"Come on then, Monochrome!" She put her face close to Lars', and Moss could feel the intense hatred between them, "Let's dance."

Chapter 2

Imp gave one last hard push to Lars' face, making sure that he got a mouthful of dirt. She stepped gracefully off him, a complete contrast to the harsh act of violence she had just committed. The moment she was completely off of him she disappeared, punk clothes and all.

Lars was up in a flash, his eyes sweeping the ground. Moss wondered if he should run, but Lars ignored him completely, not even seeming to take into account that he was there; his only target seemed to be Imp. Moss shuddered a little. No wonder Imp was constantly being chased. Just this one teenager seemed to be obsessed with her.

Lars whirled around and slashed, making Moss jump. What was he-?! A second later Lars' legs buckled beneath him, sending him tumbling onto his face. Imp's shrill laughter filled the air, sounding like thousands of twittering birds. Lars tried to get back up, pushing himself up as quickly as he could using just his hands. But it wasn't fast enough for Imp. She delivered a painful-looking kick to his back, making him groan and roll onto his side.

A sword-wielder came at Moss, surprising him. He stumbled out of the way of the swordsman's first strike. He obviously wasn't as skilled as Lars; Moss could see the white-knuckled tension that contrasted with his well-tanned skin, and the newness of his uniform. But there probably was a reason that he was with such a high-powered group.

Suddenly Moss' knee gave out, sending him tumbling to the ground. He saw the swordsman advance slowly, as if he was sure of victory. For a second he thought that Imp had attacked him, but then he remembered the poison. He'd forgotten about it completely! His whole left body was numb, and he was having trouble breathing. How could he have forgotten about that?!

Pheonix burst out of nowhere, delivering a nasty kick to the swordsman face. He stumbled back, looking surprised and gingerly bringing up a hand to his bruised visage. She took that moment to whack him hard on the back of the neck with her fist, knocking him unconscious.

Moss' vision began to fade, Pheonix's face going a little blurry when she leaned over him, gently taking one of his arms and slinging it over her shoulder.

"You're in bad shape." She murmured.

"'Bout time you noticed!" Moss grumbled. His voice sounded a little slurred, as if he were about to pass out.

Pheonix scowled at him. "Yeah, well at least I did notice! It was really tempting to just leave you there!"

Now it was Moss' turn to scowl. Pheonix led him to the safehouse. No one tried to attack them. It looked like the Police were either unconscious or trying to attack Imp.

"You sure we should leave Imp alone with them?" Moss asked, realizing that Pheonix wasn't calling her to retreat or anything.

"I think she can handle Lars by herself." Pheonix answered, and Moss swivelled his head to see if she was right.

Obviously she was handling him quite well, and having fun too. Every time Lars tried to stand up, he'd fall back down again, and Imp would laugh like a madman. He tried to swing his sword at her, but it only bit into empty air, to no avail. It just made her laugh harder.

Pheonix kicked the door open, and Moss realized that he was right about the safehouse being tiny. One wall had a small bed propped against it, a large cabinet dominating the other. The back wall was left empty, probably for other bunkers to sleep against.

Pheonix threw Moss down onto to the bed, opening one of the drawers. She took out a machine, something that Moss didn't recognize.

It was shaped like the safe house, a slanted metal shape. The face of it was covered in buttons, a small screen sitting at the middle top. There was a test tube coming out from beside the screen, and Pheonix took out a dart. Moss recognized it as the one that had been used against him, and wondered when she had managed to get a hold of it. He hadn't noticed her searching for it.

Pheonix hung the dart over the vial, and Moss watched a little drop of poison fall from it. The machine whirred to life, making a small binging sound as the drop was absorbed into the hole. Something appeared on the screen, but Moss couldn't read it from his position. Pheonix frowned, then opened one of the doors to reveal shelves upon shelves of small glass vials. She lifted the vials one by one, looking at the labels on them closely.

"What the heck is that machine?" Moss asked as Pheonix picked up another bottle, scowled and picked up another.

"You've never seen one? It's a poison tester. It analyses the poison and recommends an antidote."

Moss was silent. Pheonix looked over at him, only to see that he was completely unconscious.

"Useless." She mumbled, still flipping through the flasks. She finally found the right one, reading the numbers on the label. They matched what the little machine displayed on the screen.

Pheonix looked over at Moss and sighed. He was wearing the same grey pullover sweater as when she had last seen him. Now she would have to try and get it off.

He didn't even wake up as she struggled to pull it off. He was still in a deep sleep by the time she had managed to get it off completely.

Sighing again, she took out one of the cloths from the drawer labelled "Cloth scraps", wetting it a little with the water from the purifier in the corner. The vial screwed open easily, and after reading the instructions, Pheonix dabbed some of the liquid onto the cloth. She started to rub Moss' arm with it, careful not to hurt him too much.

Pheonix grimaced at her fingers; they were turning reddish, the same color as the antidote. With a big sigh, she cleaned off the cloth, trying to scrub at her fingers. Why wasn't it coming off?! It was no use. It seemed like the colour would stay on her fingers forever.

"I hope you're happy, Moss." Pheonix grumbled under her breath. She was going to have to wash them off in the river. And somehow, she was going to have to avoid all the fighting...

"Are you going to check up on Imp?" Moss asked, sounding groggy.

Check up on Imp?! He's delusional! But instead of telling him that, Pheonix just went silent.

When she looked at him, Moss was rubbing his eyes. He looked exhausted, but somehow was still clinging to consciousness.

"Go to sleep, idiot." Pheonix muttered.

"Don't leave her alone with him. Stuff happens."

"Are we actually talking about the same person here? I'm pretty sure that Imp's handling it well enough by herself."

"But *still*. C'mon, Pheonix! Please?" Moss whined, sounding exactly like a little kid begging for ice cream from his mother.

"Fine!" Pheonix snapped. "If it'll make you shut up and go to sleep, then I'll go!"

"Yay." Moss smiled tiredly, his eyelids fluttering. He was back asleep in an instant.

What an idiot. Pheonix thought with a sigh, but this time it was tinged with a little feeling of warmth. *Honestly, he's too kind-hearted.*

"Monochrome!" Imp chanted, laughing crazily, "Monochrome! Monochrome!" Her voice echoed off the trees dizzyingly, so much so that it was impossible to tell where it was coming from.

Lars was grovelling on the ground, moaning every time he was kicked. His armour was probably protecting him from bruises, but it didn't stop the blows. He was going to be sore tomorrow.

The rest of his troop was lying on the ground, all of them unconscious. Only three of them had been taken down by that one Cinnamon Flavour. Imp had taken out the other one when they had tried to save him from Imp.

She kicked him again, this time aiming for his revealed stomach. He groaned at the blow, spitting up a little bit of bile.

Damn her! Whenever she was like this, it always meant that he was going to get beaten to the ground. He liked her better when she was normal, not so sadistic and a lot gentler. She usually just ran away when he appeared. If he backed her into a corner, she fought her way out and left. But when she was in 'Berserk Mode', as Lars liked to call it, she took her time and tortured him for a while.

He heard the door of the safehouse open, for a second wishing that the positions could be reversed and he'd be the one taking shelter in it. He saw black armour boots from the corner of his eyes; it was that Cinnamon chick again.

"Imp!" She called, trying to sound cheerful even though you could hear the shaking in her voice, "Uh...It's time to go in now!"

So even the Flavours were afraid of her.

"Bite me!" Imp yelled, suddenly materializing in front of the other girl. She jumped, sticking her hand in her mouth to probably stifle a scream.

Lars suddenly felt Imp's foot pound into his back, and he yelled in pain. He hadn't seen it coming, and wasn't able to prepare for it.

He tensed, waiting for another hit, but none came. After a few tense moments of silence, he relaxed a little. Imp must have been gone.

"I'm bored of this!" Imp yelled, "I'm going inside!"

Imp appeared as she turned the door handle, slamming it as she stepped inside.

Lars moaned as he stood up, gingerly putting a hand to his bleeding nose. It hurt really badly.

"She always has to get the last word!" He grumbled, mostly to himself. But he saw the Cinnamon Flavour tense, as if she was expecting him to attack her.

"Don't worry." He tried to sound reassuring, looking at her from the corner of his eye. She was watching him warily. He walked over to one of his fallen men, putting a finger to his throat to sense his heartbeat. It was normal, so he started to move on to the next one. "I'm not going to attack you. The moment I start to charge, you'll be in that safehouse in a flash. Stupid safehouses."

She still looked untrustingly at him, but he expected that. The hate between Flavours and Police went back many years. Simple words, no matter with what sincerity they were spoken, would never cause them to trust each other, even for a second.

The girl edged back towards the safehouse as Lars checked up on his bow-woman, never turning her back. She was a smart one. The moment she was at the safehouse, she was inside.

Is Imp done with her little fit? Lars had to wonder, *Probably... Whenever she's Berserk, she never backs down. I hope so, for those Flavours' sake.*

Chapter 3

The cool, musty air of the shack greeted Pheonix. The smell of safety: rotten wood.

Moss was passed out on the bed, and Imp was slumped in the corner, her eyes closed and head against a wall. At least her little fit was over.

Pheonix actually liked Imp when she was normal. But it was the fear of saying something wrong and causing one of her fits that kept her from properly befriending her. To tell the truth, everyone was scared of Imp. Not because of how rare her powers were, but because of her...moments.

Pheonix checked on Moss' wound, more out of not knowing what to do than necessity. She had no idea what to do with herself. She didn't want to talk to Imp, especially if she was still suffering from the side-effects of her fit. She couldn't go outside, because that Lars kid and his goonies were still there. She didn't want to go sit down, because the only open space was right beside Imp.

You're just going to have to suck it up, She reminded herself, holding back a sigh, *You can't ignore her, especially considering you're going to have to spend the night, and she probably is too. Plus, you managed to survive her all of yesterday, when it was just you and her alone...*

Pheonix summed up her courage, going to sit beside Imp.

"I'm sorry." Imp murmured so quietly Pheonix almost didn't hear her.

"Uh, it's okay." Pheonix answered.

Awkward! She thought.

"I've been trying to control it, you know." Imp was really talkative today.

"That's always good." *Wow, I fail at small talk.*

Imp smiled slightly, her eyes never opening. "I suppose." She chuckled.

Suddenly Imp got up, heading towards the wooden counter. She opened a drawer, and, not finding what she was hoping, closed it and opened another. And another. And another. And another...

All the drawers were opened, and Imp stood there, staring at them. She sighed. She looked extremely disappointed, and a little worried.

"What's wrong?" Pheonix asked, wondering what the heck she was doing.

Maybe she hasn't completely recovered from her little fit. Opening and closing drawers definitely isn't normal!

"There's no Cream Soda gummies."

Pheonix winced. Running out of gummies was about the worst thing that could happen to a Flavour. Gummies were their lifeline, the thing that gave them their powers. Most safehouses always had refill bags for gummies, but apparently the supply runners hadn't gotten to the safehouse yet. It was pretty isolated...

If Imp were to run out of gummies, it would spell disaster for her. Especially if the next safehouse was far away, and she ran out when she was halfway there. It would be even worse in the middle of a battle.

Imp looked tough, but she didn't have weapons with her. According to her, it was because she didn't believe in weapons. Pheonix thought it was more because Imp was afraid of what would happen if she had a knife during one of her fits.

"How many do you have left?" Pheonix asked, although from the hopeless look on Imp's face, it was going to be a bad number...

"Three." Imp answered, opening another drawer. She re-checked all of them, but looked even more disappointed when she was done.

The gravity of Imp's situation settled on Pheonix like suffocating snow. With only three gummies...That would only last one battle, at the most! The nearest checkpoint was a week's walk away. That kind of distance would usually result in at least two Police encounters, probably more in Imp's case.

"Sometimes I hate being a Cream Soda." Imp sighed.

Cream Soda was the rarest of all Flavours. Extremely powerful, they dealt with the intangible, while all other Flavours dealt with elements. Cream Soda controlled dreams.

Pheonix wasn't exactly sure how it worked, but she had a basic idea. When Imp used a gummy, she could sense people's dreams, or their deepest desires. She probably could just pick or choose which one she liked, and use it for herself.

Imp's desire was to be invisible. Apparently, Imp's master had found a way to train someone to actually be able to control their dream. It was supposed to be extremely harsh training. But because of that training, Imp could always depend on invisibility when she used her powers.

Even though those were wonderful powers, Pheonix never wanted to be a Cream Soda. It was a tough life. All Flavours were wanted by the Police, but Imp had the biggest bounty of them all. She was constantly on the run, always having to move from place to place.

And there was a terrible rumour about why Cream Sodas were so rare...

Pheonix shuddered, definitely not wanting to think about that.

Imp rubbed her fingers over her temple, like she had a headache. She was starting to look more determined than hopeless. Pheonix wondered where she got all that inner strength. Imp looked frail, mostly because of her incredibly pale skin and quiet demeanour. But she must have had some kind of amazing perseverance, to be able to keep going after thousands of capture attempts. In a way, Pheonix admired her.

But she would never want to be her.

Pheonix dipped the black t-shirt into the stream.

The slow current threatened to pull it from her hands, but she held tight, watching thin rivulets of dirt come off the shirt and merge with the water.

The walk to the nearby stream had been stressful and slow-going, because she constantly had to stop and listen to any sounds. But she made it without incident, and was now washing the clothes as quickly as she could.

Imp had volunteered to do the chores, but Pheonix didn't want her going outside. Especially considering that Lars creep that had attacked Moss was really after Imp the whole time... And with Imp still suffering from the side effects of her little fit, it would be too easy for her to get captured. No matter how uncomfortable Pheonix felt around her, Imp getting captured would be the end of the line for the Flavours.

Sighing, Pheonix took out the shirt, wringing it out and placing it back in the laundry bag. She took another shirt out, this time scrubbing it so that it would wash faster.

It was good to be with Moss again. They had been together ever since they had made it to the FTA, but sometimes they were assigned separate missions. Like this one had been. Moss had been assigned to a public display in Tiyuk, while Pheonix had been assigned to one in Lotis. But they had promised to meet up again at this checkpoint, and together they were going to move on to the next town checkpoint to get new missions assigned.

I wonder where Imp's heading, Pheonix wondered, *I've never seen her attend any public displays. Does she get secret missions or something?*

Pheonix dipped another shirt into the water, this one her own. It wasn't really a t-shirt. It had the short sleeves of one, but it ended halfway down her stomach. The coloring was the same as Moss' t-shirts; simple black, meant to keep her from overheating when fighting.

Pheonix finished cleaning up the laundry. It wasn't much of a load. Flavours only carried around one extra set of clothes, cleaning it and using those when the current clothes they were wearing got dirty. There was no point in carrying a lot of clothes around. There were plenty of streams along the way to the checkpoints. It was simple to just wash a shirt, if there was time. She filled up multiple canteens, wishing that they had a Blueberry flavour along for the trip. Water flavours were always useful because they could just generate water out of thin air. And that water was always pure and delicious, like it came straight from a glacier.

Pheonix finished up the laundry, taking the short trail back to the shack. She admired the forest but was always ready for an ambush. As she reached the shack's door the sun was setting, painting the sky with orange and purple hues. Pheonix opened the door, greeted by the sight of Moss snoring on the bed and Imp setting up her sleeping bag, their semi-refilled packs open on the floor. After checking on Moss' wound, she curled up into her own sleeping bag and fell asleep.

Chapter 4

Imp hoisted her backpack onto her back, pushing the shack's door open.

It made a tiny creak, the sound of old hinges needing to be oiled. Imp glanced over her shoulder, hoping that Moss and Pheonix hadn't been woken up by the tiny squeak. But they were both still in a deep sleep, Moss even snoring a little.

Imp smiled as she stepped out into the clearing, listening for any sounds. The sun was slowly rising, gracing the treetops with a pale yellow light. It was time to get traveling.

She crossed the clearing in a few easy steps, keeping her ears and eyes open for trouble. Even though Police couldn't enter the safehouses because of the law magic protecting them, this safehouse had no control over the surrounding area. It was impossible to claim territory in a forest. And, knowing Lars, he would exploit that and be camping out nearby.

Although, from the way Pheonix kept glancing at Imp in fear, she must have given him a pretty good beating while she was in 'that' state...

Imp shook her head, trying to rid herself of those kinds of thoughts. What's done is done. She preferred not to dwell on her past experiences. It was not a happy subject.

Imp took a deep breath, walking towards the trail that led north. She loved mornings. The air was always the best, cool and fresh and easy to breathe. It was always so quiet, and the bird calls in the forest were the best at that time. The whole effect was spectacular.

"Hey, Imp!" A hand landed on her shoulder, startling her. She hadn't even noticed anyone, so deep were her thoughts. Imp turned around, coming face to face with Pheonix and Moss.

"Where do you think you're going?" Moss asked, scowling. He looked angry, his hair and clothes rumpled, almost as if he had just woken up. He obviously wasn't happy about it.

"We're not going to let you travel alone when you only have three gummies!" Pheonix said, trying to keep her face full of innocence but failing, "You idiot."

And that was how Imp gained two more temporary companions, starting off her day in a good mood.

"Let's stop here." Moss puffed out, his breathing ragged and unhealthy sounding.

Imp felt a twinge of annoyance, but it instantly died down when she looked at Moss. His face was red, and it was obvious that he was pushing himself the most he could. She remembered Pheonix mentioning something about poisoning, and she had seen the dart and empty vial of antidote on the counter of the shack.

"Good idea." Pheonix said, shooting a worried glance at Moss, "It's lunch time anyway."

Imp didn't quite want to stop, but she admitted that they needed a rest. They didn't want to run themselves ragged, especially with Moss in that condition. She was still worried about the Police, even though Pheonix and Moss seemed to have forgotten about them completely. But Imp knew Lars well. After being chased for a couple years, she got to know him a bit. He was tenacious, almost to the point that he could keep himself going by sheer willpower, even though he was wounded or exhausted. Pheonix seemed sure that he had been telling the truth when he said that he was 'done with this place'. But Lars was tricky.

They each brought out a packet of jerky from their bags, along with a canteen of water. Imp remembered a time when she used to love beef jerky. But that was a long time ago. After living off it for a couple of years, she got tired of it.

Moss chewed on a piece of jerky, looking like he was about to pass out. His breathing was slowing down a little, but it was still ragged compared to Imp or Pheonix's. Pheonix looked really concerned, handing him an extra slip of jerky and forcing him to drink more water.

"Here." Imp rummaged in her bag, pulling out something round, wrapped heavily in paper towels. A heavenly smell wafted into the air, and Imp started to unwrap it carefully. Slowly, a peach revealed itself. It had perfect ripe colors; Moss' mouth watered at the sight of it.

"I find that fruit helps healing." Imp smiled, watching as Moss reverently took the peach from her hands. Fresh fruit was extremely rare for Flavours. Fruit bruised too easily, and it would usually rot. Apples were the most common fruit for Flavours, and even those were pretty rare.

"Where did you get that?" Pheonix asked, staring at the sweet juice dribbling off Moss' chin. He looked like he was in heaven right now.

Imp shrugged. "I hid out in someone's barn for a bit. He was willing to let me stay the night. He was also having a bit of a bad crop. All of his trees were unhealthy, and he was having trouble growing his peaches to official selling size. His dreams were full of ripe peaches and healthy trees. So I helped him out to show my thanks. He gave me a bunch of them. That was my last one, though."

Pheonix was struck silent by how *weird* that was. Growing peaches using dream power? Talk about ridiculous! Pheonix never expected Imp to be able to use her powers like that. She always imagined it as stuff like turning invisible or flying. But growing peaches? C'mon!

Moss laughed. "Okay, *that's* weird, even for a Lime Flavour!" He wiped the peach juice from his chin, "But thanks."

"You're welcome." Imp answered with a smile, and for a second Pheonix wondered why everyone was afraid of her. But then she remembered how she had looked yesterday, appearing right before her eyes with such a look of hatred on her face, and the fear began anew.

"Maybe we should get moving." Pheonix suggested, shuddering a little. Imp looked at her curiously, as if she had an idea why she looked so spooked. She started to pack the leftover packets into her bag.

"Aww! We just got here!" Moss complained, "I'm still tired!"

"Don't be such a baby." Pheonix glared at him, but smiled a little when she saw Moss' teasing smile, "Plus, if you have energy to complain like that, you can walk."

Suddenly Imp tensed, her hand freezing halfway to her bag. She dropped her canteen into it, putting her fingers to her lips.

"Shhh..." She whispered as both Pheonix and Moss looked up, tensing when they realized why she had frozen in place. It was quiet for a while, Imp still frozen in a crouching position while Moss and Pheonix slowly reached towards their gummy bags. After five minutes of nothing but silence, Imp straightened up with a confused look on her face.

"What was it?" Pheonix asked, her voice only slightly louder than a whisper.

"I thought I heard something." Imp said slowly, looking intently into the woods. Her search done, she turned back towards Pheonix, "I think I might've been imagining it, though..."

"Good." Pheonix adjusted her bag onto her back, "Then let's get out of here."

"You idiot!" Lars hissed, glaring at his fellow swordsman, "You need to be quieter!"

"Sorry." He whispered back, looking ashamed. He was new to the Police. Lars could tell by how pristine his uniform was, and by how nervous he seemed.

"It's alright." Lars answered grumpily, making it completely known how *not alright* it was, "They didn't notice us. Just be extra careful from now on. Imp will be listening for everything now."

He looked back at his group, each member hidden behind trees. He had sent the dart-spitter back because of some burns, but he had stayed. He had brought a salve with him that was good for healing bruises, only available to the elite. One of his bow-women now wielded a dagger because of the fire-girl...*Pheonix*, he reminded himself, *They called her Pheonix.*

Lars had hoped that he would've been able to mount a surprise attack on Imp, but now she was traveling with friends. It was troubling. She was more the loner type, which had always been good when he tried to capture her. But now he needed to get her alone.

And she only has three gummies. Lars grinned, signalling to his group to start moving again. Pheonix had practically yelled it out to the world in the morning. It had been easy for Lars to overhear that conversation.

He knew that Imp would only use those gummies if she absolutely needed to. But with her weapon-less state, it would be easy to capture her. And if she used a gummy, he just needed to keep her engaged until she used another, and another...

She would never make it to the next checkpoint.

Imp was on edge.

Pheonix and Moss walked ahead of her, completely oblivious to her misgivings. She was listening for every sound, anything from the snap of a branch or the sound of footsteps. Whenever they would step on a branch in the path, Imp would jump.

"Hey Imp!" Moss looked back at her, smiling, "Why are you so quiet?"

Imp didn't hear him at first, having completely ignored his and Pheonix's chatter to listen for sounds. She looked up after awhile, wondering why he was looking at her like that. She was starting to feel a little self-conscious.

"What is it?"

Moss sighed, repeating his question. It took a while for Imp to answer.

"I dunno... I just don't like it. Lars just couldn't have given up. He's just not like that." She looked in the shadows of the trees, as if she wanted to see into them, "He's a lot more persistent, usually."

Moss shrugged. "Whatever you say. But shouldn't you be happy that he's not bugging us?"

"Not really...When he's 'bugging' me, I know exactly where he is." Imp answered slowly, "I hate forests. It's too easy to get snuck up on in them."

"That's a weird way of thinking!" Moss exclaimed, "On two counts! Just be happy that Lars isn't following you. He probably ran away with his tail between his legs! And..." Moss gestured to the forest around them with wide arms, "What's not to like about a forest?! There's seriously something wrong with you if you don't like them!"

Imp smiled a little, even though she never stopped looking from tree to tree, watching for any sign of movement. Moss shrugged and started talking to Pheonix again, who was watching Imp from the corner of her eye.

*Maybe Imp's right...*Pheonix wondered, *Who do I believe? Moss, who's too easygoing, or Imp, who's too uptight?*

They were making good time. Another six days of walking like they had done that day, and they could easily make it to the next checkpoint. The question, though, was whether Moss could make it that long. He was trying to hide it, but it was obvious that he was getting tired. He was subconsciously rubbing his arm now and then, where the dart had hit him. The antidote might have neutralized the poison, but it couldn't easily repair the damage he had taken because of it. Numbing poisons were really difficult to heal completely, especially with just a little vial of antidote instead of actual medical treatment.

Maybe we shouldn't have left so quickly. Pheonix thought, *But...If we had waited, then it would have given that Lars creep time to recover and get more troops...We would've ended up in more danger!*

Pheonix sighed in frustration. There were so many different scenarios, so many ifs and buts. Sometimes she really hated being a Flavour. But most of the time it was the best thing in the world.

Night fell, and the group decided to sleep under the branches of a large pine tree. After a bit of digging, they managed to dig a pit large enough to fit three people; albeit tightly. But with all of them crammed together like sardines, it quickly warmed up and they were all comfortable.

At first, Imp insisted on taking watch duty for the whole night. For a while Pheonix argued with her, and eventually she conceded to only taking a half-night watch, with Pheonix taking the other. The moment Moss spoke up to volunteer, he was put down by both of them.

Moss muttered crossly under his breath, but the moment he curled up into his sleeping bag, he was asleep. Pheonix sighed with a small smile, taking the spot next to him and closing her eyes.

Imp positioned herself so that she could peek from under the branches, but still remain in the warmth created by the overhead and her companions. She settled herself into a comfortable position, resting her head on knees drawn tight to her body, and watched.

It was a quiet night. She heard an owl hoot, and for a second she was surprised that she heard it. Then again, they were deep in the forest.

There was another bird-call, and Imp's mind started racing. Why were there so many birds? Could it be...a signal? Could it be Lars?

Imp took a deep breath, trying to calm herself down. She was going crazy. She listened attentively, but she couldn't hear anything that remotely sounded like footsteps...just another bird call. Imp bit her bottom lip, a sure sign that she was stressed.

She had always had an over-active imagination. Even when she had been at home, every little creak could've been someone sneaking about in the house, every groan someone opening a door. But, then again, in her home, she had a reason to be scared...

Imp brought up her hand and whacked herself in the head, surprising even herself. All dark thoughts flitted from her mind, and she once again concentrated on her watch duty.

Why do I feel so worried? Imp thought, glaring into the shadows in a vain hope to see through them, *Why do I feel like I'm being watched?*

By the time she woke up Pheonix for her turn, she was feeling less reassured than before. The night had been too quiet.

She couldn't shake off the feeling of uneasiness, even as she slept.

The next morning, they set out again.

After a tiny breakfast of beef jerky they hit the trail. This time it was Imp in front and Pheonix and Moss in the back. They could see how tense she was. The only thing they couldn't see was the tired look in her eyes after spending a restless night.

Moss and Pheonix exchanged a look, and they both tried to get Imp to talk. At first, she would only answer with monosyllables, but by noon they managed to have a conversation with her, starting to get familiar with her slow smile.

And by supper-time, they had managed to convince Imp that Lars was gone.

Mistake number one.

Imp was so convinced that she volunteered to go get firewood. They had decided to sleep out in the open that night, and Imp had readily agreed to a small fire.

Imp set off in the woods, scouring the ground for downed, dry branches. After gathering an armful, she noticed how far away from camp she was. It was time to head back. She had plenty of branches for a small fire.

She froze when she heard a branch snap behind her. When she turned...

"Hello, Imp." Lars said, a devilish grin on his face.

Mistake number two.

Chapter 5

Imp felt her body seize up, instantly dropping the branches in her arms. She reached towards the bag of gummies in her pocket, but froze. She only had three gummies, and they were only two days into their journey...

*Then use me...*The *thing* inside her whispered deep in her mind, filling her with the deep terror it always brought.

No! Imp thought, trying to be brave, *I can do this myself!*

Really? It asked quietly, in a dangerous and seductive voice. A second later, *it* filled her with all the self-doubt she'd ever felt, a huge, tumulus emotion building up inside her.

"No, I can do this!" Imp whispered desperately, trying to fight back the negative emotions. Lars blinked in confusion, but he drew his sword, ready to advance. Imp felt a twinge of fear.

A second later she realized her mistake, trying to squash the little bit of real fear. But it was the only opening *it* needed. *It* took control, pushing her into the back seat as it struggled to take control.

"No!" Imp yelled out loud, making Lars jump back with a startled cry. She clapped her hands over her ears, her whole body shaking as she waged a desperate struggle against her inner demon.

She was slipping, the flashbacks beginning. She started to whimper, wanted to hide from them. But she couldn't when they were inside her...

Blood! It's everywhere!

Lars didn't know what to do, watching her with confusion clearly written on her face...

She's dead! It's his fault! He killed her!

It was pointless. She couldn't fight against the negative emotions pent up inside her, every regret she had ever had and every fear she had ever faced. It was just too strong.

The blood...Her mother was lying on the ground, dead. Her father had a knife. He killed her with it.

"Damn Flavours." *He murmured, looking unfeelingly down at his wife, her mother. She was crying.*

"You won't betray me, will you?"He asked her, his voice soft and tinged with madness, "You won't make me mad, right? You'll do what I tell you, won't you?"

She nodded, so afraid of him. Her mother's blood reached her hands and feet, still warm.

"Good girl." He said, smiling. He tousled her hair with his bloody hands. She could feel it drip down her forehead...

No! Stop it! She fought desperately, for a second seeing Lars, his face stunned.

"Knock me out!" She yelled to him, seeing him jump.

"What?!" He spluttered.

...and into her mouth...

No! Please! "Just do it!"

...it tasted like copper, warm and delicious...

Lars hesitated, and Imp waited desperately, trapped halfway between nightmare and reality.

Lars seemed to make his decision, bringing his blade up so the hilt was ready for use. With strength that Imp was surprised he had, he brought it down on her head. She crumpled instantly, not fighting against the cloudy darkness starting to fill her mind.

*That's gonna bruise...*Imp thought, joy filling her as she felt consciousness and monster receding, *But no more flashbacks...I'm safe now...*

And she slipped into darkness.

Lars looked at the unconscious figure of Imp.

What the hell?!

His swordsman walked up slowly, as if afraid Imp would suddenly rear up in Berserk mode and rip his throat out.

"Did you see...?" He asked Lars, not bothering to finish his sentence. Of course he'd seen it. They'd all seen it.

She had changed for a second. It was the form that Lars was all too familiar with...Berserk Mode. But the next second she had been back to normal, albeit looking like she was being tortured. And she had begged him to knock her unconscious.

What's going on?

It was as if she was trying to stop Berserk Mode. But why would she? Lars admitted that there was no way that Berserk Mode could be her real personality...He always thought it was more of a split personality kind of thing. The little data they had about Imp said that she was bipolar, but that sort of condition wasn't something that people could just stop like she had tried. Imp made it look like she was trying to stop it from happening.

*I don't get it...*Lars thought, giving up trying to understand for now, *But you can't argue with results!*

He ran his fingertips lightly over her eyelashes, trying to check if she was truly unconscious. They didn't even flicker, something that would have been impossible for someone who was conscious.

Too easy. Lars thought with a feeling of triumph, *Way too easy.*

"Did you hear that?"

Lars shook his head. The newbie swordsman had been jumpy all day, as if he was trying to redeem himself for making Imp suspicious of their presence. Lars had already gotten over it, forgiven him because he knew he had been exactly like that when he had first started out. But now he had just put himself into Lars' official 'never be put on my team again' list, all thanks to the countless false alarms and the countless apologies.

"Relax." Lars told the jumpy swordsman, "There's noth—Waah!"

Lars was suddenly knocked over, the air whooshing out of his lungs and black spots clouding his vision. There was a hiss from his attacker, and he suddenly wondered if he was being attacked by a feral cat. He could no longer feel Imp. She had probably gone flying from his shoulder when whatever it was had knocked him over.

Lars blinked furiously, trying to clear the spots so that he could see his attacker. *Alright, there's some red...black, and white...What the heck!*

It was Pheonix!

Chapter 6

With a shocked hiss Pheonix jumped back, instantly sliding into a fighting stance. Her head spun dizzyingly, and for a second she wondered if she was going to fall over. She had hit her head hard on the Police-boy's armour, at top speed no less. No wonder Lars was still able to follow them after Imp's beating. That armour had probably hurt her more than it had hurt him.

Moss took a bit longer to get up. At least the swordsman seemed unconscious. Pheonix could see the offending tree root under the swordsman's head. He must have had a soft head; either that, or Moss had hit him hard. Pheonix didn't think he was *that* heavy.

In one fluid movement, Lars jumped up and drew his sword. Pheonix was impressed. She didn't really think that he was that agile; he was wearing heavy armour, and Imp must have hurt him a little bit. It was no wonder that he was in charge of Imp's capture. His age was probably what the Police had been looking for. Someone young enough to still have considerable speed, yet still be able to take a hit. Pheonix doubted that an older Police officer could hold their own against Lars.

"Karma." Lars commanded, and one of the bow-women looked inquiringly at him. Pheonix had to wonder what it would be like to work under someone half her age. It was hard to estimate someone's age when they were covered in dirt from the forest, but just from her height and figure Pheonix could tell that this 'Karma' was probably older than Lars by fifteen or twenty years, "Grab Imp."

That was when Pheonix struck.

She hoped that she could catch them off-guard. And she did, partly. Karma flinched, her hands busy with Imp's arms. It was Lars who countered. He grabbed Pheonix's wrist, avoiding her flaming fingertips. Pheonix lashed out with a kick, forcing him to let go of her wrist and stumble away. Instantly she had a fireball formed in her palm, flinging it at Lars. He blocked it with his sword, something that she didn't see coming. The fireball exploded into tiny sparks against the metal.

No way! Pheonix thought, shocked, *I heard rumours that the government had found some kind of metal plating that protected against fire attacks...But I didn't think it could protect to that extent. I can't fight long-range anymore...He'd just use his sword to stop my attacks. I'm going to have to fight close-range, as stupid as that is against a sword.*

Lars took advantage of her surprise, slashing at her horizontally. She leapt easily out of the way. Before she could even call upon her fire he slashed again, and she barely stumbled out of the way. He attacked again, and Pheonix was forced to weave out of the way of his sword thrusts with no time to strike back.

Moss wasn't having much luck either. One of the bow-women came at him with a dagger. She slashed at him, lightning-quick. He kept dodging, realizing with a small feeling of dread that the mere centimetres she was missing by was slowly dwindling with each slash. He wasn't as fast as Pheonix, he knew. He was more the type to stay away from the battle and attack from afar, sometimes depending on others to distract his foes before he could entangle them in his roots. But Pheonix had a tendency to rush into battle, and he was forced to follow her. And that had resulted in him dodging for his life.

Moss dodged another slice, barely evading the blade. His back hit against a tree, the dagger-woman advancing on him, ready for the final blow.

Honestly? Moss wondered, wanting to laugh, *Have you already forgotten what my powers are?*

He took control of the tree's bark, stripping it from its trunk and wrapping it around himself. He watched her triumphant look turn into one of surprise, instantly reeling back as a root came up to try to snag her dagger. She slashed instead, advancing on him. Her dagger didn't even make it halfway through his armour.

The bow-woman sprang back, but she was too slow. A monster root shot up from the ground, swatting her aside like a fly. Moss grinned inside his cocoon. She was sent flying by the monster root, hitting the ground hard, skidding towards a bunch of thorny bushes. She stood up in anger, picking thorns out of her skin, and Moss smirked inside his bark cocoon, watching the action from tiny slits in the bark.

She took so long to recover it was easy to sneak a root around her ankle. When she tried to move, she found that her foot never left the ground. The expression on her face... classic. Even more so when a whole army of tree roots wrapped around her, trapping her as effectively as a Chinese finger trap. Except she wouldn't be getting out of that one so easily.

Moss turned to see that Pheonix wasn't having such luck with Lars. He was pressing her so hard that she was having trouble counterattacking. She narrowly dodged out of the way of his sword, but he took too long to strike again. A fireball formed in Pheonix's hands, and she threw it, catching Lars in the stomach. He stumbled back, probably hurting more from the blow than the actual flame.

An arrow sunk into Moss' bark cocoon, its point piercing the bark and coming extremely close to his forehead. Too close for comfort. He dissolved his armour, figuring that he would have to keep moving against this bow-woman. Sure enough, the moment his armour retreated back to the tree he had to dodge another arrow. The bow-woman—Karma, Lars had called her—had propped Imp up against a tree and was aiming another arrow, this one at Pheonix. She saw it coming from the corner of her eye, and burnt it to a crisp with a fire shot before it struck.

Lars had recovered, and was advancing towards Pheonix. Moss rushed to her, going back to back as they faced off against their two enemies.

Imp slowly opened her eyes, dazed.

Her head was throbbing. It felt like there was a whole marching band playing in it. She tried to bring up a hand to rub her temples, but she couldn't. She blinked in confusion, trying again. That was when she felt cold metal dig into her wrists.

Handcuffs, Imp's body went cold.

There was something towering in front of her. She blinked a lot, trying to clear her mind and eyes. Eventually two pant legs came into focus, followed by the still slightly blurry figures of who Imp guessed was Lars, Pheonix, and Moss. She could hear a twanging sound, and she watched as little bursts of flame burnt thin sticks to cinders. Arrows.

They need my help, Imp thought, struggling against the handcuffs, *But how?* She couldn't reach her gummies. Her legs were folded in such a way that she couldn't move them without falling over herself, *What can I do?*

There was only one thing she could do.

This is gonna hurt, She thought, closing her eyes.

Karma suddenly screamed, making Lars jump. He whirled towards her, wondering what the heck she was doing, only to see Imp slung over one of her legs.

Instantly Lars felt something rough twirl around his wrist. He looked at it in confusion, his stomach dropping. It was a root. He didn't need to look to know that there were other roots on their way. Sure enough, in a matter of seconds, they were all over him, restraining his wrists, legs, even his torso. Pheonix grinned at him triumphantly, giving a thumbs-up to Moss.

"That was anticlimactic." Pheonix chuckled, a smug smile on her face. As she walked past Lars her grin only grew wider, which made anger flare within him. He struggled against the trap, but to no avail. Escape was impossible in his condition. The tree roots were as strong as the trees they came from.

"That hurt." Imp groaned, even though she was smiling, "Her boots are really hard."

Pheonix laughed, helping Imp to her feet as Moss secured the bow-woman to the ground with roots. With a simple slash by Pheonix the chain of the handcuffs melted.

Lars looked on hopelessly as the trio walked away.

"That was so awesome, Imp!" Pheonix laughed as they headed back towards camp, "I can't believe you took out a Police by *falling* on them!"

Moss was also grinning. "All I wanna know is how the heck you ended up in handcuffs in the first place!"

"Yeah, I'm kinda curious, too." Pheonix shoot Imp a questioning look.

"Uhhh..." Imp paused, the smile leaving her face. She obviously wasn't expecting that question. She looked like she wanted to run away, "It's a long story..."

Moss raised an eyebrow. "We still have a week together. How long will it take?"

"Good point." Imp smiled a little, "Maybe tomorrow? I'm a little tired."

Moss shrugged, clearly a little peeved with her answer. "Whatever."

Pheonix was silent.

What doesn't she want us to know?

They reached their semi-built camp, Imp instantly starting to unroll her sleeping bag. Pheonix had to admit that she did look a little tired. No, tired was the wrong word. She looked...*haunted*.

"Do you think Lars will go home for a while? You know, to regroup or something?" Pheonix asked, hoping that a change of subject would chase away the little feeling of malaise that she felt.

"Maybe." Imp answered, unrolling her sleeping bag completely before looking at Pheonix, "But his pride was hurt. He'll be back, no matter what. And he'll probably bring more guys with him. We have to do something so that he loses our trail."

Moss groaned from his sleeping bag. He had already set it up before they had had to rush to Imp's rescue, "Why can't we talk about something *not* depressing right before bed?"

"Because if we don't we'll most likely never talk about it." Imp answered simply.

"So? That's perfectly fine with me." Moss moaned, pulling the sleeping bag over his head, as if it could shield him from bad news.

"Stop being such a baby." Pheonix scolded tiredly, slipping into her sleeping bag, "Imp is right. We need to talk about this."

"Whatever." Moss answered. Imp was quickly learning that this seemed to be his favourite word. She shuddered at the thought of having to deal with him without Pheonix.

"Lighten up Moss. You know what they say at the Academy..." Pheonix started, obviously waiting for Moss to finish her sentence. When he didn't, she sighed and continued, "Ignorance is going to get you killed!"

Moss groaned, putting his backpack over his head instead of the pillow he had been using it as.

"Do you see why we always fight, Pheonix? That's just because you're so damn annoying."

Pheonix laughed, snuggling farther into her sleeping bag. "Love ya too, Moss!"

Chapter 7

"Imp. Imp!"

Her mother was crying her name. But it didn't make any sense. Imp was the one standing at the doorstep, watching her walk away. Imp was the one screaming, even though it was in her mother's voice. It was wrong, all wrong. It shouldn't be her mother leaving her. Her mother was dead. It was supposed to be her father leaving her behind.

"Imp!" Her voice was changing, growing louder and louder, "Imp!"

It was unbearable, as if someone was yelling in her ear...

"Wake up!"

Imp's eyes flew open, and she sat up suddenly. Pheonix barely had time to move, narrowly avoiding their heads bashing together.

"Geez, Imp." Pheonix looked a little surprised, "You're a loud sleeper! You—"

But she stopped talking when she saw the look on Imp's face. She looked completely spooked, even though it seemed like she was trying to calm herself down.

"Hey, are you alright?" Moss asked from behind Pheonix. He had been hovering behind her the whole time, impatiently waiting for her to wake Imp up so they could get going. He wanted to make up for yesterday's little delay.

"I'm fine." Imp tried smiling a little, though it was shaky. She pushed her sleeping bag away, and Pheonix noticed that her hands were trembling.

Whatever she was dreaming about really freaked her out. I've never seen her so unhinged—excluding her little fits, or course...And with Imp, that's saying something.

"Ready to go?" Imp asked, as if she wasn't the one holding them up. She was looking at Pheonix intently, as if she had a clue about what she was thinking.

Pheonix nodded anyway, standing and picking up her backpack.

Without another word, Imp set off down the trail.

Pheonix, Moss and Imp traveled well for three days, making excellent time. No Police tried to stop them. For the moment, they were under the radar.

The closest checkpoint was only another two days away. If Lars had headed back to Tiyuk City, which was pretty much a given, he would never be able to catch up to them in time. Pheonix did a mental calculation. The next town was four days away. It would be impossible to catch up if he came from that direction, either. They were home free.

Imp never did tell them what happened. Pheonix was the only one who noticed. But she didn't dare ask Imp. Every morning, she woke up shaking. And even though she tried to hide it, Pheonix could still see the spooked look in her eyes. She didn't want to make Imp even more uncomfortable, no matter how curious she was.

They camped out for the night. They didn't need a watch. This time, they were absolutely sure of it.

The next morning came quickly. Pheonix was glad when Imp woke up with little more than a shudder. She actually ate that morning, something she had been skipping ever since Lars' ambush. The moment they were done, they hit the trail.

There were very little breaks. Even if they were certain of their escape, if they could press that advantage and make it to the safe house, then hide their trail, it was worth tiring themselves out. It was dangerous to get cocky, and not bother with things that should always be done. The Flavours knew that, and that was why they had stayed so strong for so long. They were hard to catch because of that.

A little bit after noon, the reached a fork in the road, one leading east and one leading north. Pheonix and Moss immediately set off on the east road. They had walked for quite a while before they noticed Imp's absence.

They turned back, and found her still standing at the fork of the road, looking uncertain about something.

"Aren't you coming, Imp?" Pheonix asked, intimidated by the silence and Imp's intense eyes, "East is this trail."

"I'm not going east." Imp murmured. Pheonix almost didn't hear her. "I'm going north."

"What do you mean you're going north?" Moss asked, "The safe house is this way!" He whipped out his map of safe houses that all Flavours had. "The safe house that way is still four days away!"

"I need to head to the capital." Imp answered simply, "That's my mission. I need to get to the capital as soon as humanly possible. I'll be in huge trouble if I'm late."

"But, four days!" Was all Pheonix could say.

"I can cut it down to two if I use a gummy. Lars dreams of flying, and being so close to him, even if I was unconscious, was enough for that power to last for a while. Flying doesn't actually take that much energy. I could travel two days worth on one gummy."

"But...Lars..." Pheonix tried to protest, but it was useless. Lars wouldn't be able to travel that fast. Imp would most likely make it to the safe house without incident.

"Don't worry. I'll be fine. I'm used to traveling alone." Imp smiled reassuringly, "It was really nice travelling with you guys, but I can take it from here. Bye." She waved, still smiling. She walked down the north trail without looking back.

Moss and Pheonix just stood there, watching until Imp slipped past a bend in the trail, disappearing behind the trees.

"I don't like this." Moss murmured.

"Me neither." Pheonix groaned, "But what can we do? She just practically dumped us here. We can't exactly fly after her, you know."

"Yeah." Moss answered, disappointed.

They stood there for a while longer, staring into the distance.

"Let's go." Pheonix said finally, "There's no point staying here. Let's get to the safe house."

"Right."

And they walked down the east trail.

"Come here, Lars." General Salem said, looking over his shoulder.

Lars just nodded, following Salem through the door.

It had taken Lars one day to get back to the safe house, and another day to get back to Tiyuk city. He was angry. He had been called on his cellphone, told to come back shortly after he and his group had managed to escape from the tree roots. And now, Imp was getting away, slipping through his fingers like sand. He was furious.

What could be so important in this stupid lab, anyway? Lars thought angrily.

"Take that scowl off your face, boy!" General Salem commanded, smiling mischievously, "You are going to love this!"

Lars liked General Salem. He was the only general who would actually talk to lower ranks, and was quite friendly with the younger members. He treated them like some kind of extended family. He especially liked Lars. According to him, he "reminds me of me, you know, when it was the good ol' days."

But now Lars was beginning to doubt the man, hoping that he wasn't just going to show him some kind of new sword, or something. His sword was fine enough, and it had a little bit of sentimental value to it. When Imp had carved Monochrome down its middle...that was when Lars became personally involved in catching her. It was no longer just a mission, it was his personal goal.

They rounded a bend and came upon a solid steel door, guarded by two armed Police. General Salem dug out a card from his pack, flashing it to them. They opened the door for him, but looked at Lars questioningly.

"Sorry sir, but no one under the rank of General is allowed into this area of the lab." One of the guards proclaimed.

That's when Lars *really* became interested.

"Oh, I'm sure it will be fine!" General Salem laughed heartily, "It's just Lars. You know, he's pretty high ranked for his age."

The guard still looked at Lars doubtfully.

Suddenly the General got a serious look on his face. He leaned over, whispering something in the guard's ear. Instantly his eyes darted to Lars, with a look of both admiration and pity.

"Uhhhh, sure." The guard's voice was a little shaky, "Sorry for all the trouble."

By now Lars had a huge case of the shivers. What was that expression again? Oh yeah. Like someone was walking on his grave.

Lars and Salem stepped through the open doorway and into a highly conditioned room. Highly conditioned was an understatement. It was *freezing*. Lars almost expected snow to start falling from the ceiling.

There were screams. Shrill, terrified screams. Lars stopped walking instantly, feeling goose bumps raise on his arms. Salem stopped walking, looking back at Lars with a reassuring look on his face.

"C'mon Lars. Nothing to worry about." He said, smiling kindly.

Nothing to worry about?! There's someone screaming their head off!

He walked after Salem anyway.

They walked past scientists hard at work, some smiling and looking in the direction that the screams were coming from. They all had a little comment for General Salem.

"It's coming along great." One said.

"She sounds really terrified!" Another smiled, thrilled.

"This will bring a lot of data in." Another's eyes were bright.

Lars thought he was going to be sick.

Finally they reached the main area. There were computers stacked and inlaid into the walls, automatically displaying data. The huge, constantly changing digits were incomprehensible. Three printers were each printing, mounds of long data sheets lying on the floor beside them. They just kept printing.

One display seemed to be recording sound. Every time a scream could be heard, it peaked. Another showed what looked like a heart rate monitor. But it couldn't be. That heart rate was beating at an incredibly fast rate. It couldn't be healthy.

And there, set into the farthest wall, was a door. Screams echoed behind it. Above the door, written in red light, was 'TESTING'. A bunch of wires from the computer pierced walls, most likely hooked up to other machines inside the testing room.

General Salem turned towards Lars. "We'll have to wait to go in until the experiment's over. Make yourself comfortable." He gestured to some chairs, immediately going to sit down in one. But Lars didn't sit. The way the chairs were set up looked too much like a waiting room setting for his tastes.

Suddenly the screams died down. A couple of suspenseful minutes later, the red light turned off, and the clicking of bolts could be heard, the door swinging open a little. Salem stood up, gesturing to Lars to follow him, and opened the door.

Inside, it was even colder than the rest of the laboratory. And, unbelievably, there was *snow.*

It was sparkling white, still unstained by boots. It sat on the floor in huge mounds, looking almost like clouds.

A scientist looking guy was handing a big winter jacket to a girl. She was shivering, and there were tears frozen onto her face. But she seemed happy enough.

She looks a lot like Imp, Lars thought. It was true. She had black hair, minus the highlight, and seemed to be about the same age. She was a bit shorter than Imp, though.

The scientist stuck out his hand, and she took it.

"Thank you so much, Luna." The scientist grinned, shaking her hand vigorously, "The experiment was a total success! Here, just take this slip to the pharmacy outside this building, and you'll get the counter-acting pills."

"Thank you." Luna answered a little shakily, taking the slip of pink paper and holding it as if it were a lifeline. She was still shivering, despite the huge thermo jacket and the rising room temperature. But Lars doubted that the cold was the cause of her shivering.

She walked past Lars and out the door, giving him a curious, yet pitying look as she walked by.

What exactly have I unwittingly signed up for?! Lars wondered with a shiver.

The snow in the room was melting, the water falling into drains placed strategically in the floor. The scientist looked up, and with a pleased smile, greeted Salem.

"And who's this?" The scientist asked, looking at Lars.

"Lars. Leader of the group hunting down Imp." Lars answered stiffly. He didn't like the way the scientist was looking at him. Almost as if he was the next test subject.

"I see." The scientist answered, smiling, "My name is Lorch. I'm in charge of this operation." He offered Lars his hand, who reluctantly took it.

"What would you like, General?" Lorch asked Salem.

"Just showing Lars around. I thought I'd introduce him to the experiment. He is the one in charge of Imp's capture, after all."

"Yes." Lorch looked thoughtful, "Very true. Follow me."

And with that, he set off through the snow and puddles, towards yet another door at the end of the testing room. He opened it, coughing slightly at the stench that came from it. Lars was struck by a sudden bad feeling. But he still followed Salem into the next room.

This one was poorly lit, the only light coming from huge tubes full of glowing clear liquid. It shimmered as it rippled in the tubes, as if something inside it was stirring. It smelled absolutely rank in there.

"Welcome to the production factory." Lorch smiled, "Where, once it is past the prototype stage, we will mass produce our little experiment."

"What is the experiment?" Lars asked curiously, staring at the viscous silver fluid.

"I'm sure you heard Luna's screams." Lorch asked, bypassing the subject, "And you saw the snow. Luna's terribly afraid of freezing to death. She has nightmares about it."

It only took one second for Lars to understand. He felt himself go pale.

It was wrong. Terribly, terribly wrong.

"We have created the Flavourless gummy." Lorch's face morphed into a savage, feral grin, "The power of nightmares."

Chapter 8

It had been a while since Imp had flown. She had almost forgotten how great it felt.

With the wind rushing through her hair, ice cold air invigorating her skin, she felt at home. Almost as if, maybe in some past life, she had been a great bird, like a hawk. She would have liked that. Or, maybe, she had been born into the wrong family, and should have hatched from an egg into a bird's family.

I should have trained myself to dream of flying. Not invisibility.

She should have listened to her personal tutor at the FTA. He had said that she should choose her dreams wisely and carefully, and that he was only willing to train her for one dream. He had recommended flying, but she had decided for invisibility, because the training for flying seemed too difficult. That was stupid of her.

But it was too late now. She didn't have time to train herself to dream of flying, and her invisibility was more useful in general. Flying was more for traveling, while invisibility could be used in battle or in stealth missions. Oh well. She would just have to rely on Lars' presence, and the fact that he never gave up the chase to get her gift of flying.

Imp kept her height well above the trees, hoping that anyone who might possibly see her would think that she was some kind of eagle, or something. If she was caught, it'd be hard to explain why she was flying. It would be even harder to explain how she got this mystical power. Especially if her ability to fly comes from her Flavour powers.

Imp sighed. There were still so many people against Flavours, but the world was starting to wake up. More and more people were helping Flavours in need, and their public displays were getting more and more support. The world was shifting towards free will.

Participating in public displays used to be one of Imp's favourite things to do. Her job was usually to go among the crowd and find potential Flavour recruits, handing them little slips of paper with instructions on how to get to the FTA. She had never given a wrong slip. It was pretty hard to, actually. Most people who honestly wanted to be a Flavour had a certain *feeling* to them, almost as if their desires had manifested into something tangible, something real. The official name for it was an aura, a strange mist that seemed to float around humans. All Flavours had one, and it was usually the color of their potential Flavour.

Learning about auras and how to see them... that was one of the optional courses at the FTA. Imp, being the next potential Cream Soda, was forced to take all the classes possible, but she didn't mind. Most Flavours did, anyway. Knowledge was essential in their high risk lifestyle. It could be a matter between life and death. It could mean the difference between getting captured and wishing you'd taken that course, or escaping thanks to that knowledge.

Most people didn't understand that their Flavour was based on their personality. Most of the people who showed up at the FTA were under the impression that they would get to choose their Flavours, but it ended up being more like their subconscious chose it for them.

But it was different for Cream Soda Flavours. No one knew exactly how they were chosen. Cream Sodas had a strange aura, one that only the best aura readers could actually see. Imp couldn't even see her own aura.

It was getting late, and Imp could feel her power draining. By tomorrow, she was sure that Lars' dreams of flying would be gone, and she would have to resort to plain foot walking for the rest of the way. She had covered half the distance to the next safe house, located in the town of Diyo. There was no way that Lars would be able to catch up now.

With an awkward landing, Imp set off to find someplace to set up camp. After ten minutes of searching she found a pine tree with overhanging branches, similar to what Pheonix, Moss and

Imp had slept in a couple of nights ago. Imp liked to sleep under trees. The projecting branches provided a perfect shelter and kept in heat. Plus, it was hard to find someone who was hiding under them. Imp knew that from experience. They made her feel safe, as if someone was wrapping their arms over her in a warm embrace.

She set up her sleeping bag, propping her backpack beside her head, where she could easily reach it. She burrowed deep into the bag, snuggling herself into a cocoon of heat. From there she watched the sun set, admiring the bright hues the sky turned. Finally, the sun finished its descent, sinking below the horizon. Night fell and the forest came to life, thriving under the starts. Imp slowly fell into a restless sleep.

The nightmares were waiting for her.

She watched her father go, turning his back on her.

She hadn't betrayed him. She hadn't done anything bad. Why was he leaving?

The man in the lab coat looked down at her with emotionless eyes. He had no facial features; he wasn't someone important. She didn't remember him. She didn't need to. She hated him.

She was put in a cell. There were no toys. She was angry at them, so she hid when they came to find her. It took them a long time to find her, putting their experiment behind by a couple of hours. They got angry. They hit her. She never did that again.

They brought her to a different room. This one had a bed in the middle, surrounded by strange machines that glowed in angry colors. They set her on the bed, and they told her to go to sleep. But she couldn't fall asleep. Not with them watching her. And she was afraid. She didn't like sleeping. They brought nightmares of blood.

The faceless doctor went to hit her, but a woman stopped him. She was important. She had pretty green eyes and long brown hair. She reminded her of her mother. Imp called her 'second mother'.

The woman sat beside Imp, cradling her hands between her own. She closed her eyes because the woman told her to, and ignored the strange plastic cups that were attached to her head and arms. The woman told her to go to sleep. She told her that everything would be okay.

But it wasn't okay. The nightmares were there, and when she woke up screaming the woman held her in her arms. The doctor got angry, yelling at the woman to get her back asleep. Imp tried to fall back asleep as the woman comforted her, and the doctor only grew angrier. It took ten minutes before she fell asleep again.

Now Imp was in a nightmare within a nightmare. She saw the scene she had seen so many times... Her mother, on the ground bleeding. Her father, with his wicked looking knife dripping blood. Her mother's blood. But the scene was different this time. Her father was no longer important. The focus was on her mother. Her green eyes were glazed over, yet they looked at Imp with a strange emotion, a mixture between burning hatred and deep sadness.

"Why didn't you save me?" She asked, her voice infinitely sad, "Why didn't you save me?" Suddenly her face distorted into one of savage anger, her eyes shooting daggers and lightning, "Why didn't you save me?!" She yelled, "I hate you! Why didn't you save me?!"

Imp woke up in a cold sweat, a silent scream on her lips. She whimpered, rubbing at her eyes, covering her ears, hoping in vain that that would stop the echo of her mother's savage yelling voice or the scene of her angry face.

The sun was beginning to rise as Imp packed up her meagre belongings, carefully and slowly.

Why are my hands shaking? Her inner voice sounded weak and pathetic compared to her angry mother's, *I've always had this nightmare. I should have gotten used to it by now.*

She kept telling herself that as she finalized her packing and walked away. She kept telling herself that until her shaking subsided and her tears stopped flowing, until the sun rose completely and warmed the earth, chasing away her fears.

Pheonix and Moss finally made it to the safe house. They had made up their minds shortly after Imp left. They ran themselves ragged the whole way, quickly refilling provisions and packing extras, grabbing a bag of Cream Soda gummies just in case.

They didn't even spend one night at the safe house. They ran until they reached the fork in the road, heading down the north trail.

They were going to find Imp.

Easier said than done.

They had run for a day, but their stamina was running out. Imp was just too far ahead.

"Maybe she'll stay at the checkpoint for a while." Moss panted.

"Yeah." It was possible. The next safe house was at a small town named Diyo. Imp might indulge herself and spend more than one night there. Maybe.

It was just as possible as Lars getting to Diyo before they did.

Don't say that. It could actually happen, Pheonix thought, *He could take a car.*

It was true. Flavours disliked cars because it was hard to get somewhere undetected. They would be driving illegally without license plates, and as soon as it was revealed that the Flavours were using a certain car, the Police would be all over them immediately. But Police had no qualms against using cars. In fact, it was their favourite mode of transportation.

But he can't get at us while we're in the forest, at least. But in town...

Pheonix didn't talk about her fears with Moss, of course. She didn't want to get him worried. He was already upset enough about his condition, and the fact that they had to keep stopping for breaks because of him.

Moss wasn't worried at all. He was sure that Imp could handle Lars on her own. She hadn't been escaping him for two years to be suddenly caught in his and Pheonix's absence.

Sheesh... Pheonix had only been with Imp for a couple days, and already she was beginning to act all motherly! Moss had experience with Pheonix's mother spazz attacks. He hated them, and he was fairly certain that Imp wouldn't enjoy them either.

Encouraged by those mildly depressing thoughts, they took off at a tired, half-hearted run, trying not to trip over their exhausted and sore limbs, and trying to run in a relatively straight line. They managed to only run into each other a couple of times, which was an accomplishment.

If the first words out of Imp's mouth when she sees us is 'Why are you here?', I'm seriously gonna punch her, Moss thought angrily.

Imp could see the light of Diyo farther ahead, glistening in the night like fireflies.

She had finally made it. It had taken her longer than expected because of her restless nights and tired body, but she had finally made it, with only two gummies to spare. She smiled.

It wasn't safe to enter Diyo at night. That would immediately set off warning bells in peoples' heads, especially because (she hoped) they wouldn't recognize her. She definitely did not need that.

The next morning, not too early, Imp set off at a leisurely, unhurried pace towards the town. She had replaced her telltale punk clothes with a black t-shirt, jeans, and running shoes, doing her hair specially so that very little of her pink highlight could be seen. Her classic normal disguise.

She stepped through into town without incident. Imp walked down the main street, drinking in the sights of the town.

Everything's the same, Imp thought, staring at the buildings of Diyo, *It's barely changed since the last time I was here.*

Home sweet home.

Chapter 9

Imp walked calmly down the streets of Diyo, surprised at how the buildings hadn't changed at all. There was the ice-cream store, where she and her mom would always get ice-cream! Oh, and the library! The video store, the convenience store, city hall! Nothing had changed at all since she left, 6 years ago.

Stop admiring the view, and get to the safe house! Imp reminded herself, *You can sight-see later, when you get your gummy refills!*

So she headed in the direction of the safe house. She had never been there before, so she had to follow her map through the streets, keeping her head down in case someone might notice her. That was the last thing that she wanted.

Imp rounded the next bend and her heart skipped a beat. She quickly ducked behind the wall of a building, her heart pounding.

The safe house was swarming with police!

There were four police cars parked outside the house, and at least 20 officers patrolling the area around the house. None of them could enter; the Law magic prevented that. But nothing stopped them from watching the house.

They know I'm here! Imp began to panic, *I need to get out of here, fast!*

Imp frantically turned the corner, not watching where she was going. She rammed straight into someone, making them squeal, and making Imp fall on her butt.

Imp was about to blurt out sorry and take off, but was stopped when she looked at the person.

"Siria?!" The lady exclaimed, "What are you doing here?! It's been so long..."

Imp was paralyzed.

Of all the people I could run into, why did it have to be Mrs. Ately?!

"Oh, I've missed you so much!" Mrs. Ately exclaimed, enveloping Imp in a hug, "Oh Siria! Where did you go? Why—"

Mrs. Ately stopped short, looking behind Imp. She must have seen the safe house.

"I knew it." Mrs. Ately whispered, shocked, "I knew it! You're a Flavour, aren't you?"

Imp was still too shocked to answer, preferring silence. Mrs. Ately was piecing everything together just too fast. She had to get away, and out of town.

"I'm sorry Mrs. Ately. I need to go." Imp said quickly, pushing Mrs. Ately away, "I'm sorry. I just can't stay here."

She got up to run, but stopped when a hand clamped down on her wrist.

"Oh no you don't." Mrs. Ately said wickedly, "You're not leaving this town until you get proper rest." She began to drag Imp away.

"No!" Imp cried, "I can't stay here! I'm wanted by the Police!"

"That's too bad." Answered Mrs. Ately, "In that case, the Police can bite me."

Like all the buildings in Diyo, Mrs. Ately's house hadn't changed a bit. The same red, overstuffed couch was sitting in a corner, the same TV showing the same news channel, the same rug sitting on the floor.

The only difference was the sandy haired boy sitting in the middle of the living room, tinkering with a skateboard. He looked at the board with intense concentration, his black t-shirt full of name brands soiled by the dirt coming off the skateboard. He wore simple jeans and boarder shoes, wielding a screwdriver with great skill.

"Delyn!" Imp exclaimed the moment she set eyes on him.

He looked at her, temporarily confused. Then his brown eyes grew huge and happy. He threw aside his skateboard and stood.

"Siria!" He rushed up to her, giving her a huge hug, "I can't believe it's you! Where the hell did you disappear to?!"

All Imp could do was laugh and hug him back. She had temporarily forgotten how to speak.

Delyn had been her childhood friend back when she used to live in Diyo. Mrs. Ately, his mother, had been her mother's best friend and they visited often. She was the one that Imp's mother would ask to babysit her when the tension between her mother and father would reach a breaking point. Imp would stay over as long as it took for her father to cool down. Sometimes she would stay for a week at a time.

Imp loved the house at the border of the town. She and Delyn would always explore in the forest behind the house, playing hide and seek. Some of their favourite activities would be sword fighting with branches, making the forest a war zone as they tried to mount surprise attacks on each other.

"It's so good to have you back!" Delyn said, stepping away from her, "How long are you staying?"

"Just for the night." Imp answered, wincing at Delyn's disappointed face, "I need to move on. I can't be late."

"Can't be late for what?" Delyn asked all innocently.

"I need to make it to the capital."

"Why?"

Imp desperately wanted to tell him. But she just couldn't. "It's kinda...secret."

Delyn clapped suddenly, surprising Imp. "A top secret mission! I knew it! That means you've joined the Police, right? I knew that you were destined for it. I always got whipped during our sword fights in the forest."

"Not exactly, dear." Mrs. Ately said, coming from the kitchen, "Siria isn't with the Police."

"She isn't...?" Delyn's brow furrowed, "Then what—" Delyn went pale.

"What is it?" Imp asked, surprised by his sudden silence.

"Don't tell me you're a Flavour." Delyn's eyes were begging her to say no. Imp winced.

Delyn suddenly slammed his fist against the coffee table by the couch.

"How could you, Siria?!" He yelled, his eyes shooting daggers at her, "The Flavours?! I thought you were better than that!"

Imp was shocked. Delyn, her best friend. He hated Flavours. She couldn't believe it!

"What do you have to say for yourself?" Delyn yelled, sounding like a scolding parent.

Imp was paralyzed. *What do I say?*

"My name's not Siria anymore." Imp whispered, her mind completely blank, "I'm called Imp now."

With a brutal roar Delyn picked up his skateboard. With a powerful toss he sent it flying in the air at Imp. She yelped and dodged it. Delyn stood there for a second, glaring. Then he ran out of the house, slamming the door.

Mrs. Ately was standing there with her mouth wide open.

"Oh dear." She looked pityingly at Imp, "Don't listen to him, Siri—Imp. He just has a bit of a temper."

Imp could only stand there, staring off in the direction of the door, where her best-friend-turned-enemy had gone.

Delyn was *furious*. How could she? How could Siria turn to a group like the Flavours?

He savagely punched the wall of the convenience store, ignoring the pain of his knuckles and the prick of tears forming in his eyes.

How could she?

How could she just turn her back on him? How could she turn her back on the Police, the government, who had done so much for the world? How could she turn to a group that was trying to destroy the peace, the order?

I'm going to stop her, Delyn thought, *I'll tell the Police, They'll capture her, and then she'll admit that she was wrong! That's what I'll do.*

Delyn found himself in front of the Police station, as if his subconscious had directed his feet there.

Proof that what I'm doing is right.

He pushed open the glass doors of the Police station, holding onto his belief that he was doing the right thing like it was a lifeboat.

"Where are you going?" Mrs. Ately asked, looking up from her book.

Imp felt slightly guilty, looking over her shoulder. "I'm...pretty sure you know where I'm going."

Mrs. Ately's expression softened. "How long has it been since you last visited her?"

"Too long." Imp sighed, opening the door.

Lars watched Imp leave the house.

He had reached the small town of Diyo by car, shortly after his slightly disturbing meeting with General Salem. And, thanks to a tipoff by one of the house's residents, he had easily found her again.

And now, here she was, obviously trying to blend in. She had discarded her Flavour clothes, probably because they were flashy and obvious. Punk clothes stood out in a small town like Diyo.

Lars checked his watch. It was shortly after 6. The moment he had been phoned, he had rushed into a Police car with its lights flashing. They had managed to make it to Diyo from Tiyuk within an hour, saving half an hour thanks to their speed.

And now Imp was stupidly leaving the house.

She had to know that the Police were on the lookout for her. The Police cars parked outside the safe house should have given her a major hint. She had had to have seen them, to have chosen to stay in a non-safehouse instead.

Yet here she was, leaving the house and walking calmly down the sidewalk.

What is she doing? Lars wondered, watching as she turned the corner. Only then did he exit the car, his temporary partner following, counting to a minute before walking around the corner after her. He watched the swish of her hair disappear around the nest corner before he followed again. And he did this until they reached the cemetery.

A cemetery? Lars wondered, watching as Imp tried to open the gate. It was locked. Undeterred, she placed one of her feet into a chain link and hopped over.

Lars and his partner ducked behind one of the trees lining the outside of the cemetery.

"Sir?" His partner asked, "Should we attack? She would be easy to trap in here."

Lars hesitated. It was true that it would be easy to trap her. But he wanted to figure out what she was doing first.

He watched Imp weave through the graves as if she was in a trance. She didn't even look at the names; it was as if she had memorized exactly where her destination was.

The cemetery was so small that Lars could see it completely from his position behind the tree. Imp stopped at one grave, standing completely immobile.

"Sir?" His partner asked again.

Lars closed his eyes. It was easy to figure out what Imp was doing now.

"No." He answered. His partner looked surprised, but he didn't say anything.

She stood there for 10 minutes, soundlessly and without movement. Then, just as suddenly as she came, she left, making Lars quickly duck farther behind the tree to avoid being seen.

Only when another five minutes had passed did Lars leave his hiding place, heading into the cemetery. He was curious.

He reached the grave Imp had been mourning, crouching down to look at its inscription.

AURA TANALI
1978-2007

LOVING WIFE TO ... TANALI AND MOTHER TO ... TANALI

Lars frowned. The names of the husband and son or daughter were savagely scratched out.

What does Imp have to do with this grave?

Imp heard the door of Mrs. Ately's house close quietly.

She couldn't sleep. According to the clock in the guest room, it was 1 in the morning. Delyn had been out for a long time. He must have been really angry.

Imp crept downstairs in time to see Delyn's sandy hair disappear into the hallway next to the living room. She followed him on tippy toes, watching as he disappeared into the bathroom.

She needed to talk to him.

She followed the hallway until she found his room. He wouldn't be able to avoid her there. More importantly, if Imp changed her mind at the last second, he would still see her. She sat on his bed, the only thing that had changed in his room, although it was still shoved against the wall. The same old desk sat in the corner, even though he had probably long outgrown it. He would never get a new one. His dad had made it. It was something precious to him.

The door creaked open, and Delyn's hand reached in, looking for a light switch. The room flooded with light and Delyn entered, rubbing his eyes sleepily. He paused when he saw Imp.

Please have calmed down a little, Imp thought fervently, *Please.*

"What are you doing here, *Imp*?" He asked angrily, saying *Imp* with the most possible venom. Obviously he hadn't calmed down.

"We need to talk." Imp answered calmly. She didn't even know what to say. She hadn't planned that far. Luckily Delyn was the first to question.

"Why did you join them, Imp?" He pleaded, "Why *them*?"

The tone of his voice surprised Imp. He sounded desperate, and sad.

"You don't know what the Police did to me."

Delyn frowned. "What do you mean?"

"When my mother died...My dad immediately donated me to a government funded lab—"

"Wait, what?" Delyn's nose wrinkled in confusion, "Your dad didn't abandon you! You ran away."

Now if was Imp's turn to say what. "I didn't run away!" She spluttered angrily, "He 'donated' me to a lab! *He* abandoned *me*!"

"That's not what he told us."

Understanding hit her like a train. Of course he wouldn't have told the truth! He probably had made up a bunch of lies to cover his ass!

"Siria." Delyn said, looking her straight in the face. Something in his voice confused her. Sadness and...longing? "Why did you abandon *me*?"

Imp gasped. "I didn't, Delyn! I never abandoned you! I told you, my father—"

"I'm not talking about that!" Delyn yelled, most likely waking Mrs. Ately up, "You abandoned me when you joined the Flavours! Don't you get it, Siria?" He hunched forward over her, his face inches from hers. She tried to back away, but he grabbed her neck, digging sharp nails into her skin.

"Stop it Delyn! You're hurti—"

"Shut up! Don't you realize how much you've hurt *me*? Don't you realize how much it hurt when you just disappeared, and I never heard a peep from you for six years! Six years, while you paraded around the country as a *Flavour*, of all things!"

He pushed her against the wall, her head banging it painfully. But what he did next surprised her.

He *kissed* her. He pinned her arms against the wall with his hands and kissed her. His lips pressed against hers with a savage rage, and he bit down savagely on her lips, as if to punish her. She was too surprised to react. He left her mouth, biting painfully at her shoulder. She squirmed, trying to get away, but her arms were trapped against the wall, and her legs kicked uselessly at thin air.

"Stop it Delyn!" She sobbed. He looked up, angry eyes meeting hers for a second, but he just attacked her neck, biting it over and over again.

"Don't just sit there!" He growled at her, "Fight back! Stop me, if you're so desperate!"

She could only cry more as he kissed her lips again, trying to shove his tongue between her lips.

She bit it, hard.

He screamed, throwing himself off her and off the bed. Imp crumpled, tasting Delyn's blood in her mouth, mingling with that of her torn lips.

"Get out." He hissed, eyes both angry and hurt, "Get out!"

She obliged, slipping off his bed and out the door. She snuck up the stairs, amazed at how Mrs. Ately hadn't woken up from all the commotion downstairs.

This house held no comfort for her anymore. Not even the familiar covers on the guest bed could cheer her up.

She didn't need to stay and eavesdrop at Delyn's door to know that he was crying. She knew him too well.

He was her best friend, after all.

Chapter 10

"Why are you crying?" Imp asked the blond boy.

He looked up, his eyes full of tears. The fresh earth was starting to stain his shoes, matching the ones on his hands.

"Does it hurt?" She continued, gesturing to the bandages on his neck, "Is that why you're crying?"

The boy rubbed a hand absent-mindedly over the white bandage, staining it brown. "No." He answered, sniffling, "My neck doesn't hurt."

"Then why?" She asked, curious. She had never seen someone cry like that, "Does it hurt in another place?"

He sniffled again. "My...heart hurts."

"Your heart?" Imp was bewildered, "How did you hurt that? Isn't it in your chest?"

"Yeah. But I'm not hurt...physcly..." He stumbled over the word, "I'm hurt...mently. That's what my mom said."

"Mently?" Imp murmured, "What does that mean?"

"My mom said that my heart hurts because I loved my dad. And now he's gone."

"Gone?" Imp asked, "Well yeah, they put him in the ground!"

That just made the boy start to cry again. Imp just stood there awkwardly, not sure what to do.

"Well...maybe your dad isn't gone?" Imp tried to comfort him, "Wounds leave scars, right? So maybe, because your heart's hurting, it will scar. And, because you loved your dad, it will be a scar of love!"

He stopped sniffling, looking up at her hopefully. "You think?"

"Yeah!" Imp smiled, feeling good since she had somehow managed to cheer him up.

He smiled back.

It was at that moment that his mom came back, taking his hand and leading him away. He waved at her as they drove away.

It was only later that she learned that his name was Delyn.

Imp woke up with tears in her eyes. Strangely, she couldn't remember what she had dreamed about, although it left her with a feeling of warmth.

For breakfast Mrs. Ately made Imp's favourite pancakes: banana chocolate chip. And, just for Imp, she brought out a case of peaches. Imp ate most of them, devouring the sweet fruit like there was no tomorrow. When Mrs. Ately wasn't looking, she would sneak a couple of the delicate fruit into her backpack for later.

Delyn and Imp ignored each other completely, not even looking at each other while they ate. Mrs. Ately was clearly confused, but she didn't ask any questions. She knew that it would do her no good. She had experience with them. Whenever they were angry at each other, they pretended that everything was all right, despite their silence. And when she asked, they'd look at her like she was crazy, asking why she thought that they were angry at each other, although they clearly were.

It was only around noon, when Imp was getting ready to leave, that things began to go wrong.

Mrs. Ately was in the kitchen, preparing soup for lunch, when the first announcement came. A loudspeaker echoed through the house, making Imp's heart skip a beat, and Delyn smile.

"This is the Police. Ately family, if you refuse to give up the Flavour hiding in your house, we will break down your door and enter by force."

Mrs. Ately dropped the dish she was cleaning and it shattered, sending white porcelain pieces skittering across the floor.

Imp was halfway to the door before Mrs. Ately caught her, roughly knocking her to the ground.

"What the heck are you doing?!" She hissed, "I'm not letting you out of the house!"

Imp glared, hoping that Mrs. Ately's resolve would waver. She didn't even budge, calm blue eyes begging Imp not to go. She didn't need to use words. Her eyes were expressive enough that talking would just ruin the effect and undermine her message.

"Fine." Imp grumbled, "But as soon as they starting threatening you, I'm giving myself up."

"That's my girl!" Mrs. Ately beamed, "Now wait here and stay down."

She went to the door, tentatively opening it. There were four Police cars lined up on her lawn, with a youth holding the megaphone. He had brown hair, freshly groomed, that reached down to tickle his neck slightly. He looked too young to be wearing the Police uniform.

"She's not here!" Mrs. Ately yelled, "She left!"

The youth picked up his megaphone, fooling around with the dials before speaking into it.

"You realise, Mrs. Ately, that lying will do no good." He threatened, "It's still enough for me to put you under arrest for helping a Flavour."

"I'm not lying!" Mrs. Ately yelled back.

"So be it."

The youth gestured towards one of his cars, and three Police came out of it, armed with swords that menacingly glinted in the noon sun.

"If you resist, you will be charged!" The youth warned her, "Let us willingly enter your home and search."

"Mrs. Ately!" Imp whispered from her position of the floor, "I'm turning myself in."

"No!" Mrs. Ately screamed, slamming the door.

"What the hell are you doing?!" Imp shrieked.

"Shut up and help me keep the door closed!" She yelled, fire in her eyes, "Delyn, get down here this instant! Help!"

"No!" Was Delyn's answering cry, his voice echoing from upstairs, "Just give up, Mom! Imp isn't worth it!"

"Mrs. Ately..." Imp began.

"Shut up Imp!" Mrs. Ately glared at her, "I'm keeping you safe whether you like it or not!"

The door buckled as one of the Police kicked it, and Imp pushed harder, struggling to keep it closed. She was positioned right beside the door handle, and she could see how much the door opened with each kick. Only a tiny crack, but she had no doubt that it would get worse.

"Get away from my house! This is abuse of power!" Mrs. Ately yelled to the Police outside. Imp never expected this quiet, motherly woman to become such a savage under pressure.

A fierce blow nearly toppled Imp and Mrs. Ately, but they somehow managed to slam the door closed again. The Police outside swore, coordinating another pound at the door. There was someone yelling angrily at them, commanding them to get the door open, wondering why they hadn't done that already. The voice was also calling them harsh names, questioning their competence, especially when being put up against 'two women, both of them weak!'.

"Mrs. Ately...I'll be fine, really!"

"No, Imp." Mrs. Ately whispered, all traces of brutality gone from her voice, "I want to help Flavours. I know what that lab did to you. Your father couldn't hide it from me."

"Are you sure, Mrs. Ately?" Imp asked, "Do you really want to help all Flavours?"

"Yes! Of course!" Mrs. Ately turned to Imp, her eyes passionate, "There's a way to get these Police away from my house, isn't there?"

"Yes." Imp answered tentatively, "But don't take it lightly. If you do it, then you must help all Flavours that ask entry into your house."

"Just tell me, Imp!" She said, bracing herself against another kick, "Stop dodging the subject!"

"It's Law magic." Imp spoke faster than before, "If you say certain words, then no Police can enter your home."

"What are they?!" Mrs. Ately yelled back, "If you haven't noticed, Imp, we don't have all day!"

"I declare this house a safe house for all Flavours." Imp quoted, "Say it, and the Police will be blown away a couple feet, and they will never be able to enter the house again."

"I declare this house a safe house for all Flavours!" Mrs. Ately yelled, loud enough for the Police outside to hear.

The pressure on the door suddenly eased up, and screams could be heard. Imp peeked through the window of the door, seeing a bunch of Police sprawled across the lawn a safe distance from the house. They had shocked expressions on their faces and some of them were pounding the ground, angry that they had been beaten.

"How the hell did that work?" Mrs. Ately asked, sinking to the floor with a sigh of relief.

"It's Law magic." Imp answered, "Very ancient and powerful. It was put in place with the first Charter. It worked because one of the laws was 'That all groups shall be granted freedom to create peaceful meetings under a roof, and no authority figure can enter that building with intent of destroying this right.'"

"So, because the Police intended to capture you, a Flavour, designating this house a safe house for Flavours means that they can't enter if they intend to capture a Flavour." Mrs. Ately said, with awe in her voice, "Maybe the ancient government actually did something right!"

"There's one last step, though. You need to assert yourself as a supporter of the Flavours, to stop the Police from capturing you for interrogation."

"What do I say?"

"I declare myself a supporter of the Flavours."

"Simple enough." Mrs. Ately shrugged, repeating what Imp had told her, "I like Law magic now." She grinned.

Then she frowned. "But why doesn't it protect Flavours?"

Now it was Imp's turn to shrug. "No one has any idea. Some people think that it has to do with the fact that the gummies contain chaos magic, and it kinda neutralizes it. I'm not sure."

It was quiet for a while. Imp and Mrs. Ately were still recovering from the shock of the Police attack.

Delyn walked down the stairs calmly, as if nothing had happened.

"Where were you, mister?!" Mrs. Ately was on him in a flash.

"I was in my room working on my skateboard. Do you want to see it? I added some cool decals." Delyn answered nonchalantly.

Mrs. Ately's slap echoed throughout the quiet household, along with Delyn's shocked cry. He stumbled back, rubbing his reddened cheek.

"Is this all a game to you? Don't you realize that as soon as Imp gets captured, she'll probably be given a life sentence?!"

"So?" Delyn answered fiercely, "She has no right going against the Police!"

"She has a right to do anything she wants! Don't you get it, Delyn? The government is controlling everything, messing with the laws set down by the ancient government until no one has free will anymore!"

"Maybe it's better that way!" Delyn yelled back, "Maybe that way, everyone is safe and protected!"

"Are we safe?" Imp piped up, softly, "Are the Flavours safe? Isn't one of the fundamental laws that of freedom of speech, or freedom of beliefs? Yet, the Police are killing Flavours because of what we believe in. Is that fair, Delyn?"

Delyn was shocked into silence.

"Safety and rules are something that people need. But we also need freedom too..." Imp's voice grew intense, "But this government has taken the rules idea to the extreme, and has hurt us instead of making us safer. After all," She paused, "Why am I declared illegal because I made the choice to become a Flavour?"

"Shut up!" Delyn yelled, and he stormed off back the way he came.

"Mrs. Ately." Imp said, continuing in the same quiet monotone, "You know I can't stay here forever. I need to leave. For both of our sakes."

"You're right, Siria." She didn't bother to correct herself. She sighed, "I'll distract them. You can leave out the back door."

Imp nodded, reaching into her bag and taking out a Cream Soda gummy. She needed to use it. There was no way she could escape the watchful gazes of the Police. That would leave her down to a grand total of one gummy. Fantastic.

I'm cutting it close.

Imp moved towards the back door, waiting for Mrs. Ately's distraction. She opened it just a smidge, ready to throw herself out of it when it came time to. She placed the gummy in her mouth, slowly chewing it as she waited.

"I'm going to kindly ask you to leave my property!" Mrs. Ately yelled, and Imp ran, allowing the gummy's power to fill her as she turned invisible. The Police hadn't noticed her yet. She was half-way there...

"She's over there!" Imp heard Delyn yell from a window, leaning out of it and pointing. "I saw a bush rustle!"

Dammit, Delyn! Imp mentally cursed him. She dodged an arrow that whizzed past her ear. She could sense the dreams of the Police, feeling the familiar dream of flying nearby. But there were a lot of people that dreamed of that.

Many more arrows split the air, but they were shots in the dark; most she didn't need to dodge, the others she dodged quite easily.

"She'll head for the forest!" The voice from the megaphone yelled, and Imp recognized Lars.

What's he doing here?! I thought I left him behind!

He charged towards her, guessing luckily where she was, his sword flashing in the sunlight. She ran for the forest, dodging branches and finding trails from her childhood, when she and Delyn had been friends.

When she had been happy.

Chapter 11

Imp rushed through the undergrowth, following a trail that she had often used when she had branch-sword wars with Delyn. She could hear the Police off in the distance, completely lost. They stumbled through the forest like elephants, making so much noise it was easy for Imp to avoid them.

She stopped at a tree, learning her back up against it and catching her breath. She was strangely calm, even if she was being chased by Police because her best friend had betrayed her. It was obvious. The only reason the Police could have known that she was here was because of Delyn.

Next time I see him, I'm gonna have a serious talk with him. Unless I strangle him first.

A crunch came from behind, followed by a soft swear. Imp froze. Even if she knew that whoever it was wouldn't be able to see her, she needed to keep quiet. Her great gulps of air from earlier must have given her away.

"I know you're here, Imp." Lars' voice sounded from behind her. He was pretty close, "Come out."

Imp stayed as quiet as she could, suddenly wishing that she wasn't so out of breath. It was impossible to hold her breath for so long. She was too tired.

She heard Lars chuckle. "I know where you are! You better move, or I'm going to get you!"

Imp stayed where she was, hoping that she could just melt into the tree. She thought that he was bluffing, trying to flush her out of her hiding place, so that she would make noise and be revealed. Lars' voice had come from just behind the tree...

Imp screamed as a thick wire swung around the tree, trapping her. She tried to struggle, but the thick cables were too strong.

It was a wire trap, a simple but tricky invention. It looked like a small black ball, but with one press of a button, or, in some cases, when it would sense movement, thick wires would surge out and wrap around its victim.

Lars came around the tree, grinning. He drew his sword, slowly and menacingly, its silver flashing in the light. It was the same sword he always used. She could faintly see the 'Monochrome' she (well, her raging side) had carved into the blade while Lars was unconscious.

"You better appear, or else I might miss and accidentally hit you." He warned, raising his sword a little, aiming it at the tree.

Imp materialized, glaring at him with her blue eyes. She was wearing everyday clothes for once, and Lars was struck by how normal she looked with them on. Almost as if she was just an average kid going to school...Not some kind of devil in punk clothes, on the run from Police officers all over the country.

"I warned you to move." He smirked, not in the least disturbed by her venomous glare, "You should've listened."

Lars turned, looking in the direction of where the sounds of struggling Police were coming from. "It's all good! She's over here. I captured her already."

Cheering came from the woods, and Imp struggled some more. Lars looked at her, that smug smirk still on his face. She felt angry, a rage burning inside her.

No, calm down! Turning into...that...won't help you out of this situation! Think!

She reached into Lars' dreams, finding his favourite one. Flying. She began to hover a bit off the ground, but Lars looked at her with a bored expression on his face.

"Don't bother trying that." He pushed a button on the wire trap shell he held in his hand, and the ropes tightened around Imp. He waited until they were tight enough that they cut off her air and she collapsed. Then he loosened just a little bit. No point in strangling her.

"Where are you?!" Lars called out to his troops. They were taking too long.

The woods were strangely quiet. No more cussing or breaking of branches could be heard. Lars frowned. Where were they?

Something pounded his head and he fell, dazed. Little stars and black spots blossomed before his eyes as he hit the ground. His sword flew out of his grasp, and the wire trap rolled away, out of reach.

"What are you guys doing here?!" Imp asked, staring at the spot over Lars. He couldn't move his head to see who she was looking at.

Suddenly, her head snapped sideways, a fist following in its wake.

"Moss!" Someone gasped. Pheonix.

"I can't believe that those are the first words you said!" Moss yelled at Imp, "We save your sorry butt, and all you can say is 'What are you guys doing here?' Seriously?!"

Imp's face looked as stunned as Lars was. He reached for his sword, where it had clattered a few centimetres away from him. A tree root immediately anchored his wrist to the ground. Pheonix bent down to his eye level, her green eyes sparkling with laughter. "Don't even try, Police-boy."

She whacked him in the back of the neck, knocking him unconscious instantly.

Moss was still chewing out Imp as he felt Pheonix take the wire trap from his hand. A second later, he heard the familiar clinking noise of the wires returning to their spherical container.

"We're outta here." Moss announced, his footsteps crunching the leaves.

"Moss, north is *that* way." Pheonix chided.

"Right." Moss said, recovering his dignity, "That's where I meant to go."

Imp giggled, trying to hide her laugh behind a cough. Pheonix just laughed straight out.

"Alright compass." She said sarcastically, "We're following you."

And they abandoned Lars as he carefully opened his eyes, his unconsciousness faked.

"Make me a Police officer!" Delyn slammed his hands on the desk of the Police chief for Diyo.

He glared at the boy. This young man had charged into the Police station, brushing past the secretary and pushing his way into his office. Then, he had demanded that he be made a Police officer in charge of hunting down Imp.

"Even if you were worthy of becoming a Police officer, " The Chief stressed the word worthy in a cool, hard voice, "You would still need months of training and you would have to pass an extremely difficult test."

"Just give me the test! Anything!" Delyn glared at the stubborn chief, "I *need* to become a Police officer! I need to find her, and bring her to justice!"

"Sorry, kid." The chief growled, annoyed, "Start treating your superiors with respect, not banging on their desks, not making ridiculous demands, and not yelling in their face, then maybe someday you'll become a Police officer." His voice clearly stated that he didn't think that that would be possible.

"You don't understand!" Delyn yelled in frustration.

"I do understand. I understand that if you don't get out of my office right now, you will be removed by force."

Delyn gritted his teeth, shooting one last baleful glare at the officer as he stormed out of his office, past the surprised secretary and out the door.

He stood in the street in front of the Police station for a couple of seconds. It began to rain, but Delyn didn't move, letting the water drip down his head and into his eyes.

"Are you really that desperate to join the Police?" A boy asked, about Delyn's age. He was leaning against the wall of the Police station, seeming to size him up with his grey eyes.

"You're...you're that kid that was commanding the Police!" Delyn gasped.

The youth winced. "Don't call me kid. I'm probably older than you, and definitely your superior." He stuck out his hand to Delyn, "I'm Lars. I'm in charge of Imp's capture."

Delyn shook hands with Lars, almost reverently.

"Why are you so interested in Imp's capture?" Lars asked, pulling the hood of his uniform over his head to prevent the rain from soaking his brown hair any further.

"She was a childhood friend of mine. But then, she ran away from home—" Delyn was suddenly struck by the memory of Imp telling him that her father had abandoned her to a laboratory. But he decided that she was lying, "And joined the Flavours."

"A childhood friend, you say?" Lars frowned a little, "So she lived in this town?"

"Yes." Delyn answered, "Most of her life. Up until 6 years ago. She was nine when she left."

Lars' frown got deeper. According to the Police data, she officially became a Flavour at the age of 12. One year of training was to be expected...But three years were still unaccounted for.

The Police believed that knowing a Flavour's past was a valuable weapon. It was possible to make a Flavour pause long enough to subdue them if you randomly blurted out an event from their history. Many Flavours had been captured this way, by using life-changing events in their life to make them turn themselves in. They were like the classic, emotionally distraught people in the movies. Just spouting random junk like 'I believe in you' and 'I can help you' was usually enough for them to change their minds. Redemption was always a tempting offer.

"What about her parents?"

"Her mother was murdered when a burglar broke into their house and found her alone. And her father disappeared shortly after she ran away."

Lars was disappointed. Another good way to wheedle Flavours into letting themselves be captured was by mentioning their parents, and how much they missed them. Even if all you could do was mention their name, most Flavours gullibly believed that their parents had actually expressed their longing worldwide, or something. It worked best on the younger ones.

"What's her real name?"

"Siria." Delyn answered.

Siria. A pretty enough name. That was valuable info. Usually Flavours would hesitate when they heard their name. Especially if it was spoken by someone close to them...

"Lars, sir?" Delyn asked, noticing Lars' silence, "Why are you so interested in Imp's past?"

Lars looked at the young man, who seemed so desperate to hunt, and possibly capture, his used-to-be best friend.

"Knowledge, especially about your opponent is a powerful weapon." Lars answered, "You'll learn that as my apprentice."

It took a second for Delyn to understand what Lars had said. "You—you mean...?" His eyes grew wide, "You're joking, right?"

Lars smiled, pleased with his enthusiasm. "No. I'm not joking. We're leaving tomorrow. You better pack your stuff."

Delyn's face morphed into that of happiness, joy filling all of his features. He rushed off towards his house, leaving Lars alone on the street.

Tomorrow, we're headed north, He smiled, *Thanks for the little tip, Pheonix.*

Chapter 12

Moss and Pheonix trumped ahead, crashing through the underbrush like there was no tomorrow. Imp hung back, like always, admiring the view while they chatted.

Imp had to admit that traveling with Pheonix and Moss was fun. Even if she barely said anything and let them do the talking she was still enjoying herself. The way they kept glancing back to make sure she was still following them made her feel important, almost as if they'd miss her if she left. She was like the girl who would hang out on the sidelines; silent, but still enjoying herself, and still being wanted.

Maybe I've finally found friends, Imp smiled. She winced as an image of Delyn flashed in her mind, and she temporarily felt guilty. But that guilt disappeared when she remembered how he'd betrayed her.

How ironic. He gives me a lecture on how I abandoned him, then goes and tries to turn me in to the Police! Sheesh.

"Imp..." Pheonix said in a sing-song voice, "You've gotten awfully quiet..."

Imp could only managed an 'uh' as Pheonix grabbed her arm and squished her between her and Moss. Imp tried to move her arm out of Pheonix's grasp, but she dug her nails into her skin, sending pain down her arm.

"So, Imp." Pheonix warbled in an innocent voice, "How the heck did you create another safe house? I'm curious."

Imp looked at Pheonix's face, searching for any sign of malice.

Wait, why am I looking for malicious intent in Pheonix, of all people? She and Moss backtracked just to catch up with me!

"I knew the people who lived there." Imp explained, "Once she discovered that I was a Flavour and the Police attacked the house she declared it a safe house." She remembered Mrs. Ately's kind face. She hadn't even said good bye to her!

"I see." Pheonix murmured, "Then who was that awfully cute boy?"

"What?" Asked Imp, completely clueless.

"He was yelling at some Police, trying to convince them to let him go into the woods after you. They wouldn't let him." Pheonix shrugged, "Well I guess he's cute, except for the Flavour-hating thing going on. Otherwise." Pheonix smiled dreamily.

Imp just stared blankly at her.

"Uh...he had sandy blond hair...Just a bit taller than me. Jeans, boarder shoes, t-shirt. Does that ring a bell?"

"You mean Delyn?" Imp made a face in disgust, "Don't even try Pheonix. He's a total jerk."

"Really?" Pheonix sounded disappointed, "That sucks."

"Well, he kinda does look like Moss." Imp pointed out, much to Moss' approval.

"Yeah, but Moss isn't as cute as he was."

"Ouch!" Moss yelled, fake stabbing himself in the heart, "That was really mean, Pheonix!"

"The truth hurts." Pheonix grinned.

Moss made a strangled sound, making Pheonix laugh. Imp smiled a little.

Pheonix kept bombarding Imp with questions about random things. Imp started to notice that she was forming a trend. Question, question, question, question about Delyn. Question, question, question, question about Delyn.

I wonder if I should just tell her about what he did to me that night. That might put her out of her misery. But, then again she'd probably start asking me a bunch of questions about how great a kisser he is, or something, Imp thought, disgusted.

The sun began to set, and they found a camping spot to settle in for the night. They had found a lean-to: a bunch of branches leaned up against another tree. It was quite large, obviously man-made. Tiny bits of string held the branches together sturdily, and a small hole in the roof was aligned with a coal-filled fire pit. Little bunches of moss were used for extra padding, and all thorn bushes had been picked out.

"Wow." Moss wolf-whistled, "It's like some super luxurious natural house." He was rubbing the leaf litter on the ground, assessing its softness, "We might not even need our sleeping bags tonight."

"We will need them if you insist on sleeping in your underwear again." Pheonix rolled her eyes.

"When did I ever do that?" Moss gasped, "I never did that! You're lying!"

"You did too!" Pheonix retaliated.

"Nuh-uh!" Moss whined back. A war of yeahs and nuhs ensued, each side seeming equally matched.

They're like little kids, Imp looked on, completely unimpressed, *Like brother and sister.*

Eventually the bickering stopped. Moss having fallen asleep half-way through a nuh-uh.

"I win." Pheonix said contently, drifting off to sleep. Imp was the only one left up.

I wish I could fall as easily asleep as them, Imp sighed, *Sometimes I hate being an insom...*

And Imp too fell asleep. It was a dreamless sleep, but she was fine with that, so long as there were no nightmares.

The next day they left as the sun rose. Imp had insisted on it, and Pheonix and Moss reluctantly agreed. They were starting to get used to Imp's strange habit of waking up extremely early, travelling with barely any rests, and only getting a small amount of sleep.

Maybe that's why she's so elusive, Pheonix wondered, *She never stops moving!*

It was true. Whenever they stopped for a snack break, Imp would sit and watch, discontent, as Pheonix and Moss caught their breath. They'd force her to eat something, just a little strip of jerky, something, because she only ever ate tiny portions at meals. Pheonix was worried for her health. This much walking, and all she ever ate were a few strips of jerky and a bit of water each meal. It couldn't be healthy.

No wonder she's so small, Pheonix though, staring at Imp. She hadn't noticed it before, but her arms were almost like toothpicks. She had no doubt that she could probably see her ribs against her skin.

She isn't lean; it's more like she's emaciated, Pheonix shivered. She vowed that at every possible opportunity, she was going to stuff Imp's face with food.

Imp caught her looking, piercing Pheonix with her bright blue eyes. They seemed almost unnaturally bright, and Pheonix found herself lost in them. Eventually Imp looked away, looking embarrassed.

Why is Imp so mysterious? Pheonix wondered, *I don't understand her at all!*

They ate in silence, Pheonix constantly offering Imp little slips of jerky. She would take them and eat them slowly. It was as if she had an inkling of Pheonix's plan, trying to drag the process out long enough so that she could still take the pieces of jerky offered and still only eat a few slips of it per break.

Eventually they finished their snack and moved on.

"So...Imp." Moss said nonchalantly, "Why are you headed north?"

She looked at him slightly shrewdly. "That's...secret."

"Really?" Moss seemed disappointed. He sighed, "It's some kind of secret mission, isn't it? How come I never get secret missions?!"

"Because you're whiny." Pheonix replied, bonking him on the head.

"Well, you're kinda helping in the secret mission by travelling with me." Imp suggested.

"Really?" Moss grinned, "You're right! I'm your top secret bodyguard!"

He dashed ahead a little bit, humming the tune from a spy movie. He used his arm like a sword, slashing at invisible enemies that had come to threaten Imp.

"I can't believe he's older than me! I swear. Sometimes he's so kiddish!" Pheonix said, rolling her eyes. Imp just giggled.

A little bit later they stopped again, and Pheonix took out her map.

"If I can ask Imp, where exactly are you headed?" She asked.

Imp pointed at the capital of the country, a city named Otta. "I need to talk to the Flavours there before I continue on with my mission."

Pheonix looked thoughtful. "That's pretty far away." She stared at the map with intense concentration, "If we follow the Piyese River, we can get a pretty direct route there, with a couple stops in towns and cities along the way."

Moss looked over Pheonix's shoulder. "There are a lot of trails along the river." He was running his finger over red lines etched into the map, "That's good. I hate backpacking through the woods. It's painful."

"You hate it? I'm the one wearing shorts!" Pheonix protested, "You have nice jeans to cover your legs!"

"Well it's not my fault that you wear shorts, is it?"

"It's not my fault either! Fire's hot. If I was wearing jeans, I'd overheat when I'm using it!"

Imp tried to blank out the ensuing argument, instead studying the map and plotting a trail in her mind.

"Let's keep moving." Pheonix suddenly said, sounding sour. She must have lost the argument, based on Moss' smug expression.

They made it another couple kilometres before night fell. This time there was no nice lean-to made for them, so they made a little shelter.

"I liked the other one a lot better." Moss said dubiously, staring at the perilous set-up. The branches were leaned against a tiny tree trunk. It reminded him of a house of cards: one little movement, and the whole thing would come crashing down.

"Don't be such a baby." Pheonix groaned. Imp was starting to notice that she said that a lot around Moss.

"I'm not." Moss sighed, "Why do you always call me that? It's annoying!"

"Oh, *that's* annoying?!" Pheonix yelled as she pushed into the lean-to with Moss, "How about all the time you complain about everything?!"

Imp sat outside the lean-to, watching as Moss and Pheonix hit each other, both with words and fists.

I can already tell where this is going, Imp sighed. As if to prove her point, the shelter came apart, showering Pheonix and Moss with sticks.

"Now look what you've done!" Pheonix screeched at Moss, "You kicked down the shelter!"

"I kicked down the shelter?!" Moss exclaimed, "I bet you a thousand dollars that the fort came down because of your foot!"

"Could you please stop fighting?" Imp raised her voice a little.

Pheonix and Moss stopped immediately, looking at her, shocked. Apparently they had never heard her raise her voice before.

"Then..." Moss got a wicked look on his face, "Why don't you tell us what you need to do in Otta, and in return we stop fighting?"

Imp looked thoughtful, "Could you guys actually stop fighting?" She asked, incredulous.

Moss got a pained look on his face. "Of course! You think we fight because we hate each other? No, we fight because it's fun!"

"Real—?" Pheonix began to say, but Moss clamped a hand over her mouth.

Imp considered. Well, they did deserve to know. They'd already helped her so much. And plus, at the moment a quiet trip seemed like heaven to her. "Deal, except every time you get close to fighting, I get to whack you with a stick. For the rest of the trip. Those are my terms."

"Deal!" Moss grinned, but it faded as Imp startling rifling through the fallen lean-to. She eventually found a huge stick, picking it up with little more than a small smile.

That's a walking stick worthy of a giant! Moss went pale at the thought of it impaling his head. Pheonix seemed to be thinking of the same thing, because she turned and glared at Moss. Luckily she didn't open her mouth and bring the wooden wrath upon them.

"Okay, Imp." Pheonix muttered, crossing her arms, "Time for your part of the deal!"

"Right." Imp acknowledged, "But you better settle into your sleeping bags first. It's pretty long, and scary."

Chapter 13

Lars had to admit that he was impressed with Delyn's progress.

They were training on the run. During breaks, Lars would teach Delyn the art of the sword. While they were walking, he'd drill him on knowledge, asking questions about different ways to disarm an opponent, stealth, and tips on getting behind a Flavour without them noticing.

"Flavours may have the powers of the elements, but they can't control it beyond where they see. A Fire Flavour can shoot flames in her field of vision, but she can't control them if they're behind her. Same with all elements." Lars lectured.

Delyn looked thoughtful. "But what about Imp's powers?"

Lars shrugged. "I've never seen her create solid from her dream powers. I've only ever seen her turn invisible or fly, which has no form and definitely doesn't need to be seen by her, because it is applied to her body. If she were to create something solid, the same rules as elemental creation would most likely apply."

Delyn nodded, and Lars was once again impressed by his progress. He had never thought about Imp's powers creating something. He'd never seen it happen. There had been reports of it, but it was hard to tell.

"Pop quiz." Lars suddenly said, looking for the expression on Delyn's face. Instead of one of horror, like he had expected, Delyn looked eager, "Name the 35th sword fighting pattern. Show it to me."

As Delyn swung around his sword perfectly, Lars was struck by the possibilities for this boy. Someone with that much skill was guaranteed a good spot in the Police forces. Better yet, Delyn had knowledge about how Imp thought and acted in different situations. Perfect.

Lars nodded in approval as Delyn finished the pattern. The boy beamed at Lars, obviously happy at being on the receiving end of his praise.

Delyn had begun to treat Lars like an older brother, worshipping him even though they were almost the same age. Delyn acted like Lars was the man to be: studying everything he did as if that was the only way to live. And Lars had come towards treating Delyn like a younger brother, giving him advice and acting as a tutor.

Delyn sheathed his sword, falling into step beside Lars. It was pretty ambitious of them to travel alone together: Imp was travelling with two others that had proved how competent they were by taking on Lars' previous group by themselves, with barely any of Imp's help.

I just need to get Imp alone again. I don't know how many gummies she has...but if I can get her alone with Delyn and I, we have a good chance of capturing her.

With those encouraging thoughts Lars set off on the trail, Delyn walking beside him like a dog and his master.

"It all started six years ago." Imp began her tale, her eyes serious and morose, voice quiet and sad, "The government was conducting testing. They were testing how they could defeat the Flavours. At first it was a just a dream. Something that most people thought wasn't possible. Some scientists would try, but it was in vain. The others would laugh at them, calling them crazy, even if they wished that something like that could be created.

"But the government finally took interest when a human being was donated. She was nine years old at the time, and her father no longer wanted her. The government gratefully accepted her, oblivious to that fact that she didn't want to be tested on. They only cared about her father's decision, and her feelings didn't matter.

"The girl was used for minor experiments, testing out new medications and new breakthroughs when they couldn't find people stupid enough to willingly try them. She was nothing more than a common lab rat." Imp said a little bitterly, but she composed herself almost immediately, continuing in the same monotone.

"She wasn't needed for another year. The government was still brainstorming how they could create a weapon to use against the Flavours. The idea was suggested by one of the keepers of the girl, who had noticed that she was having a lot of nightmares, and fits during which she would scream strange things about her past."

Pheonix shivered. Now she got it. This wasn't Flavour intelligence gained from spying. This was Imp's past.

"They thought that these fits could help their research. So they monitored her, day and night, testing out different methods to cause a fit. They ignored how much the fits tortured her, how much she thrashed and screamed... They didn't even realise that they were the ones that had been the initial cause of the fits, a reaction to something they had implanted into her during a past experiment. But that's not important to this tale.

"For one whole year this continued, an ordeal that seemed to last much longer to the girl. There were so many attempts to escape the cruel doctors, all met by a painful hand. It didn't take long for the girl to become so exhausted she turned into nothing more than emotionless husk, submitting to their orders. All she wanted was for it to end, to curl up in a corner and die."

Imp's voice trailed off, and for a second she seemed to be lost in thought, as if contemplating the horrible treatment she had received.

"The scientists slowly began to unravel the secrets of dreams and nightmares. They needed to discover how to induce nightmares on human targets. Can you imagine? A tool that could stop someone in their tracks, forcing them into a state where they imagine their nightmares, their greatest fears, into reality? Do you even realise how terrible a weapon that would be?

"Prototype 1 was created. It was pill, that, when eaten, would cause slumber and nightmares. But they couldn't use that as a weapon. Perhaps as a torture tool, but not a weapon in real battle. They needed something that could cause nightmares from afar, without needing to force the target to do anything.

"It was only when they were shipping the girl off to a more advanced lab did she get a chance to escape. The truck was driven by a traitor, a kind woman who had always treated the girl with gentleness, the only one who was at her side when the nightmares started to merge into reality. This woman brought the girl to the FTA, where she learned how to be a Flavour.

Imp's eyes suddenly grew bright, despite the darkness as light fell.

"The government has almost completed the weapon, and they're shipping it off to the capital for final testing and completion. That's my mission. I need to destroy it."

They spent a restless night plagued with nightmares. They were gone before the sun even rose.

By mid-afternoon they could hear the river, hidden from their view by trees. Within an hour they had come beside it, admiring the crystal clear waters.

After two days of travelling along the river, the novelty of it ran out.

At first Imp, Pheonix and Moss had been amazed and overjoyed about being able to spend time beside the river, walking beside it as it gurgled along. Whenever the going got warm, they'd dip their feet into the cool water, looking for fossils as they chewed on stale jerky. The river had become their companion: a gurgling, enjoyable companion that would playfully spray them with water when they got too close.

But eventually the fun ended. It became stressful when pebbles would skitter under their feet and they would almost lose their balance. Sometimes the river would turn into a muddy bank and the going would get tough. The mud would stick to their shoes and boots, sometimes nearly pulling them off their feet, and forcing them to scrape off huge amounts of mud before they could start to move again. Often Moss' socks would get dirty: Pheonix and Imp's feet were more protected, but their feet became extra heavy and hard to move when they finished walking through the mud. Mist coming off the river would chill them instead of invigorating them, and tempers rose. The only thing that kept Moss and Pheonix from fighting with each other was the threat of Imp's stick, which she clung on to like it was a lifeline.

They found the first destroyed safe house three days later.

Where the safe house should've been was a black crater of burnt wood. Little pieces were strewn everywhere across the valley, almost as if it had been blown up from the inside. A mattress had flown halfway across the clearing, some cabinet drawers were in pieces in a pile far away from the original site.

"It looks like some kind of bomb." Pheonix murmured sadly, gazing at the pieces. It almost looked as if she was trying to put the safe house back together with mind power alone, "Why would someone do something like that? There must be a traitor!"

Imp was extremely pale, her eyes intense on the pieces, almost as if she were scanning it for something. "I don't think a Flavour did this."

"What?" Moss exclaimed, "But who, then? No Police could get in there, right?"

Imp was silent.

Moss ground his teeth. "You know something, don't you Imp? Why won't you ever tell us anything?! Are we not trust-worthy enough for your tastes, or something?!"

Imp was still silent. Her brow furrowed. She began to move towards the safe house, looking around for Police.

Moss turned to Pheonix. "This is upsetting!" He complained, "Why does she have to keep everything to herself?"

"Don't be such a baby." Pheonix told him half-heartedly. She was watching Imp pick through the destroyed house.

Imp looked up at them, her blue eyes serious. She gestured for them to come.

"Oh, now she wants to talk to us." Moss grumbled.

As they got closer, Imp knelt down and began rubbing the burnt grass absent-mindedly.

"What is it, Imp?" Pheonix asked, kneeling down beside her.

"I didn't tell you the whole story last night." Imp ripped out a charred piece of grass, crumbling it in between her fingers. Pheonix and Moss were silent. They had learned that Imp didn't like to be questioned.

"The government is being slightly hypocritical with this weapon." Imp explained, "It's a gummy. A nightmare gummy."

"That's very nice, Imp, but what does that have to do with this?!" Moss exclaimed, gesturing towards the burnt house.

"Everything." Imp said simply, "Safe houses work by law magic. The reason only Flavours can enter safe houses is because of chaos magic contained in the gummies, and the fact that they are supporters of a different belief, and the Police are trying to squash that belief. Usually chaos magic and law magic can't react together."

"Thanks for the lesson in magic, but we already knew that." Moss answered sarcastically.

"That's not the point." Imp sounded frustrated, "Safe houses work for Flavours because the law magic in them is created in a way to allow chaos magic inside. That's the beauty of law magic: it's neutral, and if it's used right it can allow it's complete opposite to be protected by it. It's neutral, like all powers should be."

"I still don't get it." Pheonix moaned, "What are you trying to get at?"

Imp sighed. "The government has created a gummy to use against Flavours. Safe houses protect Flavours because of law magic, despite the chaos magic in the gummies."

Pheonix gasped in horror, understanding finally setting in.

"I'm still confused." Moss muttered crossly.

Imp looked at Moss, her eyes intense. "Any Police carrying a Nightmare gummy can get into safe houses. They're going to destroy us by getting rid of our safe points."

"Oh." Moss went pale, his brown eyes huge, "That's not good."

They decided to spend the night next to the ruins of the safe house.

They had set up a small camp far enough from the ruins to feel comfortable. The trees around the clearing provided plenty of shelter from the wind, and the river nearby was soothing. It would have been a beautiful setting: sleeping under the stars, a gentle river nearby, no wind, but the fact that there was such horrible destruction in the same clearing wrecked the ambience.

They quietly settled into their sleeping bags, worried that speaking would wreck the fragile peace, or somehow insult the sobering wreckage.

It was around midnight that Imp woke up.

She woke up alert, listening for sounds. She vaguely felt that something was wrong, almost as if she were being watched.

She kept lying down, trying to see through the dark, looking for some kind of movement. But her eyes were taking a while to adjust. She tried blinking up a storm, but she could barely see past where Pheonix was laying down, a couple of feet away. After that, it was completely dark.

Imp began to sweat. She had woken up many times this way, believing that there was some kind of monster beyond the shadows. But that had been just a slight feeling of malaise, a feeling of unreality, which, despite knowing that there was nothing there, was enough to resist falling asleep just so that that imaginary being didn't attack while your eyes were closed. This feeling felt more real, as if there was a palpable threat beyond her imagination.

I don't like this at all, Imp thought, shivering despite herself.

She tried to see into the shadows, finally deciding that lying down would just disadvantage her if whatever it was tried to attack. She struggled to get up, trying to untangle her arms from the sleeping bag.

Suddenly a hand was felt on the back of her neck. A painful electrical shock racked her body. Imp groaned in pain as her world faded to complete blackness.

Chapter 14

Imp's eyes fluttered open. She groaned in pain, a splitting headache forming deep in her skull. She was face down on the ground, her arms tied together behind her back. She tried to roll over, but icy gloved hands positioned her back into a face down position.

"Don't try to move." A chilling voice warned.

"Why are you being such a jerk, Snow?" A female voice asked. The voice sounded like someone who was standing right next to Imp, looking down on her. Sure enough, Imp could see a pair of boarder shoes from the corner of her eye.

"He has the right to be a jerk!" A male voice said, this one talking so fast it almost sounded like gibberish, "They destroyed a safe house!"

"No we didn't!" Pheonix cried, and Imp turned her head to see a bound Pheonix lying beside her. Imp could almost see a bit of Moss' hair behind Pheonix, "Why won't you listen?! We're Flavours, we would never do such a thing!"

"It's no use, Pheonix." Moss grumbled, "They're too damn stubborn."

"Trust me." A different female voice said, sounding threatening, "You're in no position to be insulting us." Imp could see a bit of golden hair, leaning over Moss. She heard him growl.

"Imp, why don't you try talking some sense into them?" Pheonix mumbled, turning her head towards Imp and gazing at her with her green eyes.

"Wait!" Another female voice exclaimed, and Imp was struck slightly by a sense of recognition, "Did you say Imp?"

Suddenly copper hair came into view, and Imp was staring into stormy eyes.

"Pyra!" Imp exclaimed, "Is that really you?"

Pyra's face turned into a grin. "Wow Imp, you sure get into a lot of bad situations, don't you?" Her eyes were sparkling.

Pyra was a friend from the FTA. She was the first one to talk to Imp, in a period when everyone had been afraid of her and when she had been constantly having fits. They had quickly become friends, but had split up when Pyra was assigned to a different group than Imp.

"You know her?" Yet another male voice asked, "How come you didn't notice who she was?!"

"Hey! It's hard to tell who they are when people are unconscious!" Pyra said, temporarily looking up at someone. She moved out of Imp's sight. Suddenly, the rope around Imp's wrists began to loosen.

"Are you sure we can trust them?" The frosty voice asked.

"Positive!" Pyra chirped.

"Oh, alright." The voice answered.

The binds let go completely, and Imp kneeled, rubbing her wrists. Now that she could get a good view of the group, she saw six members, including Pyra. Pyra was working on Pheonix's binds, and Moss was being assisted by the golden-haired girl.

Six Flavours were strewn around the small clearing, all with different expressions on their faces. Standing beside Imp, staring disinterestedly at her feet was a girl with black hair and blue streaks. She had a huge silver butterfly on her black shirt, sparkling every time it caught the sun.

Standing next to this girl was who Imp assumed was the one who spoke with such a chilling voice. She guessed that he was the one who was named Snow, mostly due to his snow white hair, black and white clothes, and black leather gloves. He met her gaze with arctic blue eyes; and, for one of the few times in her life, Imp was the first to look away. He was a Mint Flavour, based on his aura.

The one untying Moss had hair that reached to her back. Imp couldn't see her eyes, although the rest of her extravagant outfit was very apparent. She was wearing a skirt, something very unusual for a Flavour.

Another was standing beside a dying fire, moving up and down slightly, like he was vibrating. He had brown, slightly curly, hair, and a long yellow-orange scarf that seemed to tangle at his legs, though it probably looked really cool in battle. He never stopped moving, no matter how long Imp watched him.

The last male of the group was sitting on the ground, staring at Imp. He smiled slightly when he caught her looking, and Imp furrowed her brow in confusion. He had a blue tuque with a brand logo on it, looking like one of Delyn's logos. His green sweater had the same design on it, and she noticed that his feet, adorned with black and red flip-flops, were full of dirt.

Last was Pyra. She was wearing a similar outfit to the one that she had been wearing last time Imp saw her. Her hair had stayed the same curly copper, reaching to her shoulders. She was wearing a red halter top, a black fanny pack was tied around one leg. Imp knew that that was where she stored her explosive objects, her specialty as a Cinnamon Flavour.

"Sorry about that!" The golden haired one said as Imp stood up, "You surprised us. I'm Aqua."

Blueberry, Aqua's aura was a vivid blue.

Imp shook her hand, and Aqua moved on to introduce herself to Pheonix and Moss. Pyra came beside Imp, giving her a fierce hug.

"I can't believe we've finally found each other again!" She exclaimed, "How long has it been? About two years?"

"That's about right." Imp confirmed, smiling.

"Wow." Pyra whistled, "Way too long. Here, I'll introduce you to everybody."

Pyra pointed at the silent one. "This is Snow. He's kinda quiet."

So Imp had been right. Snow offered her a black gloved hand, but he didn't say anything.

"I'm Dustorocks." The brand-loving one walked up, giving Imp a dazzling smile.

Chocolate...Earth, It explained all the dirt on his feet.

"We call him Dusty." Pyra whispered in Imp's ear.

"Hmmm..." Dusty looked thoughtful, gazing into Imp's eyes long enough for her to feel uncomfortable, then suddenly gazing up at the sky, "Do you know why the sky is so gray?"

"Uhhh...Why?" Imp asked, expecting a joke.

"Because all the blue is in your eyes." Dusty said, once again smiling at her.

"Uhhh...Thanks?" Imp answered, completely oblivious. Dusty looked disappointed as Pyra quickly directed Imp towards another member of the group.

"This is Aria." She said as she gestured towards the butterfly-shirted one. Aria waved, though she got distracted halfway through by a fluttering piece of fluff. Imp didn't have time to read her aura before she chased the fluff away.

Last but certainly not least was Tric. When he was talking, Imp had to concentrate on making out what he was saying. He talked too fast. Pyra explained that he was a Lemon Flavour, Electricity, which was what caused his hyper activity.

"Welcome to SOFT." Pyra smiled, "Special Ops Flavour Travellers. Dusty obviously came up with the name."

"Cool." Was all Imp could say.

"You might as well stay for supper." Aqua said from her position on the log, stoking the fire into life, "We didn't bring your packs with us, so I sent Tric to go get them. It'll take a while for him to get back, but it would probably have taken you longer to go get them. He runs so fast, it's scary. Too energetic." She rubbed a spot beside her, which Moss promptly took. She looked at him in confusion for a moment, but quickly went back to playing around with the ashes with a stick, until Dusty brought over a couple logs and twigs and got it going.

Tric returned with their packs as supper was finished cooking. It was a simple stew, but Aqua had added some spices to make it tastier.

"So," Asked Pyra, looking at Imp, "What are you guys doing?"

"I'm heading towards the capital." Imp replied immediately.

How come it was so hard to tell us that, but as soon as Pyra asks she gets answers? Moss wondered sourly.

"Why?" Pyra's eyes were full of curiosity.

"That's a secret." Imp got a pained look on her face, almost as if she were extremely disappointed that she couldn't tell Pyra.

"Imp." Snow said slowly and coolly, "We are...SOFT." He winced at the name.

Imp was silent, waiting for him to continue.

"Special Ops Flavour Travellers. We're in charge of investigating how the safe houses are being destroyed. I believe that you have some valuable information about that, so we need you to tell us." Snow's pale blue eyes were intent.

Imp bit her bottom lip. She didn't like giving out information like that. The only reason Pheonix and Moss knew was because she trusted them. She trusted Pyra, but the rest of the group...She wasn't sure about them yet.

"Oh, for Pete's sake." Moss grumbled, "If you won't tell them I'll tell them." He glared at Imp. She glared back with equal venom.

"She's travelling to the capital to destroy a weapon that the government is using to destroy safe houses." Pheonix spoke up.

"Not exactly." Imp sighed, "I think they're just testing out the weapon by destroying the safe houses. They created it mainly to fight against Flavours."

"But how did they get in the safe house?" Pyra asked, looking confused, "I know my explosions, and the house was definitely blown up from the inside."

"It's a gummy." Imp answered, "A Nightmare gummy. Do I really need to explain this? I already had to explain this to Pheonix and Moss."

"We had theories." Dusty said, looking straight into Imp's eyes and smiling slightly, "We knew that it had to do with chaos magic. I thought of that theory by myself."

"No you didn't!" Aria exclaimed, bonking Dusty's tuqued head, "Tric did! Stop trying to show off!" Imp looked at Tric, recently returned, who grinned cheesily and gave her a thumbs-up. Even though he was sitting down, he still was in motion, swinging his legs and seeming to bounce off the log.

"Owww..." Dusty complained, rubbing his head.

"Yeah." Pyra nodded, ignoring Dusty's pain, "We had a basic idea of what the weapon needed to have to work like that. It was either chaos magic or something impervious to law magic."

"We're headed to the capital too." Aqua smiled, "You could travel with us for a while. Strength in numbers."

"I like that." Moss grinned.

"It would be a good opportunity to get to know each other better." Dusty looked at Imp, winking.

"Don't be an idiot." Aria groaned, hitting Dusty in the shoulder. Imp was starting to see a lot of similarities between Pheonix and Aria, "Why must you flirt with every new girl?"

Imp looked completely confused.

"You didn't notice?" Pyra grinned, desperately trying to contain her laughter, "He was flirting with you the whole time!"

Imp's face went beet red.

"She didn't notice?" Dusty looked like he was about to cry, "I can't believe she didn't notice..."

Chapter 15

It didn't take long for Dusty to recover from his failure at flirting with Imp.

For a while he vainly hoped that maybe now that Imp was aware that he was flirting with her she might actually hook up with him. Instead she remained oblivious and a bit more wary of him. She was avoiding him, and it hurt for a while. That lasted for a day, during which Pyra and Imp would share tales of their adventures, with Moss shyly trying to get to know Aqua better, and Pheonix just generally chatting with everybody, especially Aria. They seemed to get along quite well.

By day two Dustorocks had moved on. This time his target was Pheonix. Aria had warned Pheonix of Dusty's general attempts to flirt with every girl, and she was ready. His first move was met with a fist, causing a chipped tooth, and a whole day of moaning on Dusty's part.

The next and final attempt ended with a kick to the groin and a punch to the face, which managed to keep Dusty quiet for the rest of the trip.

Imp was quickly discovering that travelling with SOFT was going to be a loud and tiring ordeal.

But at least watching Dusty get beat up is funny.

Imp had tried to get to know everyone in the group better. Aqua, she discovered, was a very motherly character. In the morning she would nag at people to make sure they ate. It got annoying, but it paid off when they were more energized and had to take less breaks. She also had a tendency to sing under her breath and to play with people's hair.

Tric was hard to understand. Imp had trouble keeping up with how he spoke, because he spoke really quickly. But he was good at making jokes, and his energy was kind of catchy. He would always give high fives to everyone, and would give thumbs up randomly.

Snow...He was quiet. Imp couldn't really get much out of him. He was sometimes a little annoying with his uncaring, annoyed-at-everything attitude, but Imp learned from Pyra that he was really skilled in battle.

Aria was a bit of an air-head. She had a short attention span. She was quite friendly to everyone, and she loved to talk. She would sometimes hit people when she was angry, although it was usually Dusty that was the victim of her rage.

The reason Dusty was constantly getting beaten was because he made corny jokes, usually ones at the expense of Aria. He would also come up with random nicknames for things. He called Imp 'Blue' for some strange reason. Imp had to admit that he was quite nice when he stopped flirting.

Last was Pyra. Pyra hadn't changed much since Imp had last seen her. She was still an optimist at heart, and loved to laugh. Observant, she was usually the first one to warn everyone of a sound, though it always ended up being a jogger or backpacker following the trail.

Imp was quickly learning how easy it was to feel at home with SOFT. Despite the strange nickname and tough-sounding occupation, they were all quite friendly and inviting. They didn't seem exactly...competent. Usually detectives had this kind of serious air to them. The only one who would fit that description was Snow.

That will probably all change in battle, Imp reminded herself, *Usually the most fierce ones in battle are the most docile out of it. It's misleading.*

Imp knew for sure that Pyra was a tough one to beat. She was an expert in bombs: she had trained herself to ignite things from a distance. Sometimes it was leaves, sometimes it was paper. Anything combustible. She would just have to throw this object at an unsuspecting person, then blow it up in their face. Imp had only ever seen her use her Special once: Pyra would form bombs out of pure fire that, when thrown, would cause a huge explosion.

I can't wait to see how the others fight. Hopefully I won't have to see them though.

That reminded Imp of Lars. How far behind was he? He probably had spent a day in Diyo restocking his supplies and forming a plan. Maybe he had waited another day for reinforcements? She never knew with Lars, which is what made him so dangerous. He was too unpredictable. The only constant with him was his pursuit of Imp.

Lars swore under his breath.

He and Delyn had finally caught up with Imp only to discover that she had gained an even bigger following.

"It's no use." Delyn murmured, "There's too many of them..."

Their numbers had gone up to 9. Nine against two weren't great odds, especially when one of those two had never gone into real combat against Flavours before.

"There's a town nearby." Lars ground his teeth in frustration, "We'll grab a car, travel to Otta and get some reinforcements. A big group."

A plan was already forming in his head. Delyn looked at him with adoring eyes as Lars thought.

"Let's go." He gestured to Delyn, walking off to where they had come from.

I'll get her, Lars thought, *This time I'll definitely catch her.*

"Lars?" Delyn suddenly said, looking at him with his brown eyes, "What's your plan?"

Lars grinned a devilish grin, "That's a secret."

"It's almost complete, sir." Lorch said to General Salem.

"Excellent." General Salem grinned, showing sparkling white teeth, "But where is Lars?"

"No one knows." Lorch sighed, "He last checked in at the small town of Diyo, but he left quickly before we could contact him."

Salem harrumphed. That was troublesome. They needed him soon. The prototype was going through final testing before they could officially use it as a weapon against the Flavours.

The safe house destructions had been part of the plan to test the prototype. But the man who had been in control of the gummy had gone crazy, killing himself after only destroying six safe houses.

The scientists were now too scared to test the gummy on humans. They didn't want to lose more testers. They were using human analogs, but it was proving difficult to program the computer brains to use its emotions. The brain thought like a human, but they hadn't yet discovered how to get true emotions out of it.

This was troubling because the reports indicated that the man had killed himself because of nightmares he was having. If they couldn't get the brain to react to its emotions, no matter how realistic and sophisticated its internal organ imitations were it just wouldn't get the right test results.

Salem ground his teeth in frustration. They had heard rumours that the Flavours were planning something big at the capital. The government didn't know what, but they were certain that they needed to stop it before it happened.

But we need to get the prototype testing done before we can use it. We're running out of time.

"What do you think caused our dear tester to kill himself?" Salem asked, almost to himself.

"I'm not sure." Lorch replied, "We think it was either the chaos magic, or just a huge amount of stress. We're doing research into whether he had been affected by mental problems before he became an eligible tester, but we aren't sure if that's the problem."

"You never know with the donated ones." Salem sounded disappointed.

They'd finally gotten the desired effect that the gummy would have on others, and now this setback. At this rate the gummy wouldn't be finished in time.

Right now it was sitting in the middle of Otta's lab after being moved from Tiyuk. The journey had been slow and tenuous, because the mix couldn't be shaken around too much. They were worried that it would somehow disrupt the ingredients and cause the mixture to lose its desired effect. But they had finally made it to Otta and unloaded the mixture.

There they had created copies of it, turning the liquid into an actual gummy by moulding it into shape by hand. That had been another hard thing to do, because the mixture had a tendency to just fall apart. But after much handling it eventually became a blob that could pass for some kind of candy.

Then the gummies had passed into the hands of the tester, who was accompanied by Police as he went to different safe houses. Bombs were laid in the houses, and the explosions that followed were nothing short of spectacular. Even General Salem, the veteran of many explosions, was impressed.

But now they had a major setback to deal with.

We need more time.

The issue was found three days later.

"General Salem!" Lorch cried as he burst into the General's office, "We've found the problem!"

Lorch was little surprised to find Lars sitting in a chair across from Salem, with another boy sitting beside Lars. This one looked about the same age as Lars, with curious and slightly nervous brown eyes and sandy hair.

"That's great news!" Salem beamed, "Let me introduce you to the newest member of Imp's hunting group! Lorch, this is Delyn." He gestured at the boy.

"Nice to meet you." Delyn smiled a little, not offering his hand. Lars was as serious as ever, his grey eyes piercing Lorch.

Lorch answered with his pleasantries, then he turned to Salem. "It seems that the cause of the tester's madness was because there was a madness gene in the DNA we used as a base for the gummy." Lorch smiled grandly, "You know that girl, Siria? Anyway—"

"Siria?!" Delyn exclaimed, standing up so quickly he knocked over his chair. Lars visibly started, thought whether from Delyn's sudden movement or the mention of Siria was unknown to Lorch.

"Uh, yes." Lorch looked a little frightened, "I believe her name was Siria. Her father donated her because she was mentally unstable, and had tried to kill him. She tried to deny it." Lorch chuckled, "But she had the look of someone who had seen murder. So we took her in and tested on her. Turns out she had a lot of nightmares that greatly helped our research."

Delyn looked like he was about to be sick. Lars' face was as impassive as ever, but his eyes were calculating and confused.

"Then that means that we can continue with the production?" Salem asked eagerly, looking sideways at Lars and Delyn. He didn't understand their reaction.

"Yes." Lorch answered, adjusting his glasses, "If all goes well, we can destroy the madness gene in the DNA. We should be ready by the time the Flavours get here."

"Excellent." Salem grinned, "Incidentally, Lars has some info on the Flavours and a plan to stop them before they reach the capital." He nodded towards Lars, "Go on."

Lars looked from Lorch to Salem, his eyes serious once more. "I do have a plan, but I need a lot of people for it. How many can you muster within a day?"

"This is the capital of the country, and the headquarters for the entire military." The General got a malicious smile on his face, "You can take as many as you need."

"Good." Lars grinned, and Delyn couldn't help but smile also. "I'm setting a trap."

Chapter 16

"Fentek is next." Aqua said, pointing to its location on the map, "Do we need to stop for supplies?"

"I think we'll be fine." Snow answered in his slow, cold voice.

"Then next stop is Otta!" Pyra grinned, "This is so exciting!"

They were close, and Imp was beginning to feel excitement and apprehension. Only another week more until they arrived in Otta, if all went well.

But why is Lars so quiet? Imp frowned, *I don't like this at all!*

"Why are you frowning, Imp?" Pyra asked, playfully punching her in the arm, "Cheer up! We're almost at Otta!"

"I'm worried—"

"Don't be!" Pyra grinned, "We're making good headway! Nothing could go wrong!"

Imp scowled. That was one disadvantage to Pyra's optimism. She was so optimistic that she never stopped to take a look at the harsh reality of things. She would just skip over it like it was a commercial break in a great TV show.

"Maybe Imp's right." Pheonix murmured half-heartedly, "Last time she had misgivings we ignored her and forced her to stop worrying. Then she almost got captured by Lars and his goonies."

"Still." Pyra shrugged, stubborn as always.

"We'll be on the look-out." Tric reassured her with a smile, "I have great hearing!"

"I thought you were just incredibly hyper." Aqua remarked.

"Don't be such a hobo!" Tric replied with a mocking grin.

"Me?! A hobo?!" Aqua lunged at Tric, who dodged easily out of the way, screaming his head off like a little girl. Imp giggled, covering her face with her hand.

Why do I always get stuck with the crazy groups? Snow sighed.

"Can we get moving?" Aria asked, tapping her foot to an unknown beat, "Daylight doesn't last forever, you know!"

"Smart as always, Aria." Dusty grinned at her.

"Don't even try." Aria warned, punching Dusty's arm.

"Oww." Dusty murmured half-heartedly.

"Aria's right." Moss said, ignoring Tric's screams and Aqua's yells of anger, "If we want to make it to the capital in good time, we should get going. Plus, we don't want to give Lars any time to catch up with us."

"Wow, Moss." Pheonix remarked, her eyes wide and full of innocence, "You're actually thinking!"

"Don't be a jerk!" Moss cried, glaring at Pheonix.

WHACK!

The sound echoed against the trees, along with the sound of the branch clattering on the ground. Pheonix and Moss cried out in pain in harmony, falling as if in slow motion. They landed on their faces, still conscious but in a lot of pain.

It became very silent in the clearing, all of SOFT looking at Imp or Pheonix and Moss with shocked expressions on their faces. Imp grinned.

"The deal was that you wouldn't fight." She shrugged, her innocent smile tinged with maliciousness, "You did, so here's the stick."

Pheonix groaned, moving into a kneeling position. She was rubbing her head, in the spot where Imp's branch had so expertly struck. She could already feel a bump rising, and a headache forming. Moss followed her, looking very, very hurt emotionally.

Moss rubbed his head, tears in his eyes. "Now I know how Dusty feels."

"Join the club." Dusty sighed as he helped Moss to his feet.

One day away from Fentek, night fell and the group decided to stop.

Moss immediately collapsed, tired, onto the ground. Others sat down for a bit to catch their breath, while Tric just immediately strode off to find firewood.

"Too much energy." Aqua sighed, taking in deep breaths. Imp agreed, nodding because her throat hurt too much.

They had run for the whole afternoon, preoccupied with getting to Fentek quickly, and eventually, moving on to Otta. It was easy to plan out that they would run for the trip, less easy once they actually got to it. With such a large group, they would sometimes stumble into and over each other. Tric was always a few metres ahead of them, trying to encourage them. It seemed more like he was mocking them. They were all grumpy by the time they had set up camp, but it was obvious that most were pleased with having gotten so far.

They sat around the fire for a while, making small talk. The most tired ones went to bed early, curling up in their sleeping bags. Imp was one of them.

She had always found it easier to fall asleep when others were still awake. Somehow the thought of her being the only one up would cause her to panic. But, hearing the reassuring murmur of voices and seeing the light from the fire was enough to calm her down. She burrowed deep into her sleeping bag, her cocoon of warmth. She tried to listen to some of their conversations for a bit. Eventually sleep came to her, and she welcomed it with open arms.

That night she slept one of the most restful and peaceful nights of her life.

It was a quiet trip by car from Salem's office to Fentek. Lars was in his calculation mode, sitting quietly in his seat, looking out the window in deep thought. Delyn sat behind him, clearly uncomfortable. His mother had had a car, but definitely nothing as fancy as this one.

It looked like a run-of-the-mill white SUV from the outside, except for the Police decals painted onto the black door sides. The doors slid open like a sports car, rising so that they looked like giant bird's wings ready for takeoff.

Inside, one of the walls was completely covered in TV screens. Three of them showed the news, most likely available to show different stations if need be. The biggest one had a giant webcam attached to the top. It was blank now, but Delyn had no doubt that it would probably fill the whole car with light when it turned on. The driver and passengers were separated by a black, soundproof glass wall. Delyn had seen this wall appear to magically retract into the floor.

The other wall was lined with windows, like that of a plane, and seats arranged in a straight line beside each one. These chairs could swivel, and for a good part of the trip Delyn had experimented with them.

It reminded Delyn of a demented cross between a limo and an army vehicle.

Next thing I know, Lars is gonna tell me that there's some kind of Jacuzzi in the back, Delyn scoffed at the idea so loudly that Lars looked away from his window.

"What is it?" Lars asked, swivelling his seat and piercing Delyn with his eyes. He was still in calculating mode, looking as if he was only going to half pay attention to Delyn's answer.

"Uh, nothing." Delyn murmured.

Lars looked at him for a second more, then turned his seat back into normal position.

Usually when Lars is like this he ignores every sound around him, Delyn pondered, *I bet he paid attention just so that he could use the swivel seats.*

Lars was silent for a while longer, in an intense examination of the countryside. He would occasionally frown at something, then his brow would smooth and he'd smile a little. From the way General Salem had treated him, Delyn had the feeling that Lars was some kind of child prodigy.

But what was that about experimenting on Siria? Delyn frowned, mirroring Lars' current facial expression.

The night before, Delyn had had trouble sleeping. He was thinking about what Lorch said.

So Siria wasn't lying about being abandoned by her father...She mentioned some kind of testing on her, and Lorch proved that. But according to Lorch, she had tried to kill her father. Everyone in Diyo was told by him that she ran away. I don't get it! Who do I believe? I don't even know if I can trust Siria anymore. Her father is obviously a liar in every way that you look at it. It would be pointless for Lorch to lie, but he might have been misled by Siria's father. Ugh! Delyn though in frustration, *This is so confusing! I wish I had Lars' intelligence to figure this all out.*

The rest of the trip was in complete silence. Lars fleshed out his plan in a cool, calculating way, while Delyn struggled to understand his Siria dilemma.

After two hours of driving they arrived in Fentek, parking beside the Police-run hotel that they would be staying at. Lars immediately sprang out, looking back at the other troop cars that arrived soon after them.

They granted me 18 men, Lars thought excitedly, *18 men! Imp will be caught in no time. And if all goes well, I'll have most of the other Flavours too.*

Now Lars' group outnumbered the Flavours by twice their numbers, and that wasn't even including Lars and Delyn. Nine to twenty. The odds of capturing Imp were so high they even made Lars excited. The odds of capturing more than half their group were spectacular. Lars loved odds.

I've finally won, Lars grinned.

Delyn came to stand uncertainly by Lars, watching the mini-army come flooding out of the SUVs.

So many of them, Delyn thought, his eyes wide, *The Flavours don't stand a chance!*

Delyn felt bubbly and excited inside. This was his chance to see that Imp was captured. This was his chance for her to redeem herself, and come back to him. Maybe then she could support the Police, be his number one fan, and be there at home when he got back from his work. Maybe they could be friends again.

"Are you ready, Delyn?" Lars asked, turning to his apprentice, "This is our final chance to stop Imp before she reaches the capital."

Delyn nodded, smiling slightly. At this rate, capturing Imp would be a piece of cake. This 'special mission' by Imp was undoubtedly a bad thing for the Police. She must be stopped at all costs, and Delyn was willing to do anything for the cause. She might have been his best friend, but that was before she turned to the evil side. He barely knew her anymore.

"Let's start laying the trap." Lars walked away towards the forest, where a trail along the river was hidden. A bag was slung over his shoulder, and even Delyn didn't know what was inside.

I don't know what you're planning, Lars, but I hope it works!

Delyn followed after him, ready to help with anything his master asked. Even if Delyn had no idea what the plan was, he trusted Lars. He trusted Lars' experience with Flavours, especially Imp. He trusted Lars' plans to capture Imp, even if he had never been involved in one. That kind of blind confidence was what made Delyn so useful, yet so incredibly stupid.

It only took a couple hours to set up the trap.

Lars already had something in mind, he just needed to find the right spot to set it up. Once he did find it, though, the real work began. It took them a whole three hours to set up, night having long since fallen by the time they had finished.

Tomorrow, Imp, Lars thought as he crashed onto his bed in his hotel room, *Tomorrow I'll finally capture you.*

Chapter 17

The day started well.

After a tasty breakfast of spicy stewed beef jerky, everyone was energized and in a good mood. Even Snow was a little more talkative than usual, and Imp actually managed to have a small conversation with him.

They ate lunch. At this point they were in line with Fentek. Sometimes they could glimpse buildings through spaces in the trees, and a couple of times they would have to hide to avoid joggers using the trail.

Then things began to go wrong.

Aria was the first to hear them. The sound of marching footsteps, faint at first, but quickly rising in a crescendo. Most of SOFT had already slung their packs over their backs, their things safely stored in them. They already had their gummies in their hand, ready for action before Imp had even processed what was happening.

Imp swore under her breath, her hand in her pack. The fresh pack of gummies that Pheonix had supplied her weighed heavily in her pocket. She took one in her hand, ready to pop it into her mouth at a moment's notice.

The footsteps were getting louder and louder, and there was no doubt that they knew where the group was.

I smell Lars behind this, Imp groaned.

The group formed a circle, their unprotected backs to each other and faces turned to every possible angle. Even if the Police obviously hadn't gone for a sneak attack, the Flavours weren't going to let themselves be snuck upon.

It was quiet, the only sound being the faraway stomping.

From the corner of her eye Imp saw a bush rustle. She cried out in warning as a dart flew, and Pheonix incinerated it before it could hit anyone.

As if the dart was a signal, Police came flooding out from the woods, armed with a plethora of different weapons. Imp couldn't count them all: they moved around so quickly. But she knew that there were a lot of them.

She practically swallowed her gummy, turning invisible as a sword-wielder came at her. He only momentarily paused in confusion: the next second he was on the ground, knocked over by a leg swipe by Imp. He tried to get back up, but Tric was there, his hands enveloped in lightning. One quick touch to the neck knocked the swordsman out. Tric thumbed up in a random direction, missing Imp entirely.

An arrow whizzed past Imp and she looked up, spotting a bow woman in a tree. She would be hard to get to up there.

Obviously not for Snow. As the archer took aim, a sliver of ice knocked it from her hand. Another expertly aimed sliver pinned her sleeve to the tree, her bow clattering to the ground. She struggled, only resulting in her quiver slipping from her back dumping the arrows downward. Three more ice daggers followed, and the woman was completely pinned from her sleeves and pant legs.

Unnatural ice doesn't thaw for a long time, Imp thought in satisfaction. The ice would only thaw once Snow lost control of it. That would take a while.

Pyra was having no difficulty, either. Imp watched as a leaf fluttered beside an unsuspecting dagger dual-wielder, the next second exploding into scarlet flame. Her hair singed, the dual-wielder stumbled back, easily taken out by a kick to the head from Imp. Imp grinned at Pyra, but she had forgotten that she was invisible. Pyra ran off to face another enemy.

Imp took out another bow woman easily, sneaking up on her from behind and bashing her on her head. The woman crumpled and Imp rubbed her fist. It was stinging, but it had done its work. That woman had a hard head.

An arrow of...air...? Something whizzed past Imp's head, narrowly missing her. The wind blasted into a swordsman, knocking him into the tree. He fell down, unconscious. Imp turned to see Aria, aiming what looked like a bow made of tiny swirling whirlwinds. As Imp watched, she took aim, an invisible arrow notched and ready to fire. Aria let her fingers slip, and Imp could no longer keep track of the arrow, until it blasted into one of the chain ball wielders. He was sent flying in the style of the swordsman, crashing into another Police with crushing force. Both of them were knocked unconscious instantly.

*Vanilla...*Imp thought, wondering why she hadn't figured it out sooner. Aria obviously had a double meaning, both a song and based off the word 'air'.

Suddenly the ground buckled, Imp almost losing her balance. She saw Pheonix and Moss stumble, while the SOFT members seemed so used to it they barely lost their footing. Imp nearly cried out as a huge rock dislodged itself, flying towards Dusty. It blasted to smithereens in front of him. The pieces floated for a second, suddenly jerked as if by puppets strings. They were drawn to Dusty's outstretched arm, coating his skin in tiny pieces of rock.

A dagger double wielder came at him, threatening him menacingly with her knives. He took a step forward, and she went to slash. He easily blocked the blow with his encased arm, moving it and punching her hard in the stomach. She crumpled immediately, spitting up bile. She fell to the ground, unmoving.

Where's Lars in all of this? Imp wondered, *I haven't seen him at all!*

Imp materialized, startling a bowman. He shot and she dodged, stumbling as another one of Dusty's rumbles shook the ground. The bowman aimed, and Imp desperately turned invisible, knowing that it wouldn't make a difference.

Suddenly a whip of water lashed out at the man, stinging his wrist. He dropped his bow and the water circled his body. He screamed as the water sent him flying, knocking over another bowman. Tric easily zapped them into unconsciousness.

Aqua stepped away from behind a tree, grinning in Imp's direction.

"Thank you." Imp said, smiling, even though Aqua couldn't see her. Aqua nodded, looking for more targets.

Now Imp understood how battles with Soft worked.

Tric is the one who cleans up the mess, knocking the ones not already unconscious out. Aqua and Pyra beat up the Police a little, enough to allow Tric to get to them. Dusty and Aria can knock enemies unconscious without any help. Snow immobilizes them. It's a good strategy, Imp thought, *They've obviously won many battles that way.*

Lars looked on at the battle, safely hidden behind a tree far enough away. He cursed under his breath.

Only ten minutes into the battle, and already half of his troops lay unconscious on the battle field. It was pathetic. He thought that he would be able to swarm the Flavours by sheer numbers, but he hadn't anticipated the new group's skill. They dispatched his men and women like they were flies, without even doing any permanent damage.

The situation was dire, and it was quickly getting worse.

I guess it's time for Stage 2.

Only three more to go! Imp thought giddily.

The Police were suffering a harsh defeat. Only three more of them stood tall: a dart-spitter, swordswoman, and chain ball wielder. The rest of the mini-army lay against trees, on the ground, or tangled up in Moss' roots. All were unconscious. The three survivors were huddled in a group, looking terrified. Their eyes dashed everywhere, their bodies shook, and some of them suffered from small burns, bruises or scratches. They were looking at the Flavours that surrounded them with fear in their eyes. Pretty pathetic for the Police.

"Retreat!" A voice called, and Imp jumped as she recognized it as Lars'. The three Police made a break for it, running past a surprised Aria. They nearly fell over each other as they ran.

So he is here, Imp thought, *I smell trouble.*

"That was anticlimactic." Pyra mumbled, clearly displeased that the battle had ended so quickly. Snow nodded beside her, losing the air of 'This is so much fun!' and slipping back into 'I'm so bored' mode. Even Tric looked a little crestfallen.

"I don't like this at all." Aqua frowned, ever the common sense of the group. She looked troubled, and Imp was put into even more doubt.

What are you planning, Lars?

Suddenly a smoking canister landed in the middle of the clearing, making everyone jump. It began to smoke, huge grey plumes. They floated towards the Flavours, tainting the air with a surprisingly odourless smell. Imp's eyes began to tear up, and only then did she realize what they were dealing with.

"Tear gas!" Tric yelled, an unpleasant warning that made everyone go pale.

"Scatter!" Aqua cried, coughing. She ran off into the trees, trying to get away from the choking gas. The rest of the group disintegrated, disappearing into the forest. Everyone's eyes were watering, and they were all coughing.

Imp followed Pyra, trying to see her red hair bobbing ahead of her through her blurring vision, coughing all the while. It didn't take long for Imp to lose track of her. Suddenly the red hair was gone, having disappeared between two brown blurs...trees. Imp was all alone.

Imp rested her back against a tree, rubbing desperately at her eyes. She tried opening them, but they were the same teary blur. She tried blinking ferociously. But the gas acted like onions, except ten times worse. No matter what she did, her eyes remained as blurry as they had been a second before.

She didn't notice Lars at first.

He was standing there, a blur of dark blue and brown. He was staring at her, that much she could tell, looking almost as if he was debating whether he should attack her or not. Imp froze, trying to see through her tear-blurred vision, just enough to make out the expression on his face, or at least what position he was in. She needed to see him well enough to foresee his movement.

Imp coughed, surprised to feel a liquid enter through her parched throat and splatter onto her hand. She tried to see what it was, but she could only make out a red blur on pale skin. Blood.

Lars was suddenly beside her, so close that she could see the expression on his face. He was frowning. Imp flinched, trying to move away from him, making her fall to the ground with her back to the tree. He loomed above her, the grey blurs of his eyes unreadable.

Imp's vision started to clear up. Now she could make out a nose within the blur of his face, but she was still coughing up blood. It wasn't much, she noticed as she looked at her hand, but it was enough to make her feel slightly dizzy.

"Don't move." Lars warned her, taking something silver from his belt. It looked like two circles...Handcuffs.

I need to get out of here!

"We need to talk." Imp spluttered, and she saw a crease form on Lars' hazy forehead.

"What?" He asked, obviously confused. He was staring down at this girl, spitting up blood and coughing like she was dying, and now she was making demands?

"Um...Look over there!" Imp yelled, pointing off in a random direction. She couldn't even see what she was pointing at.

"Honestly, Imp?" Lars sounded exasperated, almost as if he were about to start laughing, "That's the best you can d-"

Imp kicked his feet out from under him, reaching up. She felt a branch, using it to stand up again. She managed to pull herself up to the branch, turning invisible as Lars picked himself up. He swore under his breath, following her up the tree. She was already far ahead of him, climbing like she was some kind of crazed monkey.

I can't believe she tricked me like that! Lars thought angrily, *I can't believe it...How stupid am I?!*

Chapter 18

Lars followed Imp up the tree, cursing all the while.

She easily stayed a step ahead of him, climbing the tree like she was born to do it. Even though she was invisible, he could see and hear the branches bending under her weight. He vainly hoped that they'd snap and send her crashing to the ground, making his job of capturing her much easier.

Imp began to laugh, a soft sound that seemed to blend in with the sounds of the forest, almost like a bird's chirp. A branch high above him bent precariously, swinging up and down. It looked like she was swinging her legs, as if she was always up this high, being pursued by a Police officer.

Lars looked uncertainly at the ground. He was so high up! He could faintly see Delyn at the base of the tree. Or was it just a pile of leaves? Everything looked like colored blurs from this high up.

Don't be such a wuss! You're over-exaggerating! Lars scolded himself.

Imp's laughter died down, for a second sounding like the tree leaves rustling around her. It was quiet, her legs no longer swinging. She almost seemed to disappear, and no one would notice her if you hadn't known she was there in the first place. Lars listened to the wind whistling through the trees, feeling the warmth of the sun.

"Isn't this nice?" Imp asked softly, "The sun seems so close. The leaves sound like they're singing. You can hear a bird chirping, in the distance. It's perfect."

Alright, Lars thought, *This is definite proof that she's not all there in the head. C'mon, singing trees?!*

"The sun doesn't care about the Flavour rebellion. It just keeps shining, no matter what." Imp said thoughtfully, "Wouldn't that be nice? Knowing exactly what you have to do, day after day? It sounds monotonous, but if you make a bunch of people happy, why not?"

She went quiet. Lars inched up the tree, wincing whenever a branch bent too much for his taste. As if he could sneak up on her from this height. He was more likely to accidentally ram his head into her feet. That would hurt.

Apparently Imp decided that he got too close, because the branch unbent and she appeared, hovering beside where she had been sitting before. She regarded him with impassive eyes. She hovered into a sitting position, crossing her legs and leaning back. It looked like she was on some kind of invisible recliner sofa.

Lars admired her. Flying had been his ultimate desire: something he dreamed about for his whole entire life. He dreamed of being up there in the clouds. And here was Imp, using his dream as if it was completely natural to her. In that second Lars almost wished that he was a Flavour, if it meant he could fly.

Stop it! He told himself sternly, *Remember the reason you became a Police in the first place.*

"Why are you a Police officer?" Imp asked, as if she had read his thoughts. For some reason, Lars believed that she had probably read a few minds in her lifetime. Someone out in the world must dream of reading minds.

"None of your business." Lars growled.

"No need to be rude." She muttered crossly. She hovered back to a standing position, floating away from him. She alighted on another tree, this one across from Lars. She sat on the branch delicately, leaning her back against the tree trunk, her head tilted towards the sky. Once again she was silent, as if in deep thought.

She is kinda...pretty, Lars thought. It was true. Her black hair was in good shape, and her face was expressive and smooth. Her eyes alone were enough for most to stop and pause, trying to decipher what was hidden behind them. Lars knew that he had been stopped dead by them a couple of times. She looked so calm now, it was hard not to feel a little emotion.

But Lars shivered when he remembered what she was like during Berserk mode. It was almost as if she were a different person: her eyes would lose their dreaminess and become hard blue disks, full of rage and anger at the world. She would hunch over more, like a cat ready to pounce on an unsuspecting mouse. Worst of all, she would grin. It was a horrible grimace of pure anger and superiority. It almost looked like her teeth were more pointed than usual. It was hard to believe that something so monstrous could come out of the calm girl sitting in a tree.

"Why do you Police hate the Flavours so much?" Imp wondered, directing the question more at herself than at Lars.

"You disrupt the peace." Lars responded menacingly, his voice a growl.

"How? By making people think? By standing up against a corrupt government that seems to have forgotten the ancient laws that made the world a peaceful place?" Imp's voice was full of emotion, but when she turned her face towards Lars he saw that her eyes were emotionless, "The world seems so gray and bland now, don't you think? I bet in the old world everyone was happy because they could do what they like while being protected. But now people lack drive and purpose...they live because they were born, because they have to, not because they love living. People used to live to fulfill something, to make the world a better place. But I guess that's kind of hard when the decisions have been made for them by the government."

"The world is safe." Lars answered simply, his voice full of contained emotion. It was a bad idea to get Imp angry, "Why can't you just be happy with that? Why must you rebel?"

"The world's too safe, that's why I rebel!" Imp almost yelled, her eyes shooting daggers at him, "No one has to think! The decisions have been made for them already. The good people are being restrained, and the bad people are getting away with their crimes! The Flavours are trying to free the good people so that they can do good. And maybe then the bad people will be punished."

"How can you talk of good people and bad people?" Lars was shocked, his voice angry, "People are getting arrested because of you Flavours!"

"They're getting arrested because they helped us? They're getting arrested because of their opinion? Doesn't that violate some kind of basic human right? Oh sorry, I forgot. The new government doesn't care about that anymore."

"You're putting innocent people in danger, Imp! How can you be so carefree?" Lars demanded.

"I'm not putting them in danger. They're putting themselves in danger. But the real reason they are in danger in the first place is the Police, isn't it? You're arresting and punishing people because of their opinions, not because they did something bad." Imp leaned towards Lars from her position on the tree, staring at him with intense eyes, "Yet the murderers get away without punishment. They get away with disobeying a child's free will, with lying, with knowingly abandoning their child to some kind of sick torture?"

Lars was silent. He was glowering, glaring at her with barely contained hatred.

"But," Imp shrugged, "What do you expect from the government?"

That was the final straw.

Lars gave a cry of anger, lunging at Imp. For a second he forgot that he was in a tree. For a second he forgot that he couldn't fly.

He plunged towards the earth. The air ripped his scream from his lungs.

I'm going to die! Lars thought, terror seizing his heart, *I'm going to die!*

Suddenly he felt hands grasp him by his armpits, tugging him painfully from his freefall. He stopped a few feet from the ground. He was panting from terror. He had been two feet from falling to his death!

"You're heavy." Imp panted.

Lars was in a state of shock. Imp had saved him?!

"Get off of me!" Lars yelled, flailing around. He reached for his sword, bringing it out of his scabbard as Imp dropped him. He lashed out, landing heavily on his back, knocking the air out of him.

"Well that's gratitude for you." Imp grumbled, rubbing her face. A thin cut had opened on her cheek. She glared at Lars with more pity than anger. She landed, disappearing as soon as her foot touched the ground.

Lars picked himself up.

The traps, He thought bleakly, *Any second now, the traps will get her.*

He was shaken up, to say the least. His talk with Imp had left him slightly confused. He had hoped that getting into Imp's mind would help with her capture, but it had just awoken more and more questions.

You're becoming obsessed, Lars warned himself. But it was his duty, and his desire, to capture Flavours. He owed that to his dear mother. Thoughts of her were enough to make his blood boil, and it helped him strengthen his resolve.

Any second now, He thought again, trying to reassure his fast beating heart, *Why am I shaking so much?*

Imp rushed through the bushes, whipping branches away from her without thought. She usually wasn't so careless. She was used to sneaking up on people, not crashing through the undergrowth towards an unknown destination.

That was probably what gave her away.

"Who's there?!" A voice cried out, and Imp immediately stopped, hiding behind a tree. She remembered her encounter with Lars, how he had found her even though she was invisible. But this voice was different then Lars'. She had left him far behind.

Then who's this guy? Imp wracked her brain, but she could only come up with the thought that the voice sounded familiar.

"Come out, Flavour! Where I can see you!" The voice called again, trying to sound gruff. But she could hear the nervousness hidden in it.

Suddenly a hand gripped the tree, inches from Imp's face. She held her breath. A head peeked out, slowly, mere centimetres from Imp's face. He obviously didn't realize she was here.

Imp's heart skipped a beat as the face came in to full view.

"Delyn?!" Imp cried, materializing.

Delyn screamed in fright, jumping away from Imp. He fell on his butt, crawling away from her for a second, before he regained his composure.

"It's you." He growled, picking himself up and dusting his clothes off. Imp's blood went cold when she noticed he was wearing a Police uniform.

"Delyn, what are you—" Imp was interrupted as Lars burst from behind a tree, making poor Delyn jump again.

"Delyn? What's the pro—" Lars stopped short as he noticed Imp leaned against a tree.

"You found her." He grinned, "Good job Delyn."

Delyn smiled back at Lars, and only then did Imp finally understand.

Delyn...and the Police? Imp felt sick to her stomach, *This is wrong! All wrong!*

That was when it started, a slow buzz at the back of her head.

"Do you have any wire traps, Delyn?" Lars looked from Delyn to Imp, "Just look at her! She looks like a frightened rabbit!" He was laughing, and Delyn chuckled a bit too.

That's when Imp disappeared.

"Dammit!" Lars swore under his breath, "Hurry Delyn! Let's split up." And, more quietly, he said, "Try to herd her towards the traps."

Delyn nodded, setting off in the direction that he heard some crashing of branches. Lars set off in the opposite direction.

She's already headed in the direction of the traps anyway, if my hearing is right. Piece of cake.

That was when Imp's frightened scream filled the air. It echoed through the forest eerily, and he was sure that the Flavours were probably cursing right now. Unless all of them had been captured already.

Gotcha, Delyn thought, grinning maliciously. He ran off in the direction of the scream, certain of victory.

Chapter 19

Pheonix ran through the trees, rubbing at her eyes. The farther away from the smoke the clearer her vision got, but it was still turning the world into an irritable haze. Everything was a blur of color.

She stopped, thinking that she had gotten far enough away from the smoke. At this distance, it should have been safe enough to stop and wait until her vision cleared.

She sat at the base of a tree, crying out tears that helped to gradually clear up her sight. She rubbed once more at her eyes. The world was now the sharp picture it should be. Pheonix smiled.

She sat for a bit longer, trying to catch her breath again. The group had been split up. Initially Pheonix had followed Moss, but she had lost track of him. She tried listening for him, for some kind of tell-tale snapping of branches, but she couldn't hear anything.

I'm alone, Pheonix thought, feeling a little pang of sadness, *How are we going to find each other again?*

She sighed, standing up again. She looked out from behind the tree. Seeing no one, she stepped carefully away from the tree, and got ready to run again.

Pheonix heard a tiny click.

Damn! Wire trap!

Thick wires shot out from the tree parallel to her, wrapping themselves around her and the tree. She was pinned, held in place by black, menacing wires.

Pheonix watched as a small hole opened up in the topmost wire, just below her neck. Small wisps of visible vapour began to waft out.

That can't be good, She thought, trying to hold her breath. But it was no use. Her nose was already filled with it.

The world went black.

Tric ran through the forest, coughing. His throat was raw, but he kept running. He had had experience with tear gas before. It wasn't a pleasant experience. The best thing he could do was run and get as far-away from the source as possible.

His eyes had barely teared up, unlike the others, but the gas was wreaking havoc on his respiratory system. He kept coughing, an unhealthy sounding hack. His throat was already raw, and he felt slightly sick.

He paused for a second, drinking in huge gasps of air. His throat *really* hurt. He felt like he was going to puke.

Hold on! He told himself, *Just a couple more minutes, and the effects will go away! You know that.*

He coughed a bit more, sliding to the ground. He laid his back on the tree. Head tilted back, he tried to breathe in slowly and deeply.

Just a bit longer. Then I'll start running again, It was frustrating for him. He was good at running, and almost never needed a break. But with his lungs in such a lack of oxygen, he couldn't go very far before running out of breath. He felt dizzy and lightheaded.

"So frustrating." He murmured, taking another deep breath before standing up shakily.

With a determined resolve, he started to run, slower this time. He was almost at a point where he would be far enough to be completely clear of any tear gas.

Click.

Tric jumped up, hooking his arms around a branch. The wires missed him by mere millimetres, grazing his foot and scarf. He swung himself onto the branch, perching like some kind of huge bird of prey. He was feeling triumphant.

Click.

He barely had time to turn his head, seeing the black ball nestled in the crook beside him. The wires snaked around him, pinning him against the tree that had been his saviour a moment before.

Not more gas! Tric groaned wordlessly as a valve opened, and the fumes flooded his nostrils.

He was out in a second.

Aqua could hear Moss following behind her. She turned, seeing him pant just trying to run after her. He was stumbling, struck by a coughing fit. She could see tears leaking down his face, a real waterfall caused by the gas.

It had been easy for Aqua to get rid of the gas. She had made herself swallow a lot of water, showering her face with chilling spray to wash any of the clingy gas away. Her mascara was running now, but at least she wasn't in the condition of poor Moss.

"Here." She said, offering him her hand. He took it gratefully, nearly tripping over a root. She slung his arm over her shoulders, gripping his hand. Her other arm snaked around his waist, supporting him. He coughed again, and it didn't sound too healthy.

"How much of the gas did you inhale?" She asked, incredulous. She had never seen someone so affected by tear gas.

"I kinda...gasped when Tric said tear gas." Moss smiled slightly, looking embarrassed, "Oops."

Aqua laughed, a surprisingly loud sound. She started out at a small jog, aided very little by Moss' attempt at running.

This will take a while, Aqua groaned inwardly, *Why do I have to be the motherly type? Why do I always feel like I have to take care of everyone? Sheesh.*

She tried running for a bit longer, making it a couple of feet. Moss was the one who cried out in warning as he heard the wire trap's click. They both ended up pinned to separate trees, Moss already gagging as more gas leaked from the wires.

I hate wire traps! Aqua sighed as darkness overtook her.

Delyn broke through the underbrush, suddenly finding Imp. She had somehow managed to snare herself into five wire traps: an impossible thing to break out of. Her head was bowed, arms and legs splayed into a star. She had a couple of wires snarled around her stomach, one on each arm and leg. She was in a real bind.

Delyn approached slowly and quietly. He couldn't see Imp's face: it was blocked by her curtain of black hair. He was close enough to touch her when she suddenly raised her head, eyes full of anger. He was surprised. He had never seen Imp so angry. She looked terrifying.

Lars came onto the sight of Imp's capture, stumbling slightly. He looked at the mess of wires with a look of awe on his face. But when Imp turned to glare at him, he went pale. She snarled, and it was at that point that Lars knew exactly what he was dealing with.

Crap! She's in Berserk Mode!

"You—!" She yelled, struggling against the wires, "You took him away from me!"

Delyn looked at her in surprise, obviously not used to seeing her in such a state. Her voice was so full of pain and rage, it was hard to believe that it could come from a fragile looking girl.

"I didn't take him away from you." Lars told her calmly, though he was very tense. He needed to calm her down, before she didn't anything rash.

"You did!" She screamed, and Lars' heart thudded as he realized that she was *crying*, "You turned him against me!"

"He didn't turn me against you!" Delyn yelled back, "You turned me against you when you joined the Flavours!"

Imp growled, desperately struggling against the wires. She looked like she was going to strangle them both.

"Don't get her mad, Delyn!" Lars yelled, trying to put some authority in his voice, "Trust me!"

"I'll be fine Lars!" Delyn said, a little annoyed. He turned to his tutor, "I know how to deal with fits."

"Not this kind." Lars answered, "Trust me Delyn, you don't want to mess with Imp when she's angry."

"Don't be such a scaredy-cat." Delyn grinned, putting his arm around Imp's immobilized shoulders, completely ignoring the death glare she shot him. "I'm perfectly fi—"

Lars pulled Delyn out of the way as Imp lunged, snarling. He barely managed to save Delyn from her grasping hands that would've caught Delyn's neck in an iron hold if Lars hadn't knocked him out of the way. They both hit the ground as Imp glared down at them.

Imp strained against the wire's hold, and Lars' blood went cold as he heard snapping. Little flashes of electricity flew as the wires came apart, revealing twisted wiring and tubes. Her arm came slowly towards them, the bonds that had held her immobile breaking in a terrifying cacophony. She was *angry*.

"Delyn!" Lars cried, turning to his apprentice as they both struggled to their feet, "Where's the control switch?! Get some gas going!"

"I don't have the control switch!" Delyn answered, his voice one of horror as he watched his childhood friend morph into some kind of monster. Imp's hand suddenly wrenched free, but they scrambled out of her arm's reach. She growled and began to work on freeing her other arm, using muscles that Delyn didn't even know she had.

"Don't you have a gas packet, or something? Another tear gas grenade? Anything?!" Lars looked at Delyn, his usually calm grey eyes in a panic.

Only then did Delyn remember the knockout gas mask in his backpack.

Lars had given it to him as an extra precaution against Flavours. It was powerful enough to knock out as soon as it was inhaled, even if it was only inhaled a tiny bit.

But how the hell would he get close enough to Imp to place it over her mouth?!

The wires around Imp's wrist were snapping at an alarming rate, peppering her skin with yellow sparks. Delyn threw down his backpack, digging through its contents and trying to find the mask.

Lars watched as he pulled out a ridiculous looking thing. It was a simple mask, like that used to apply anaesthesia to those getting surgery, but where the tube went, there was a pump. A little switch protruded from the entrance of the bag. Flipping the switch would allow the gas in the pouch to flow into the mask, leaking the gas.

Lars saw what Delyn was doing, nodding to him. Lars drew his sword, aiming at Imp. She stopped trying to pull out her arm, glaring at him with madness in her eyes. He charged, and she struggled desperately trying to get her other arm out, oblivious to Delyn's approach.

As Lars pointed his blade to Imp's throat, Delyn snuck behind, avoiding the thick twist of cables around her leg, the ones that were around her arm lying on the ground, still sparking. He got the mask ready as Imp crazily gripped Lars' sword with her bare hand. She had just begun to bleed as Delyn slipped the mask over her nose and mouth.

Imp struggled, gripping Delyn's arm with savage force, staining his wrist with her blood. He threw the switch as her grip tightened, and for a second he thought that she was going to break his bones. The gas whooshed out, visible against the plastic like steam. Imp struggled slightly, but her grip on Delyn's arms was loosening. Her head began to droop forward, eyes fluttering as she fought off the sleep. But it was useless. She went limp in the cords, and Delyn loosened his grip on the mask, removing it after shutting off the pouch. It was completely depleted now, and Delyn stepped away so that he wouldn't catch a whiff of the dangerous instant knockout fumes.

"Finally." Lars gave a great sigh of relief, steeping away from Imp and plopping himself onto the ground, "After all these years. Thank you Delyn."

"You're welcome." Delyn answered, staring at Imp. There was something unreal about seeing his best friend become such a monster, yet looking so peaceful while she was unconscious. Almost as if they had been fighting their imaginations, not this girl that lay limp in her binds.

"Ugh." Lars leaned up against a tree, closing his eyes. It had been a crazy day. But fighting off a Berserk Imp was worth it, if it meant he caught her and a lot of her friends. He still didn't know how many had been snared by the wire traps, but it didn't matter. He finally had Imp.

Unless something goes wrong, He reminded himself.

"What do we do with her?" Delyn asked, still staring at Imp.

"We bring her to the capital." Lars replied simply, "To a high security prison, where she will most likely be put there for the rest of the days."

"What if she renounces being a Flavour?" Delyn asked, slight worry in his voice.

Lars turned to him, his eyes serious and sad. "She'll still be put in prison for a while, but she will eventually be let free." He turned away from Delyn, looking up at the sky, "But that's very unlikely."

"Oh." Delyn responded, looking slightly crestfallen.

What if she doesn't admit she's wrong? I've lost her forever.

Chapter 20

Snow stumbled into a clearing, listening for signs of others nearby.

He couldn't find any other members of SOFT. He had heard Imp scream, but he was more worried about how the scream would cause others to flock to the scene...and most likely get captured themselves.

I need to find the others. Get a head count. See how many of us have been captured.

Snow sat down for a second, catching his breath. The tear gas had barely affected him. He was used to it, due to being the oldest and having attended the most displays. But there was no doubt that Imp would have been badly affected. She didn't attend many public manifestations, where tear gas was a common weapon against the gathered protesters.

A branch cracked behind him. Snow tensed, forming a blade of ice in his hand. He turned, seeing Aria stagger into the clearing, rubbing her eyes. Snow relaxed, melting the ice in his hand. He was happy that she was safe.

"Is that you, Snow?" Aria asked, squinting.

He nodded, hoping that Aria would be able to track the movement. He didn't like talking.

Aria sighed in relief. It was easy to tell Snow by his white hair, but it wasn't impossible for a Police to have the same color...

"Did you see any of the others?" Snow asked as Aria sat down beside him, coughing slightly.

"I had seen Dusty for a while, but we got split up. I haven't seen anyone else." Aria looked at Snow, her eyes only a little bit wet now, "Do you think something bad happened to them?"

Snow grunted. "I had to disengage some wire traps along the way. There's no doubt that that was part of the attack plan: drive us away so that the wire traps can get us."

Aria nodded. She was honestly a little overwhelmed in the battle plans. She could never concentrate long enough to understand them. But she was always the first one to notice things that were out of place. That was how she had avoided most of the wire traps, using air to blast herself out of the way of the ones that slipped her attention.

"Imp definitely got captured." Aria said, a little sadly. She liked Imp, despite her obliviousness and quietness.

Snow nodded, seemingly lost in thoughts. He slipped his black gloves back on. Aria knew that to be the signal that he was done fighting: in a battle, he always went barehanded.

"Let's try to find Dusty, then." He offered his hand to Aria after standing up, the perfect gentleman. She took it, feeling the icy coldness even through his glove.

They set off in a random direction, hoping against all hopes that they would find Dusty.

Pyra was actually the one who found *them*.

She had been fighting through the underbrush. At one point she had heard footsteps behind her, panicking and trying to make the other lose her trail. It obviously worked, because a second later the footsteps had faded in the distance.

What if that had been a good guy? She wondered now, thinking about it, It probably was...Dang.

But she had quickly moved past that thought, striding through the forest with a certainty that could only be born from optimism. Her eyes weren't *that* blurry. Her throat didn't hurt *that* much. She kept telling herself those things.

It was quite fluky when Pyra took a trail, happening to find Snow and Aria as she turned a corner. Snow had looked on, expressionless, as Aria gave a happy 'Yay!' and hugged Pyra. Pyra was just as happy to see them.

"Have you seen Dusty?" Aria asked as she took a step away from Pyra.

Pyra nodded no, and Aria looked disappointed.

"Have you seen anyone else?" Snow asked, his voice emotionless.

Again Pyra nodded no, and it was Snow's turn to look a little dismayed.

"I could send up a flare." Pyra suggested, "Give a little signal to where we are."

"Too risky." Said Dusty's voice, as he stepped onto the trail. He had a thing for dramatic entrances. He opened his arms, as if expecting someone to hug him. Everyone stayed where they were, staring at them.

Dusty hung his head, looking utterly defeated.

"He's right." Snow broke the silence, which was unusual for him, "If we send off a flare now, the Police will be on us instantly. Let's wait until later, when the Police might have retreated."

"Which they probably will, if they have Imp." Dusty finished for him. He sighed, probably thinking of how his sweet Imp was now a damsel in distress. Aria rolled her eyes, not even bothering to hit him.

They searched for a bit longer, keeping out a watchful eye for wire traps. They found no one, apparently having gotten past the barricade of the dangerous traps.

Night had almost fallen when they decided that it was safe enough to send off a flare.

Pyra ate another gummy, the one from this afternoon having long since run out of its power. She shot up a pure blast of fire, not trusting her leaves to get very high. They watched as it arched into the air, a scarlet flame against the night sky. Pyra concentrated, suddenly forcing the fire to explode. Orange and yellow sparks flew everywhere like fireworks, scattering onto the tree tops.

They didn't set up much of a camp. It the Police attacked, they needed to be able to get out of there quickly, and would rather not have to pack away a bunch of camp supplies. They ate cold jerky, deeming it too risky to start a fire. As they curled up into their sleeping bags, they were faced with the cold reality that it was most likely that everyone else had been captured. Even Pyra's optimism couldn't keep out the feeling of dread.

They awoke the next morning, hoping against all hopes to find another one of their group lying on the ground beside them.

But there was no one. If someone had come, they would've heard them, even in sleep. They all knew that, yet they all hoped.

Snow took out his map, spreading it out on the ground. He pointed at their approximate location, on the trail right beside Fentek. Still another six days of travel to get to Otta.

"They're definitely heading towards the capital." Dusty said pensively, kneeling beside the map with his elbow on his knee, his head in his hand, "If they take a prison vehicle, which they will for sure, they could get there in about four hours...Assuming they traveled at 80 kilometres per hour."

Aria sighed. "We'll never make it. Six days to four hours?"

"Unless..." Pyra started, looking uncertain, "We took a car."

Everyone looked up at her, shocked. Flavours and cars didn't mix well. They all could drive, though they had no licenses, but if they were caught by the Police, they'd get in big trouble.

"Where the heck would we get a car, anyway?" Aria asked, uncertain.

"Minor detail!" Pyra declared, "Just think. The speed limit for highways is 100 kilometres an hour. The prison vehicle can only go 80 safely. We can make it in about three hours!"

"But it would be impossible to get a car." Snow replied, sounding annoyed, "Don't forget that, Pyra."

"Maybe not impossible." She answered, already fleshing out the scheme in her head.

Pyra's face fell as another door slammed in her face.

"I don't think that anyone's going to lend us a car." Aria mentioned unhelpfully.

"We're wasting daylight. Let's get moving." Snow suggested.

"No! There's gotta be someone who will lend us a car!" Pyra screamed in frustration, pounding her fists against a lamp post.

"You need a car?"

They all turned, staring at the woman who was standing there staring at them. She had dirty blond hair that fell to her shoulders. She had just finished closing the door to her car, heading towards the nearby motel.

"Yeah." Pyra answered shyly, "Could you please, miss...?"

"Are you Flavours?" The lady asked.

"Urk!" Dusty exclaimed, "How dare you call us that?!"

"So you are Flavours?" The lady smiled a little, opening the door of her blue car, "Get in then."

"So, who are you all?" Mrs. Ately asked as they hit the road. Apparently she had been heading the same way as they were heading: towards Otta.

"Snow." Answered the one who had taken the seat beside her. He was dressed in all black and white clothing.

"Pyra. Nice to meet you!" The red haired girl answered, looking as if she was about to extend a hand.

"I'm Dustorocks, but you can call me Dusty." The tuque-wearing, brown haired one said, nodding politely.

"I'm Aria." The one with the butterfly shirt answered. She was gazing off out of the window, seemingly lost in the scenery.

"Nice to meet you all!" Mrs. Ately answered, "My name is Mrs. Ately."

They all chorused a 'nice to meet you'.

"So, why are headed towards the capital?" Mrs. Ately asked.

"We're going to help out some friends who've been captured." Pyra replied, her face full of worry, "The Police snuck up on us, and most of us got caught."

"Why are you going?" Dusty asked, "If you're willing to tell us, of course."

"I need to find my son." Mrs. Ately got a pained look on her face, "He recently made...bad choices, so I'm following him."

"That sucks." Aria sighed, "I once had a brother who thought it would be cool to join the Police. He eventually quit once he ran into me."

"It might be worth it to mention that your brother joined the Flavours, after." Snow grumbled.

"So I guess he can make good choices, after all!" Aria smiled at him.

"Well," Mrs. Ately said quietly and reluctantly, "My son Delyn made a bad choice like that too. Except he joined so that he could capture a childhood friend."

"Wow." Dusty commented, "That must suck."

"Yes." Mrs. Ately sighed, "Even worse, his childhood friend is like a daughter to me."

"Wait a second!" It was Pyra, "Delyn?!"

"Yes." Mrs. Ately said hesitantly.

Pyra looked sick. "You're talking about Imp, aren't you?"

Lars couldn't help constantly glancing back.

He was riding in the prison vehicle, an ominous looking machine. A thin grate separated the passengers from the prisoners, and Lars would look back every two seconds, making sure his prisoners were still there.

There were five in all: Imp, Pheonix, Moss, Tric and Aqua. All of them would glare every time they caught him looking. All of them, except Imp, who was gazing through the tiny window behind her with a melancholic look on her face.

The prison portion of the vehicle was sparse at best. Small, padded seats were supplied, though they didn't look quite comfortable. There were chains attached to them for the more troublesome prisoners, but the Flavours had been disarmed and they only needed handcuffs. There were eight seats in total, lined in two rows along the sides of the bus, making a cramped but walk-able alley way in between the prisoner's feet.

Delyn sat beside Lars, sinking into the plush seat for passengers. The driver was in a row in front of them, and they had the entire back row to themselves. Only Lars would look back at the Flavours, Delyn preferring the large window of scenery.

Delyn had gotten frighteningly quiet lately. In the beginning he had been quite talkative, but ever since Imp's capture he had barely said a word.

Are you feeling remorse, Delyn? Lars desperately wanted to ask him, but he could never find quite the right moment.

It was entirely possible. Imp had been his best friend, after all. Seeing her in such a state must have been hard on him.

Maybe I shouldn't have mentioned how unlikely it would be for Imp to repent. That was a little insensitive.

It was very rare for Lars to regret his words.

"Sir." The driver said, looking out into the dark night, "I think we are going to have to stop. By the time we make it to Otta, it will be midnight. The prison station there doesn't take well to midnight visitors."

"Alright then." Lars sighed, "Let's take a motel."

Chapter 21

"Why did they have to shove us into the basement?" Tric grumbled.

They had stopped at a Police-run motel, because it had gotten too dark to continue on, according to Lars. Lars, with his smug expression on his face and his triumphant look. It made Tric's blood boil, quite a feat because of his general cheeriness.

"Cuz they're jerks." Pheonix answered simply, setting up her mat, "At least they gave us something moderately nice to lie down on." She sat on the mat, sighing as she sank to the ground, "Never mind."

"I wonder what they did with Imp." Aqua wondered as she set up her own mat.

They had shoved the four of them down in the basement facility for safe keeping, while Lars had led Imp to a different room. She had looked really angry at him. When they had asked where he was taking her, he had just replied 'Wouldn't you like to know' and tugged on the chain attached to her handcuffs.

"I really hate that kid." Moss grumbled. There were groans of approval all around.

But they could do nothing. They had been freed of their handcuffs, but they were completely disarmed.

"How are we going to get out of this?" Pheonix asked, picking at the foam mattress.

"No idea." Tric sighed, "We'll just have to wait and see what happens, I guess."

Lars led Imp to a normal motel room.

It contained two beds, a small TV set and a bathroom, like all motel rooms.

"What's this for?" Imp growled at Lars, obviously not completely recovered from her Berserk mode. He decided that keeping the handcuffs on her was a good idea.

"I'm not going to let you hang around those other Flavours so you can plot an escape plan." Lars explained, glaring at her, "I'm going to keep you here, so I can watch you."

Imp just scowled at him.

"Here." Lars said, leading her towards one of the beds. He motioned for her to lie down on it. She just gave him an icy stare. He sighed, undoing one of her handcuffs and attaching it to the metal bed post. Lars was relieved when she just watched him do it. He almost expected her to retaliate.

Imp still just stood there, tugging slightly against the hand cuff. It was almost as if she didn't understand the concept.

"You might as well lie down." Lars told her, "I'm not undoing those handcuffs until tomorrow."

He left the room to go register his location with the Police, hoping that Imp would still be there when he got back.

How the heck would she get away, anyway? She's tied to a metal post!

Imp watched as Lars closed the door, having left her alone.

The moment he was out of sight, she tried to calm herself down. It was a lot easier when he was no longer there: just being in her sight was enough for *it* to feel angry.

If she turned her head right, she could see the lights of the city through the window. It was dark out, and the moon couldn't be seen among the lights of buildings. It was a depressing feeling, not being able to see one of the most beautiful of nature's sights because of humanity's need to not be in darkness. No one would admit it, but everyone was afraid of the dark. Why else would there by lampposts lining sidewalks, or neon signs that stayed on all night?

She tried tugging at the handcuff, but the metal bar was solid. She bent down as far as she could, trying to get a look under the bed. The bar was solidly attached to the floor.

Damn.

She clenched her fist in frustration, wincing immediately. When she opened her hand, she noticed that there was a deep slash across her palm, slowly leaking blood.

Imp didn't even know how she had gotten that wound. The moment she had been snared in those traps...she had become so desperate she had barely resisted when *it* tried to take over. The next thing she knew, she was sitting in the transport car, met with the morose faces of her friends.

She tried gripping one of the covers to stop the flow, but the rough cotton only made it hurt more. So instead she tried to sort through the sheets, finding the light, thin one that beds always had. She dabbed at the wound, frowning as it did nothing to stop the flow, only resulting in the pristine white sheet to turn red.

Lars, of course, chose that moment to walk in.

He was immediately at her side, roughly grabbing her hand. He bundled the sheet up, forcing it into a ball.

"Hold that there." He said gently, his voice completely different from his actions. Imp nodded meekly, stepping a bit closer to the pole so that she could use her handcuffed hand to hold the bundle down. Lars rushed into the bathroom, leaving her behind, bewildered.

Lars quickly gathered his supplies, thankful that the motel was so well equipped. He had completely forgotten about Imp's wound in all the action, and he felt stupid because of that. That was something he should have gotten treated before they left Fentek.

When he came back into the room, he noticed that Imp was sitting on the bed. But that wasn't what was out of place.

The sheet was completely red.

He was on the bed in an instant, only needing one look to know that she had lost a lot of blood; she looked dazed.

Lars pushed up her sleeve, opening the first aid kit and taking out a rubber strip. He tied it around her wrist, hoping to slow down the blood. When he took the bundle away, he was thankful that his earlier assessment of the situation had been a little overboard. The redness of the sheet seemed to be mostly from when he had just come into the room, when she had been trying to dab away the blood.

Imp said nothing as he cleaned the wound, watching him use a slightly wet cloth to clear the blood the best he could. He took some rubbing alcohol, spreading it onto cotton swabs. When he applied it to her wound, her fingers twitched, though she said nothing.

Lars spread some antibiotic cream over the wound, followed by a pad. Her hand was starting to look a little pale, so he removed the strip.

Imp shuffled nervously as he started to wrap the bandage around her hand. But when he looked at her—discretely, of course, he didn't want to make her more nervous—her face was completely expressionless.

"There." Lars said, pleased with his handiwork. He usually wasn't so great at taking care of wounds, but he thought he had done a passable job.

Imp withdrew her hand from his, not looking at him at all. She looked like she was about to flex it.

"Don't." Lars warned, stopping her mid-movement, "You'll just make it start to bleed again."

She nodded, still burning a hole in the bed with her gaze. Why was she so nervous?

In an attempt to make her feel less anxious, he took his time replacing the kit and cloth, trying to wash out some of the stains. When he came back into the room, she actually managed to look at him. At least she seemed to have recovered a bit.

"How did I get this?" She asked quietly, nervously.

"Get what?"

"My wound."

Lars blinked in confusion. Shouldn't she know how she got her wound?

"You gripped my sword...remember? When you went into Berserk Mode after being caught by the wire traps."

She looked away.

She doesn't remember! Lars thought, shocked, *So now...on top of Berserk Mode becoming something she resists, she doesn't remember what happens while she's Berserk?*

"What is it like?" He asked. Imp shot him a questioning look, "What is Berserk Mode like?"

She frowned. "I don't know what you're saying."

Oh yeah. I guess I'm the only one that uses that term...

"When you..." *How do I put this delicately?*

"I call them fits." She murmured.

Lars hesitated. "So what's it like...?"

She looked suddenly self conscious, taking a while to answer, "It's...terrifying."

Imp looked away, as if embarrassed. He assumed that no one had ever asked her something like that.

She rubbed sleepily at her eyes, and Lars glanced at the clock. It was one in the morning. From what he knew about Imp's sleeping habits, it was late for her.

"I don't know about you, but I'm hitting the sack." He said nonchalantly, trying to clear the suddenly awkward atmosphere. Hopping onto his bed, he slipped under the covers, putting his back to her. He was asleep in seconds.

What time is it? Lars wondered, turning around and squinting at the clock. The red numbers read 3:03 A.M.

Why did I wake up? He rubbed his eyes, sitting up sleepily. He had gone to bed at around one...

But apparently Imp hadn't.

Lars flipped the light switch, blinking against the harsh light. Imp was sitting there, in the exact position she had been in two hours ago. She was watching him.

"Why aren't you asleep?" Lars asked, already getting the feeling that he was going to get into an argument with her.

"The nightmares are always worse after I...you know."

"So you're going to stay up all night just to avoid these nightmares." Lars stated grumpily. He hated waking up in the middle of the night. He always had trouble falling asleep when he did that.

"That's the plan." Imp answered simply.

Lars stared at her in disbelief. He couldn't believe it. They were just nightmares. She knew that they weren't real, right...?

She looked like she suddenly felt self-conscious. "I almost always stay up all night after one of my..." She hesitated, "Fits. And it doesn't help that you're in the same room as me."

Lars laughed harshly. "I'm the one making you nervous? You're the one who plans to stay up all night just staring at me!"

She didn't have an answer for that. He sighed.

"Just go to sleep. You're old enough to realize that they're just dreams, aren't you?"

His attempt to sound patronizing was completely lost on Imp.

"My nightmares are real." She told him firmly.

"They might feel real, but they aren't."

"You have no right to say that. You don't know what my nightmares are about."

Lars was surprised to find steel in Imp's voice. What was so intense about her nightmares? He could understand having one and then not being able to sleep for a while, but choosing to skip sleep completely was just overdoing it. Even if she said that she had done it before.

"Look." He said, exasperated, "If it reassures you any, I'm a light sleeper. If you start having a nightmare, I'll wake you up."

She sat there for a minute, regarding him with her calm blue eyes.

"Fine." She finally sighed, lying down and pulling the covers over her body. She turned her back to him, apparently still mad.

Should I say something? Lars wondered, questioning the strange urge to say good night, *No. She'll probably have something to say about that.*

"Mom? There are Police outside..."

"Don't worry about it, honey." The boy's mom replied, tousling his hair before opening the door, "Why don't you go to bed? It's getting late."

"Stop treating me like a kid! I'm 10!" He complained, smoothing out his hair.

"And what a man you're becoming! But that doesn't change the fact that you need your sleep, Lars."

Lars pouted, although he turned around and went up the stairs. His mom opened the door, and he heard shouting. His foot paused midway up one step. And as his mother passed completely through the door, he was at the bottom of the stairs, heading towards the window.

What's going on? He wondered, watching as his mother stepped out across the grass, taking something small from her pocket.

"Watch out!" One of the officers cried, "She's got a gummy!"

"I have no intention of using it, mind you." His mother replied calmly, "After all, my son's watching. I don't want any ideas of violence to get into his head."

"Hey." Lars heard a voice, even though no one's mouth moved. It was a wispy voice, as if it came from somewhere far away.

The Police surrounded his mother, who willingly lifted her hands to receive the cuffs.

"Mom!" He screamed through the open window. She turned back, her brown hair catching the last rays of dusk, green eyes full of love. She smiled kindly.

"Mom!" He yelled again, tears springing to his eyes. She stepped into the Police car, the door slamming shut.

"Hey!" It was the voice again. Lars ignored it.

The Police car was driving away, the platoon following in its wake. He saw one of the officers start to walk towards the house.

He knew what the officer would say. He would tell him that he needed the phone number of a close family member. After all, he joked, Lars wouldn't be seeing his mother for a long time...

"Lars!" The voice was more insistent, more demanding. The dream was starting to fade away, leaving only a feeling of being shaken.

He sat up suddenly, making Imp jump. He grabbed her still outstretched arm, making her eyes widen a little.

"What are you doing?" He asked calmly, although he hated the little tremor in his voice.

She frowned. "I was waking you up. I thought you were having a nightmare."

"I was." He answered curtly, "But I never asked you to wake me up if I was having one."

"I was just returning the favour." She said levelly, a tone of voice Lars had never heard her use before. She must have been really angry.

They stood there for a moment, glaring at each other. He tried to force Imp to react by squeezing her wrist; but she didn't even blink, not even flinch. She had one of the most formidable poker faces he had ever seen.

Lars was the one to break eye contact, looking at her bed instead. He could see how she had strained to reach him; she was stretching, the chain only having reached halfway across her bed.

Imp stood beside her bed for a second, as if contemplating it.

"What were you dreaming about?" She asked as she stepped onto the bed, slipping under the covers without even bothering to look at him.

"Why would I tell you?" He growled in answer, lying back down.

"You were yelling for your mom. I can infer a lot of things from that. You might want to tell me before I get the wrong idea."

"That's doesn't matter to me."

"What if I told Delyn?"

Is she trying to blackmail me? Lars wondered incredulously. He had never expected Imp to try something like that. Although with Imp, he never knew. It was a pretty pathetic attempt, but for some reason he answered anyway.

"I was dreaming about my mother."

Imp was quiet, obviously waiting for him to continue.

"I was dreaming of the day she got arrested." Lars said hesitantly, not even sure why he was explaining this to *Imp*, of all people.

"Why was she arrested?" Imp asked softly.

"She was a Flavour."

Imp looked away, which Lars was thankful for. He would have hated having to look her in the eye just then.

"Is that why you hate Flavours?" Imp murmured.

"Or course it is! They took my mother away, alright?" He sighed, and was surprised to find that her eyes were full of pity, "She became a Flavour, and she got caught by the Police. She's in jail right now, and she will be for the rest of her life."

"That's sad." Was all Imp could say.

"Honestly? 'That's sad.'? You can only manage that much? The reason she's in jail right now is because the life of a Flavour seemed so much more exciting than that of a stay at home mom, raising her son." He glared for a second, then once again turned his back to her, "That's why I hate Flavours."

Lars expected Imp to protest, or at least start yelling at him because 'That's not a good reason to hate Flavours!' etc, etc. But she was as quiet as he was.

"Isn't it sad that both sides in a war think that what they're doing is right?" She said instead, "But the one who is deemed righteous is the one who wins. It doesn't matter how many people they managed to get killed, or arrested. They won, so they're right."

Lars didn't answer, and he could feel Imp look at him for a bit longer. But eventually he heard the covers rustle on her bed. It didn't take long for her to start snoring lightly.

But Lars couldn't fall asleep. He was too disturbed by what Imp had said. As he tossed and turned, he thought of his mother.

I'm so confused, He thought as he drifted off to sleep.

"Otta." Pyra breathed as the lit skyscrapers of the city came into view.

They looked even more foreboding than usual when pitched against the dark night's sky. Even Dusty, who had been a city-dweller for most of his life, was impressed by the sheer size of the steel towers.

Three hours was a short drive for the Flavours. They were used to long days of travel. But for poor Mrs. Ately, it was a tiring ordeal.

"Do you think we made it before the prison vehicle?" Aria asked, gawking at the streets full of people and cars, despite the late hour.

"Definitely." Snow answered.

"My dears..." Mrs. Ately began, sounding extremely tired, "Is there someplace that I could stop? I need a rest."

"Of course, Mrs. Ately." Pyra replied, looking at each of the remaining members of SOFT in turn. They all nodded.

"Let's go to the Flavour Training Academy."

Chapter 22

Imp gulped as she looked at the Police prison.

It was tall and foreboding, looking exactly like one from the movies. The towering walls were topped with barbed wire and metal spires to deter the prisoners from climbing over the walls. As they were led through the gate, Imp caught a glance of the courtyard, a tiny space between the walls and the main building. Everything was open there, and guards were patrolling, even when the inmates were inside.

They moved on, ushered by an impatient Lars. He was glaring at them with a cocky smile, amused by Imp's wonder at the prison. A guard opened the door and they went through, shivering as soon as they entered the building.

There was a reception desk, but instead of being manned by a woman wearing glasses there was a burly man sitting and sorting papers. He looked up at them, and Imp was surprised to find that he was actually wearing glasses: tiny things that seemed to sink into his face.

"Is this the new shipment?" He asked Lars, who nodded. The secretary grumbled, sorting through some more papers. He picked up an old-fashioned stamp, slamming it onto a paper.

Macho secretary, Imp thought, and she couldn't help but smile slightly. She saw Pheonix stare at her, obviously wondering what the heck she had to smile about at a time like this.

Lars took the papers and the guards started to get them moving again, leading them down a veritable maze of twisted hallways. Eventually they came to a straight one. It was lined with cells.

Each cell contained a small cot hanging against a wall. A tiny window was lined with bars, letting a pitiful amount of light in. There were a couple of shelves, small ones. No bathroom was in sight, which Imp was thankful for. That meant there must have been a public bathroom somewhere in the building.

Lars led his captives through more and more hallways, until the cells started extending into double ones. Imp looked at the imprisoned people with sadness in her eyes. Almost all of them were Flavours: it was easy to tell who by the way they sighed when they watched Imp and her friends being led away. The criminals would sneer at them as they passed.

Eventually they reached some empty cells at the end of the corridor. Or, at least moderately empty. Two cells were completely empty, while one of them contained a girl.

She looked rather young: at the very most, only thirteen. She had purple hair that was losing its dye, turning into blond hair that reached down to her mid-back. She was wearing the simple prison uniform that they had all been forced to change into; pale blue t-shirts and pants, looking more like a hospital outfit than a prison one.

"This is your new home." Lars grinned at his captives. The guards opened the doors of the empty cells.

Pheonix and Aqua were moved into one cell, Tric and Moss into the other. That left Imp.

Imp was pleasantly surprised when she ended up moving in with the purple girl. She had honestly expected to be split up from the others, like last night. Lars seemed to be thinking that too, because he turned angrily to the guards.

"You sure you want to do that? This is *Imp* we're talking about. She's a troublemaker."

"Are you questioning our guarding abilities?" Was the answer as the guard raised a menacing eyebrow.

"No, of course not." Lars answered, gritting his teeth slightly, "It's just—"

"Then it's fine." The guard interrupted, leading Lars away. Only the inmates saw him roll his eyes at the over-zealous boy.

"You're Imp?" The girl asked when they were out of sight. She coughed into her scarf. Imp nodded.

"Nice to finally meet you." The girl smiled slightly, her eyes still curious and watchful, "I'm Ninja, a Black Liquorice Flavour."

Lars opened the door of the Police car, seeing that Delyn was still sitting inside. He hadn't wanted to go inside to see Imp get locked up.

"Do you honestly think that Imp will ask for redemption?" Delyn asked as soon as Lars sat down.

Lars hesitated.

"Tell me the truth." Delyn said with a hard edge to his voice.

Lars didn't hesitate this time. "No."

Delyn closed his eyes as if he were in great pain. Lars watched him, feeling a sense of pity. He had experienced a similar problem as Delyn's, except with his mother. It had been a hard time in his life, and now Delyn was going through the same thing.

Delyn opened his eyes, gazing at the walls of the prison. His brown eyes were glazed over as if in deep thought.

"It's her fault." He mumbled, and Lars stared at him, "It's her fault for turning to the Flavours. She deserves it."

Lars just nodded, and the driver started the engine, heading into town.

The Flavour Training Academy was a huge, old style building made of red bricks. One section seemed to be some kind of dorm surrounded by an open field where Flavours could be seen.

For Mrs. Ately it was impossible to look at the building from the corner of her eye. It was only seen when looked at from dead on, an interesting phenomenon that reminded Mrs. Ately of some kind of ghost building.

"It's a lot busier than usual." Aria frowned, looking towards the courtyard. It was practically swarming with Flavours practicing with weapons.

"Weird." Snow mumbled.

The dwindled SOFT strode towards the door of the huge place, Mrs. Ately following behind timidly. She kept looking around, as if she couldn't quite believe her eyes.

As soon as Dusty rose a fist to knock the door swung open, and they were ushered inside.

"Welcome!" An elderly lady greeted them, her now pure white hair pulled back into a long ponytail. Her apron was full of stains, "Come in, come in! Oh, it is so good to see you again!" She boomed, looking at Aria, Dusty, Snow and Pyra, "Who is this?" She asked, turning to Mrs. Ately.

"Mrs. Ately." Was all Mrs. Ately could say, nearly squeaking it out.

"Welcome!" The old lady beamed at her, taking her hand and shaking it, "I am Rain. Very nice to meet you!"

Rain led them through a hallway, past a kitchen where delicious smells were wafting out from.

"Why are there so may Flavours here?" Aria asked as Rain led them into the dorm section of the FTA.

"You didn't get the message?" Rain turned, raising a questioning eyebrow over her blue eyes, "We're mounting an attack on the Otta Lab soon."

"What?!" Pyra exclaimed, "When?!"

"As soon as Imp gets here." Rain answered, "Come to think of it, she's late. What is it?" She asked, noticing that everyone had gone pale.

"Imp was captured." Snow answered, seemingly unruffled by the fact, "Along with the rest of SOFT and two other Flavours."

"Oh dear." Rain sighed, "That's a major setback."

Mrs. Ately was silent, looking mournfully at the ground. It was sad when someone as young as Imp got sent to a prison for a lifetime, especially if she hadn't done anything that wrong. It was a right to hold peaceful protests, wasn't it? Why were they given the same sentence as a murderer when they hadn't done anything nearly so bad?

"I guess we'll have to bust her out, then." Rain stopped walking, staring through a window at the courtyard. There were at least thirty Flavours practicing with weapons and their elements, "We already have an army in the making, anyway."

It had been an uneventful day.

As the 'new inmates', some of the Flavour captives had introduced themselves. Actually, most of them had introduced themselves. Moss, Pheonix, Aqua, Tric, and Imp didn't have time to feel lonely. It was almost as if they had dropped into some kind of happy gathering, not a prison.

How can they be so cheerful? Imp absent-mindedly thought as another Flavour introduced himself, claiming that he had been in the building for five years now, *They're in prison, for Pete's sake!*

Ninja seemed to be quite popular with everyone, despite her quietness. She was treated like everyone's little sister, but there was some kind of underlying respect in their affection. It was strange.

The day was extremely quick, unlike what Imp had expected. She thought that the days in the prison would be long and hard, but surprisingly it went by in a flash.

Because they had arrived in the morning, they missed breakfast. After breakfast was the trip to the exercise room: an hour of working out on machines. After that was free time outside in the courtyard. It made Imp feel claustrophobic. Next lunch, after that more outdoor time. Free time in cell came next which, for Imp constituted drawing, followed by more exercise. Supper, more time outdoors, then free time in cell until lights out at nine.

It's more like a demented summer camp than a prison, Then again, maybe it was just the fact that they were constantly surrounded by friendly people that made the prison seem laughably un-prisonlike.

After a very forgettable supper—Imp forgot what it was the moment she was finished eating—they were let outside for a little bit. Imp, Pheonix and Moss sat on a bench and watched as Aqua totally owned Tric in a volleyball rally. Ninja was off in a corner chatting with another Flavour, who had introduced himself to Imp as Rowan, a Lime Flavour like Moss. They were whispering, and Imp wondered what they were up to.

"Ha!" Aqua yelled as Tric narrowly dodged one of Aqua's vicious serves. He sat down on the ground, groaning. Obviously he wasn't having much fun.

"Oh c'mon, Tric! One more round!" Aqua begged, laughing.

"No!" Tric moaned, falling onto his back in the sandy court.

A volleyball impaled itself into the sand by his head, and he jumped. Another one narrowly missed his leg, and Tric jumped to his feet, screaming. Aqua kept delivering her serves at him, laughing maniacally as he barely avoided death by volleyball.

The whistle blew to signify that outside time was over.

"Saved by the bell." Tric sighed in relief as he ran off the court, coming to stand beside Imp.

"So why are you here?" Ninja asked, staring at Imp.

Imp put down her book, looking up at Ninja.

"I was caught." Imp shrugged, "Like everyone else, I guess."

"Then, how'd you get caught?" Ninja turned her head questioningly, cat-like.

"I was heading towards Otta with some friends, and Lars ambushed us. After fighting off most of his troops, they retreated and attacked us with a tear gas grenade. We were split up and got caught by wire traps that they had set up."

"Ouch." Ninja winced, "How many people were you travelling with?"

"Nine, including me. I don't know what happened to the other four who didn't get caught...Hopefully they're alright."

Ninja nodded, turning towards the tiny window. "So...you were heading towards the capital for the Flavour gathering thing, right?"

"Flavour gathering thing?" Imp asked.

"You don't know?" Ninja turned to Imp, her green eyes wide.

"No, I was going towards the capital for a mission that was assigned to me. Pheonix and Moss decided to join me, and the rest were heading in that direction anyways."

Ninja looked at Imp, her green eyes pensive. She bit the bottom of her lip, looking as if she was going to make a tough decision.

"What if I could...break you out of here?"

Chapter 23

Imp woke up in the middle of the night.

She groaned, rubbing at her eyes. Ninja had said that they would make a plan to get out tomorrow, and Imp had spent all night excited for it. Imp rolled in her bed, looking over to where Ninja was sleeping.

Or rather, where she should have been sleeping.

Instead there was a bundle of covers that probably looked a lot like a sleeping girl from the outside, but from Imp's view it looked anything but. She got out of bed, putting her hand on the covers. They were dead cold. Ninja was long gone.

What's happening? Imp thought as she went towards the door. She leaned against it, trying to get a view of the corridor.

Imp nearly screamed as the barred door swung open, sending her tumbling into the hallway. She froze, looking fearfully down the row, hoping that no guards would come see what was happening. But there were no guards, and Imp straightened.

Now what do I do? Part of Imp was tempted to go back into her cell and be a good girl. The other wanted to go outside and explore a little.

Suddenly alarms started blaring, red lights flashing in the ceiling. Imp nearly jumped out of her skin. She rushed into her cell, closing the door and burrowing under the covers.

What if I was the one who tripped the alarm?! I'm so dead! Imp thought, panicking.

She watched as guards rushed towards her cell...then breathed a sigh of relief as they continued past, heading to an unknown destination.

When all the night watchers had marched by, Imp went to the window, her eyes widening at the sight.

The courtyard was covered in pure darkness, the only flashes of light the flashlights that the sentries held. But they only illuminated a foot in front of them; the darkness was like a thick fog.

Suddenly all the guards looked up towards Imp, and she could not help but panic under their glare. One of them pointed, and she realised that they were not looking at her.

They were looking above her.

Some of the guards aimed their bows, madly shooting arrows at the unseen assailant. Imp watched as most of them bounced off the building, broken. The guards stopped shooting, looking disappointed, and the fog began to dissipate.

Black Liquorice Flavour. Darkness, Imp suddenly remembered, and it all made sense.

The next day at breakfast Ninja, Imp, Moss, Pheonix, Tric and Aqua sat together. As soon as Ninja told them the plan to get them out of the prison, they were all on board. Especially Tric, as long as it involved running.

They spent the rest of the day formulating a plan. It was rare for Ninja to break out such a large group, especially right after another group. The guards were more watchful than usual, their embarrassment over the escapees turning into a savage desire for order. Every activity section had extra sentinels, armed with swords and bows. Their hands were constantly on their weapons, as if they expected all of the inmates to suddenly go rabid and attack.

Ninja was like some kind of grand escape artist. She had every hallway mapped mentally, a great feat. According to her, there were 102 different hallways, all named by the guards. Imp almost expected her to know exactly how long each one was.

Ninja coordinated the escape so easily even Moss, who had a notoriously bad memory, could remember.

"So exciting!" Tric said, bounding up and down slightly and clapping his hands in excitement.

At supper it was noticeable that the group was excited. The guards were giving them suspicious glares, but they didn't care.

We're busting out!

"So here's the plan." Snow said, looking at the group of Flavours gathered.

"Yeah, a plan!" Screamed one of them, followed by the giggling of a female voice. Snow could already feel his blood beginning to boil.

Why did those two have to be here?! He thought, glaring at the infamous 'soul mates'.

Dark and Ness, Black Liquorice Flavours. According to them, they chose their names *before* they met each other, and that's how they knew that they were destined to be soul mates. Most people doubted the story.

Dark was a tall-ish, black haired male with a huge ego. He had a tendency to flirt with girls, even though he had found his 'soul mate'. He wasn't well liked among the females though, mostly because they thought he was slightly creepy.

Ness was the girl who was clutching his arm, laughing as if he were some kind of comedian. She had a tendency to stick her nose into things, wanting to help. Although it usually turned out worse than before.

"Please don't interrupt me." Snow said icily, grinding his teeth, "Now, on to the plan."

Snow gestured to a huge map of the capital prison. They had gained it from one of the escapees, who had been given the map to give to the FTA. In the corner was the name of the cartographer: Ninja.

"According to Rowan," Snow said, nodding in the direction of the Flavour leaning against a wall, "Imp and the others are being held in the O'Donnell wing. The same one as Ninja. We'll wait until nightfall, and picklock the gate. We'll get Dark and Ness to bend the shadows to disguise the gate opening and us sneaking in. Once inside, we'll stick as close to the walls as possible, heading through the secretary's office, and down the O'Flaer branch, then to the O'Donnell wing. Any questions?"

"Why are the branches named so funnily?" Aria asked.

"I think you missed the meaning of questions." Pyra whispered to her, "He's talking about questions about the battle plans."

"Oh. That makes sense." Aria nodded sagely, "But why are they named that?"

Pyra sighed. "I think they're named after towns."

"Weird."

"Okay, any questions *other* than stupid ones?" Snow demanded. Aria raised her hand anyway, "Good, no questions."

They waited until midnight.

Ninja pulled off her covers, seeing Imp do the same from the corner of her eye. She looked through the metal bars, listening. When she heard no footsteps, she took out her lock picking tool, put her hand through the bars and reaching for the lock.

It only took Ninja a few seconds to unlock it. She was so used to it by now. She gestured for Imp to follow her, moving on to the others' cells. They were already awake, watching Ninja unlock the doors with eager eyes.

The group followed Ninja down the hallway, their bodies taught with excitement and fear. She was leading them to the inmate lockers, where she hoped their gummies would be. She had a special wire for the lockers, too. She pretty much had some way of unlocking every door in the whole prison.

They had now made it into the secretary's office, and Imp yearningly looked at the doors of the prison. Outside those doors was the courtyard, and eventually the gate.

Ninja suddenly tensed, whirling around with a finger to her lips. She ran soundlessly towards the secretary's desk, gesturing for the group to follow her. She pushed the secretary's rolling chair out of the way, wincing at the sound. Gesturing desperately to them again, she pushed them into the space under the desk, where the secretary's legs would go. Imp was pleasantly surprised to see how spacious it was. Then again, that was probably expected of that beefy receptionist.

They all managed to fit in, tightly, and only then did they hear footsteps.

How the heck did Ninja know someone was coming? Imp wondered.

A door opened, and Imp was slightly relieved to find that it wasn't the one they had come from. But her relief was destroyed as the guard walked across the office and headed towards the door that led to the corridor that they had been held in.

"We don't have much time." Ninja whispered as soon as the door closed. She sprang from underneath the desk, moving at a quick jog. She gestured for them to follow, taking the door that the guard had come from.

They walked into the other wing, tiptoeing as quickly as they could past the sleeping inmates. They went through the door at the end of this hall, and Ninja immediately turned, going through a locked door that she opened easily.

They now stood in a room with rows upon rows of lockers, each locker with the cell number on it. Ninja ran her fingers along the lockers as she walked towards the number 382: her and Imp's cell. Next to it were the lockers 383 and 384.

Ninja once again took out her lock picking tool, using it to open all three lockers. Imp was relieved when she found her pack of Cream Soda gummies sitting in the locker, along with her backpack. There was nothing of Ninja's in the locker.

"Alright." Ninja said, popping a gummy into her mouth, "Time to break you guys out."

That was when the alarms went off.

Snow and his group of 6 Flavours approached the prison under the cloak of night.

The group was composed of Snow, Aria, Pyra, Dusty, Dark, Ness, and Bolt, a Lemon Flavour, all of them handpicked by Snow and Dusty. Despite their shared hatred of Dark and Ness, they were the only Darkness Flavours on hand, and they needed their help, as much as they hated to admit it.

The towering walls of the prison seemed to glow with some kind of evil aura, a kind of malice that was a warning to all Flavours. They approached from the back, knowing that the large, fancy gates would be too obvious if they opened.

Snow gestured at Dark and Ness. They nodded, Dark flashing him a smile so white it probably gave him away in the inky darkness. They raised their hands in unison, dark tendrils of smoke-like night coiling around their fingers like snakes. The pure blackness oozed along the ground, enveloping the gate in a shroud of darkness, a deep shadow, like that caused by the sun. They waited in anxiety for a second, but no alarms sounded, and Snow pointed at Aria.

Aria advanced towards the gate, bearing a lock pick. She walked up to the door, and cursed under her breath. The once traditional key lock had been replaced with a digital one, a fancy thing that demanded a fingerprint.

"Damn." Pyra swore as she came to a stand beside Aria, "We need another plan, Snow."

Snow frowned, looking as if he were in deep thought. "Let's go over the walls."

"What?!" Bolt exclaimed, staring at the Mint Flavour who he now decided was completely nuts.

"Aria." Snow asked, turning to her, "Do you think you could boost us over the wall?"

"Maybe." Aria was looking doubtfully at the spikes and wires perched on top of the high barrier.

"I want to go first!" Dusty exclaimed, looking excited, "I'll make the earth rise a little so you don't have to push me that far."

Aria nodded, stepping close to Dusty as the earth pitched. A mini-mountain appeared, reaching to about halfway up the wall, about seven feet.

The shadows moved to the wall, cloaking it because of Dark and Ness' will. Aria breathed in deeply, pushing towards the ground. A burst of highly-concentrated air pushed Dusty off the ground. He floated higher and higher, and the group on the ground watched as the air pitched him over the side of the wall.

The ground rumbled beneath their feet a little, and they waited once again for any alarms to sound. The prison was silent, and they all breathed a sigh of relief. Aria waved down at the group, silently asking for another volunteer.

"I'll go." Pyra said, stepping up and waving at Aria. She immediately felt her feet lift off the ground, and was surprised to find herself in line with the platform in a matter of seconds. She stepped onto the ground, waiting for Aria to catch her breath. Moments later she was in the air again, pitched over the wall. She had to hold back a scream as she saw the ground rush towards her.

Pyra landed, knocking the air out of her lungs, but nothing was broken. She felt sand on her bare skin. Dusty offered her a hand, and she gratefully took it.

Next came Dark, Ness, Bolt, Snow, and finally Aria. They all crouched down surrounded by shadows, watching as guards walked past them, unawares. Eventually Snow gestured to them to follow him, sneaking towards the front doors. He opened it, surprised to find it unlocked. They were greeted by a hallway branching off to more hallways.

"This way." Snow whispered, gesturing towards one of the hallways.

That was when the alarms went off.

Chapter 24

Ninja swore out-loud, pushing the others in front of her.

"Don't let them see my face!" Ninja hissed from her position behind Imp, "If they do, my days of busting people out are over!"

They ran, Pheonix, Moss, Tric, Aqua and Imp each chewing on their individual flavoured gummies.

"I'll scout ahead!" Imp yelled to Moss, who was currently running in the front. She squeezed past him, turning invisible and running ahead.

Some guards came at them, surprising Imp. She immediately delivered a punch to one of them as they rushed by. He fell, clutching his nose, the other clothes-lined by Imp's still outstretched fist. As the clothes-lined guard struggled to get up Tric zapped him, knocking him unconscious. The punched one aimed a kick at Tric. A water whip came out of nowhere, wrapping itself around the watchman's leg. He was slammed into the wall, sliding to the floor. He wasn't moving.

The group stepped over the fallen Police, continuing to run down the hallway. They made it to the main entrance, the secretary's office.

Ninja yelped as a guard rushed towards them, and Pheonix jumped in front of her to protect her identity.

Wham!

The guard went flying, a burst of air stirring in his wake. From the corridor opposite the locker-leading one came a sorry sight: Snow, Aria, Pyra, Dusty and three other Flavours Imp did not know.

"That was anticlimactic." Pyra yelled to them, grinning.

"We still need to get out." Snow reminded her, pointing to the door. They had blocked it with a rock, courtesy of Dusty. Banging sounds came from behind the door, and they watched as it bulged, as if someone was kicking it.

"And this is where I leave you." Ninja said, stepping out from behind Pheonix.

Imp nodded, though it was hard to see Ninja go. Even though she was young, she was incredibly brave to stay in prison when she could so easily escape.

Ninja waved to them as she went down the O'Donnell wing, which would lead to her cell and a long time in prison.

"We need to go, now." Dusty warned as another kick to the door sent a crack down the middle of the rock.

"Let's go, then." Snow nodded to Dusty, who immediately disintegrated the rock, the particles flying to his hand in preparation.

They waited for a while, surprised when no more kicks came.

"What are they waiting for?" Bolt asked, staring at the door as if it would suddenly spring open.

"This is taking too long!" Pyra complained, moving towards the door. She kicked it, amazed at how easily it opened into the courtyard.

A courtyard full of Police.

"Watch out!" Aria cried as an arrow whizzed towards Pyra's head. Aria quickly sent a blast of air, deflecting the arrow in the nick of time. Pyra slammed the door, leaning her back against it. Footsteps were heard rushing from outside, and the door bulged, nearly sending her sprawling. Aria came beside her, both of them pushing against the door.

"Is there another way out?!" Moss asked, clearly panicked.

"There was mention of a back door in the plan." Snow said, his voice as calm and collected as ever, "Follow me."

After Dusty secured the door with another rock, Snow led them down the door that led to the O'Donnell wing. There were Police unconscious on the ground, their clothes singed, ice pinning them to the wall, or bruised by either Dusty or Aria. They turned immediately, going through a door the same way Ninja had gone when she was bringing them to the locker room. Aria quickly unlocked the door, and they pushed through into the room.

This place is symmetrical, Imp realised, wondering why she hadn't figured it out before.

They came into another locker room, this one for the cells in the wing opposite O'Donnell's. Through the tunnel of red lockers they could see a rectangle shape in the shadow of the lightless room. As they got closer to it the shadows receded, and Imp's heart leapt at the sight of a door.

Aria ran forward, once again taking out her trusty lock-pick. With a skill only slightly below Ninja's she maneuvered the thin steel rod. A click sounded, and she opened the door, slowly and surely. She peeked out of the tiny crack that opened.

"They've got spotlights!" Hissed Aria, quickly closing the door.

"We need more darkness." Dusty replied, looking pointedly at Dark and Ness.

Dark gave him a thumbs up and a cheery grin, reminding Imp temporarily of Tric. But Tric did a lot better, an honest effort to cheer someone up, lacking the 'I'm so superior' touch that Dark's had.

Dark opened the door slightly, trying to keep himself hidden. It was more difficult that he expected, with the spotlight glaring down at him. He made some of the shadows rise to hide the door's crack, but he wasn't sure if it fooled the Police.

Ness came to stand beside him, gesturing with her head towards the shadow cast by the spotlight, the inky night that clung to the walls. He nodded in understanding.

The shadows along the wall began to rise, a steady, slow movement that clung to the bricks. The spotlight perched on top of the wall shone its light on the door, and the Police in the courtyard stood in ready positions, staring at the Flavours waiting inside. Neither of them noticed the darkness shifting, crawling up the walls like dark demons.

"As soon as the lights go out, we run." Pheonix warned everyone, even though they already knew. She was crouched in a sprinter's beginning position, her hand ready to push the door open.

"Yes! Running!" Imp heard Tric whisper under his breath, and she couldn't help but smile.

Dark raised his hand as the darkness began to pool onto the spikes and wire on top of the wall, roiling like smoke towards its target.

The darkness sprang up, enveloping the light. The world went black as all hell broke loose.

"Watch out for them!" Lars yelled, gesturing at his officers, who'd all cried out in surprise as the spotlight went out, "They'll try to escape in the confusion!"

He was right when he felt something brush past his face, suddenly exploding into a blinding fire. Lars rubbed at his eyes, blinking to stop the purple blotches that were blinding him more effectively than the darkness.

The spotlight came back on, temporarily illuminating the courtyard, and Lars got a good idea of where the Flavours were. Some of them were just as disoriented as the Police were, but all of them were making their ways towards the side of the building, where they would eventually circle around back towards the gate.

"Head towards the gate!" Lars yelled as wisps of blackness enveloped the spotlight once more, giving the world strange shadows before it completely obliterated the light.

He ran towards the courtyard, stumbling and knocking one of the Flavours down by accident. There was a girl-like cry of surprise, and Lars desperately tried reaching for an arm, anything to hold her down. The lights came back on, the spotlight temporarily winning the battle against the darkness. Lars nearly screamed in terror as he realized that there was no one there beneath him, even though he could feel flesh beneath his fingers.

Relax! It's Imp! Lars reminded himself. The lights went out again.

Suddenly he felt a boot connect with his face, and he cried out in surprise. He reeled back, clutching his bleeding mouth. He felt Imp move, a fist sinking into his stomach. He fell to the ground, momentarily stunned. Lars could hear Imp's footsteps as she ran away.

I can't believe I accidentally ran into her, then lost her within a minute! Lars growled, knowing that he would be beating himself up for that later.

As Lars straightened up and began to run again the lights came back on, this time seeming to have lost the darkness. He could see two Flavours ahead of him reaching into their bags, ready to eat another gummy.

They must be Black Liquorice Flavours! They're controlling the darkness!

Lars saw Delyn rush past him, brandishing his own sword, no longer the basic one Lars had given him. The hilt, black metal etched with swirls, was grasped firmly in his hand, the silver blade glowing in the spotlight's glare.

With a fierceness that Lars had come to admire, Delyn charged, flicking his wrist and scoring a stinging lash along the female Flavour's back. She cried out, dropping her gummy as she rolled, avoiding his next attack. Lars watched as the male Flavour brought his gummy up to his mouth, and Lars charged. He brought the hilt of his sword down on his wrist, spilling the gummy to the ground. The Flavour retaliated with a kick, barely missing Lars' face.

The female Flavour screamed, and Lars turned. Delyn's sword flashed, and a long scratch appeared on her face. Another sword flash left a long gash on her arm. Delyn was laughing. Laughing like a lunatic.

"Delyn, that's enough." Lars commanded him as he slashed at her other arm. Lars grabbed Delyn's arm, forcing the sword point to the ground instead of in the girl's flesh. Delyn threw him off, growling like a crazed animal. The female Flavour moved to her feet, the male coming to stand beside her with concern in his eyes, and anger aimed at Delyn. Before Lars could stop him he opened a gash on her leg, blood already seeping from it.

"Stop, Delyn!" Lars punched him in the face, hoping that a bruise would bring him to his senses, "You are my subordinate! You *must* obey me!"

Delyn staggered back a few steps, his hand flying to his face. He turned on Lars, glaring at him as he raised his sword a little, pointing it towards the two Liquorice Flavours as they prepared to swallow a gummy.

An invisible force knocked him to the ground. Imp materialized, straddling Delyn. In her hand she held a knife, probably from a fallen Police. It was held to Delyn's throat, Imp's tiny fist wrapped up in his shirt, tilting his head back. She looked angry, only a step away from Berserk mode.

"I know you have a problem with me." Imp said, her voice shaking a little with uncontrollable anger, "But don't take it out on someone else." She gestured with the blade she held, pressing it so close to his throat that Lars was surprised she didn't draw blood, "It will stab you in the back one day. Or in the throat."

Delyn gulped. There were a few tense moments as Imp just crouched there, seeming to contemplate whether she should sever his head with her blade. Eventually she withdrew, stepping off Delyn. She turned away from them, arrogantly certain that no one would stab her in the back. The two Flavours followed her almost meekly, glancing back at the fallen Delyn with a look of pity in their eyes. One of them raised their hand, and the courtyard was plunged once again into darkness, the escaping Flavours seeming to melt into it, disappearing out of the prison.

Chapter 25

Imp was relieved to see the FTA again.

She considered it her home, not the house in Diyo where her mother was murdered and her father betrayed her. Here, she was respected and loved, not treated with the scorn her father had given her.

As they opened the door, all of them weary and Ness bleeding in multiple places, they were greeted by Rain.

"You're a sorry sight for sore eyes." She murmured, ushering them inside. She immediately sent Ness to the sick room, Dark trailing her worriedly.

They might be annoying, Pyra remarked internally, *But you can't doubt that they're committed to each other.*

Rain brought the rest of them to the kitchen, boiling some water on the stove. It didn't take long for cups of hot chocolate to be pushed in front of them, and they drank greedily. She also offered them some cookies and soft bread as a little snack.

It's been so long since I've had hot chocolate! Imp thought excitedly, drinking from the frothy beverage. She loved hot chocolate almost as much as she loved peaches.

From the corner of her eye she saw Aqua drinking greedily, serving herself to a second cup before everyone else had gotten halfway through their first. She smacked her lips.

"I love chocolate." She murmured under her breath, breathing the hot steam that was rising from her cup, "Chocolate and water...my two favourite things combined in a heavenly cup."

Imp smiled slightly, still drinking hers. She dipped some of the cookies in—triple chocolate, her favourite—enjoying being in the FTA again.

"Imp." Rain said as she led Imp to her room. Everyone else had already gone into theirs, and it was Imp and Rain alone.

"Yes?" Imp asked curiously.

"We have gathered as many Flavours that could possibly help you with your mission, but we're still short." Rain frowned, turning to the girl standing in the hallway, "We need to attack soon. They're almost ready. We only have 26 Flavours gathered here, including you. Do you think this will be enough?"

"Plenty." Imp nodded, feeling a little sick to her stomach. The Flavour 'army' was meant to be a distraction as she slipped into the lab, eventually finding the gummy and destroying it. If they could only get 26 Flavours, it would have to do.

"Are you sure?" Rain asked, probably seeing some doubt in Imp's face. Imp did her best to put on a brave air, "Imp, if this attack doesn't work, then we will never get the opportunity to attack again. They will expect it the next time. We could wait another week—"

"No." Imp said sternly, "By then they will have launched an attack against us. Don't worry Rain, I already have an idea on how the lab is laid out. If we have plans of the factory, even better. I can make it exactly to where the gummy is quickly, especially if everyone is evacuated because of the attack. I'll destroy it."

Rain still looked uncertain as Imp brushed past her, opening the door to her room and closing it behind her in one fluid movement.

"We need to be armed for the attack." Dusty announced, taking a stand in front of the group of gathered Flavours, "Some of you are probably familiar with these weapons; others have never used them before. The key is to take a weapon that you think you will work best with, and it would be even better if you could find one that was different than your fighting style. If you prefer long range attacks, take a sword or dagger. If you usually fight up close, take a bow. As you can see, there are plenty of weapons here; after everyone has finalized their choice, feel free to help yourself to another one."

Imp barely listened, drifting off from her spot on the grass. In a couple of moments, she would have to choose her weapon. She already knew what she would choose. A sword. She had trained to use it when she entered the FTA. The only reason she didn't carry one around with her was because she was afraid of what she could do with it.

Dusty finished his speech, blowing into a whistle. The group scattered, each going to different sections of the courtyard to practice with their fellow wielders.

Imp headed to the sword station, noticing Dark and Pyra staring at some blades. She came to stand beside them, looking at the glittering array.

Imp watched Dark choose a sword, swinging it experimentally. The smile that lit upon his face was that of pure pleasure. Apparently he had found his sword.

Imp stepped to his place, looking at the rack. Pyra was still there, looking extremely uncertain. Imp picked a medium length blade, but it felt too top heavy. She moved on, this time taking a slightly longer one, with a hilt that tilted down at the ends, perfect for deflecting attacks. She swung it, marvelling at how light it was. A couple more swings sealed the deal. It was the perfect blade for her: light and easy to maneuver.

Imp would need to keep this blade with her during the battle. It could be her only chance to destroy the gummy, slashing the machines that created it, hopefully annihilating it in the process. She doubted that she'd be able to destroy it with her bare hands, so some kind of weapon was needed.

Imp went to stand beside Pyra, helping herself to the scabbard that had the same number as her sword. She was suddenly struck by a memory of going skiing...having to remember your ski's number, and leaving it behind to go into the chalet. Imp realised that it had been a while since she had gone skiing. It was a thing for happier days.

Pyra was staring at the sparkling blades with a hopeless expression on her face.

"Do you need help choosing a sword?" Imp asked as she buckled on the scabbard, sliding the sword into it. She felt a lot heavier than usual.

"Yes please." Pyra answered gratefully, deciding that her search would prove fruitless with her lack of experience.

It took a while for Imp and Pyra to settle on a sword. Eventually they settled on a different weapon: a wicked looking scythe. She slashed it around with a look of satisfaction.

They moved to join Dark at the small training ground for sword wielders. The moment Imp drew her sword, Dark was upon her.

"Hey." He said, giving her a flirtatious smile, very similar to that of Dusty's, "Do you need help learning how to use a sword? I'm a great partner!"

Well, he's more subtle than Dusty, at least.

Imp raised her sword, as Dark rose his, inviting her to attack with his empty hand. With a flick of her wrist she gave a painful scratch to Dark's fingers. She watched his expression change from one of superiority to horror as she sent his sword clattering out of his hand.

"I think I'll do just fine, thank you." She beamed innocently at him, "But thanks for the offer."

The rest of the afternoon for Imp was spent teaching Pyra how to use a scythe. Imp felt a little out of place, but tried her best to help her out. By the middle of the training session, Pyra could at least swing it with some potency.

Imp felt a little out of place at this point, but Pyra insisted that she continue to teach her. Apparently Imp was a lot better teacher than the ones she'd had before.

Eventually Pyra was managing to deflect most of Imp's attacks, even to the point that with an extra shield she could actually hold her own in a battle.

Pyra finally let Imp go after supper, saying that she would practice some more against other weapons, and she didn't need Imp's help for that. So she decided to go check out how everyone else was doing.

Imp watched Snow and Tric spar. Snow had chosen a dagger, although he was relying more on his ice slivers, trying to train Tric, who had chosen a bunch of shurikens. It went pretty well with his whole ninja look, what with the long scarf and the newly added gloves. They seemed to be pretty equally matched, so Imp moved on. There was no point in intruding, especially because Snow could supply Tric with two different kinds of experience: long-range and short-range.

Dusty and Aria were also sparring, pitching her arrows of air against his flying chunks of rock.

Suddenly Dusty changed tactics, the ground exploding around Aria and disintegrating into harmless dust. Imp watched in amazement as the dust flew to his arm as if to encase it, but it morphed into a huge war hammer. Apparently he had decided to form his weapon out of his element, not even taking his own advice. Aria responded by taking out her new weapon: a wicked looking halberd that had been strapped to her back. She maneuvered the pole with ease, using the long spike on top to stab, and the small axe blade to strike.

Imp moved on, spotting Aqua and Pheonix practicing. Aqua had two small daggers strapped to her waist, although for the battle she was relying on her trusty whip. Pheonix was now sending out bursts of fire, probably having taken some inspiration from Pyra. Aqua was using her whip to disintegrate the daggers, causing an awe-inspiring display of steam.

Imp realised that she needed someone to spar with. She didn't want to interrupt any of her friends' fights; they had obviously chosen their partners to gain some good practice with their new weapons.

"Hey Imp!" A voice called, and she turned to see Moss running towards her. He waved, and she waved back as he got closer.

"Do you wanna spar?" He asked, and for a second Imp wondered if he could read minds.

"Sure." Imp smiled, and Moss grinned back. It wasn't a really reassuring thing. It looked like he had something up his sleeve.

Perfect, Imp thought. The Police were always full of surprises, and dealing with them was a skill essential for survival.

"Don't make me too sore." Imp grinned at him, and Moss was surprised by how excited she looked. Could a spar really excite her that much? "I need to be in good shape for the attack!"

They found a spot clear of battlers. As the sky started to darken, they began.

Moss was the first to attack, the roots already starting to tear up the earth beneath their feet. Imp jumped as a root came up at her, slashing the top off with her sword. It shrunk back as if in pain as Moss attempted an attack on Imp's back. She landed and rolled, the root missing her.

She needed to get close to Moss, so that she could put her sword to use.

As he raised his hand once more, she charged, surprising him. She slashed, and he blocked it, using a quarterstaff he had cleverly formed from a root. He pushed her away, dodging his attack. They parried for a while, neither of them willing to let the other get one smidge of an advantage over the other.

It was only after 20 minutes of sparring did they call truce, falling to the ground, exhausted. They didn't even wish each other good night as they dragged themselves up to their rooms.

Mrs. Ately looked sadly at Imp.

Here she was, reunited with her 'daughter', and now they would be separated to go off into battle where survival was uncertain. The scene reminded her of when she and Delyn were going to school: except this time, her son had turned to the enemy and was probably trying to kill Imp, and Imp was walking into the middle of her enemy's base. Mrs. Ately felt like she was going to cry.

Imp looked up at her, having finished buckling on her sword. She looked so much older, Mrs. Ately realised. With her eyes filled with an anxious and ready glint her hand toying nervously with the sword hilt at her side, she looked more like an adult than the child that Mrs. Ately had came to love. It scared her.

As Imp's eyes met Mrs. Ately's, her eyes softened a little. She smiled, opening her arms, and Mrs. Ately rushed into them. She nearly laughed at how the roles had been reversed: instead of Imp rushing into Mrs. Ately's arms when she was hurting, it was Mrs. Ately who needed the comforting.

"Goodbye, Siria." Mrs. Ately whispered, and she was happy when Imp didn't bother to correct her.

"Goodbye." Imp whispered back, holding onto her second mother. She let go, all too soon for Mrs. Ately, waving as she turned her back and got into the car with the other Flavours.

Chapter 26

Imp gulped, staring at the Police factory.

It was huge. A sprawling centre made of a bunch of different buildings, the lab was surrounded by a huge wall that reminded Imp of the prison. According to the battle plans that they had been presented with yesterday, the building that Imp needed to sneak into was the far left one, the high security factory, where they would be producing the Flavourless gummy. To the north of this building was the indoor testing lab. The right half was separated from the left half by a large field, where the main battle would be likely to occur. On the right side were two sections: the main research lab to the south, and the outdoor testing area above it.

Trees surrounded the walls in an effort to make it seem more innocent, but the effect was ruined with the barbed wire mounted on top. It lacked the spires of the prison, but it still gave off the same message. Stay away.

The Flavours were hidden in the foliage, the leafy barrier disabling the security cameras that sat within the barbed wire. They were a large group, at least for the Flavours: thirty-eight members, all armed with at least two bags of gummies. Rain had managed to muster up a few more troops. It was a huge amount for only a couple hours of battling, but necessary for those who were planning to hit the Police hard and painfully. The commanders, and Imp, of course, were equipped with walkie-talkies. They were some kind of high-tech communicators, probably stolen from the Police. A thick black collar was attached around the neck, buttons lining it and a small section to speak into. From one side came a thin wire, at the end of which was an ear bud that projected sound so perfectly, it was only heard by the person wearing it, no matter what volume it was set at.

Imp adjusted the belt of her sword for the umpteenth time, nervously pawing at the blade's handle. Her plan had so many faults in it that it was almost laughable. Even if she was invisible, the factory was high security, probably equipped with heat and pressure sensors. Somehow she had to sneak through the building without being noticed, eventually reaching the core of the whole attack. Something so valuable had to have outrageous security measures. The Police could get pretty extreme with their traps. Anything worked, so long as it stopped the invader in their tracks. Imp had run into very primitive and very high tech traps: poison darts that shot from walls, or heat sensors that could record the fingerprints of the thief from a distance, identifying them in the database. But the absolute favourite for Police on the go was the wire trap.

Imp honestly did not know what to expect, and she was worried. She hated surprises that usually ended up in her getting captured.

Any second now, the bombs that Pyra had set would go off, destroying the wall and opening the lab to invasion. Imp already had the gummy in her mouth, not chewing it. The flavour of cream soda was seeping into her tongue, only serving as a reminder how everything was on her shoulders. Cream soda, the power of dreams, the most powerful Flavour in existence. It wasn't a blessing. It was the mark of a hard life, where the only way to survive was hanging onto dreams of better days.

Blessing or curse...It doesn't change anything. I'm still the Cream Soda Flavour, no matter what.

There was a huge boom, and they were showered with small bits of stone and metal. The bomb had gone off. It was time to fight.

How long will this war last? How many people will die because we're too stubborn to put aside our differences?

Imp chomped down on her gummy, invisibly joining the Flavours as they charged towards battle.

Lars couldn't sleep.

All night he tossed and turned, replaying the events of the prison break over and over in his mind. It was like a film reel of shame, showing him the moments that he had failed badly. The particular scene that kept sticking out the most was that of Imp holding a knife to Delyn's throat. In particularly nightmarish scenes, it was Lars on the ground. The dream was so vivid, he could feel the cold steel edge of the knife against his throat, and Imp's weight leaning over him. But the scene that by far scared him the most...It was Imp on the ground, with Lars on top of her. He had his sword to her throat, and he could see the absolutely terrified look in her eyes. The scariest of all was the yearning to slit her throat.

Lars shivered, turning to see the alarm clock on the night table of the hotel room. It was 6:30 A.M. He would've liked to sleep in a bit more, but it was impossible.

Lars got out of bed, sleepily changing from his pyjamas to his uniform. He caught a peek of himself in the mirror; it wasn't pretty. His usually bright grey eyes were glazed over with tiredness, the intense color muddied by the black bags beneath them. He had a red line on his face, and he realized that it must have been from the covers of his bed.

At least Imp didn't give me a black eye when she kicked me, Lars thought, shivering at the mental image of his eyes completely rimmed in black. Then his face would scare even the most seasoned officers.

Lars chuckled at the thought, heading to the bathroom. He quickly washed his face, rubbing it with cold water until he felt a little more aware. He took a moment to look at his face in the mirror, wondering why he was so self-conscious this morning. For some strange reason, his skin was much more pale than usual. Lars frowned into the mirror, pinching his cheek like the maidens of old. But no color came.

I'm a total wreck, Lars groaned at the thought. Today he had to be ready to fight as the defence against the Flavour's attack. It wouldn't be good for him to appear like he had lost sleep over it.

Lars stumbled out of his room in the hotel, absent-mindedly buckling on his sword and scabbard to his back. He paused outside Delyn's door while walking down the hallway. He could hear the faintest of snores coming from behind the door.

How can he sleep so well? Lars wondered, *He nearly killed a Flavour, and nearly got killed by Imp!*

The thought of it brought back the scary scenes of his nightmares. Lars put his back to the wall, trying to catch his breath.

Why am I so terrified? Lars wondered, poking at the scene of malaise that had gathered at the back of his brain.

He jumped as Delyn opened his door, and Lars felt a bit of relief as he noticed that Delyn's eyes were as tired as his. Delyn looked at Lars with a sneer, and Lars frowned at him. He had been different ever since...Lars shuddered. It was another memory that he was trying to force from his mind, ranking in scariness just as high as his latest nightmare.

But Delyn probably knows all about that, Lars thought, walking away. He could sense Delyn glaring at him from behind his back, following him as he headed down the elevator, *You probably know a lot about nightmares now, Delyn.*

As Lars walked out of the hotel and towards the awaiting car, Delyn veered off towards a different vehicle. Lars winced as he recognized one of the lab cars. It was used for transporting testing equipment.

Lars swung his sword, beheading another dummy.

He had been training for hours now, losing himself in the swinging of his sword and the image of his enemies losing limbs in defeat. Sometimes he guiltily imagined Delyn, and he wasn't proud to say that he maimed those dummies more than the ones he imagined as Imp.

This is all so wrong! Lars thought, his voice seeming to echo in his head, *Now my friend is somehow turning into an enemy, and my enemy is becoming a friend!*

Lars slashed again, taking out the final dummy of the training field. He had decided to train against the traditional straw, unmoving enemies, instead of the newest models: steel ones that moved and talked, swinging with holographic weapons that simulated pain when hit. He didn't like those. The thought of killing such realistic robots was just as bad as killing humans for Lars.

You're probably going to have to scrap that concept, Lars reminded himself, *This battle will be merciless, and I doubt that you'll be able to capture the Flavours in this big of a brawl.*

For the umpteenth time he wondered if the Flavours knew about the Police ambush. He wouldn't be surprised if they did. Whoever was in charge were master planners and knowledge getters: more than once the Flavours had known of top secret Police knowledge, and it was rare for Flavours to walk into huge, planned traps. Lars had to wonder how they got all of this info.

"Lars!" The booming voice of General Salem called, and Lars could see him striding down the training field towards him.

"What is it?" Lars asked politely.

"It's time to go set up the resistance." Salem reminded him, gesturing towards the army SUV that had been parked on the road beside the training arena.

Lars let Salem lead him into it, taking a seat in silence.

Lars crouched down, hidden underneath a bush in the sparse lab yard. It was really a wide open space, with barely any cover and full of grass. It wasn't the best place for a battle, especially one with archers that could easily send a rain of arrows onto their heads. They would have nowhere to hide.

The Police army tried its best to set up small shelters with plain wood and scraps that they had either scavenged or brought with them. It wasn't much, but it was more than the Flavours would have.

The Flavours should be here by now, Lars thought, drawing his sword. The watch hadn't reported anything. But it was hard to see with the trees that had been so stupidly planted right next to the wall. If it hadn't been for the barbed wire on top, just about anyone who was decent at climbing could get in. But after the prison break, there was no doubt that Flavours could somehow get over walls with any kind of protection.

There was a huge boom, and some of the Police men screamed. The ones closest to the strong steel gate were showered with tiny bits and pieces of it.

A bomb! Lars gasped in his mind, raising a protective arm against the debris.

With a savage roar, the Flavours flooded through the smoke of the destroyed gate.

"To battle!" He heard General Salem's voice call, strong and loud over the Flavours' screaming.

Lars charged.

Chapter 27

"Give us some shelter!" Pyra yelled at Dusty, who nodded. With a flick of his hand he made giant walls of rock in between them and the Police, effectively creating trenches that weren't underground. The archers set themselves up behind these walls, occasionally sending out arrows and crossbow bolts of all elements. Aria was the fastest of them all, knocking out the Police in bucketfuls. For every one the other archers hit, two had been felled by her arrows of air.

In this battle, SOFT were the ones in charge. They had been declared commanders by the High Council: and because of that, it was on their shoulders to keep the army fighting, and keep everyone alive.

Aria and Snow were in charge of the long-rangers, while Pheonix, who had been made an honorary member, was in charge of close combat in conjunction with Tric. Dusty and Aqua were in charge of the miscellaneous, with Pyra and Moss in control of the middle-range section.

The Flavours had known that the Police would be there. They were good at getting whiffs of plans. But that was all they were: whiffs. They knew that the Flavours were planning an attack and when, but they had no idea of their battle plans. It was one of the only advantages that they were certain of, and they stubbornly used it for everything.

The first moments of the battle was testing the enemy. Arrows were fired against each other's defences. A couple of swordsmen faced off, slashing at each other slowly in an attempt to look for weaknesses. But that was all. Eventually they retreated, waiting in tense moments for each other to make the first move. Dusty strengthened their defences, reinforcing the earthy walls and making trenches for their troops to hide in. They could see the Police watching them, their weapons ready.

The Flavours were the first to strike.

The weakest of the Police defences was chosen, Pyra and Moss giving the orders to shoot. Moss' roots tore at the metal, while Pyra used her bursts of flame to burn away the wood. Other elemental, and some weapons, followed, all trying to batter down the defences. There was a joint cry of victory as it went down in flames.

Pheonix and Tric led their wing to battle, meeting with the Police sword wielders. Element met steel as they clashed, and a volley of arrows descended upon them, both their own side and the Police side.

A Police slashed at Pheonix, his silver sword missing her as she jumped out of the way. She retaliated, slashing him across his chest with blazing fingers. A burning trail of smouldering clothes was the result, revealing steel armour underneath. Another Police tried to slash at her back. Tric stopped him, his electrified hand giving the attacker a painful shock. Pheonix barely had time to nod in recognition as another swordsman came at her. He slashed, and it was child's play to dodge and strike, a burning kick piercing right through his armour. He turned tail and ran.

Tric was having a grand time. He was running through the Police troops, using his agility to dodge and strike. Even the slightest touch from his hand could make a man unconscious. It was with an admirable effortlessness that he took out the attackers.

Where's Imp? Tric wondered, *Has she gotten into the factory yet?*

Tric slowed down his knock-out, hoping to make this battle longer and drawn-out. They needed a distraction to prevent them from noticing Imp was gone, and to keep most of them out here instead of in the factory if she was spotted.

Tric glanced at the projectile Flavours troops, watching as Pyra and Moss were attacking the defences. Another two of the Police defences were on fire and in the process of being decimated. They could see the Police trying to hold the burning pieces together.

Pyra sent another few burning leaves at the enemy, acting as a cover to Moss. He was vulnerable, concentrating on controlling his roots. He was doing a good job, the roots acting like gnarled hands that tore away at the defences. He was joined by two other slower attackers, controlling a small catapult launching bundles of rocks swathed in oil-soaked cloths that became flaming balls when lit. Pyra had commanded the rest of the projectile team to protect those three, deterring attackers with daggers for ones that came too close, walls of stone to defend against arrows, and throwing stars to prevent approaching Police.

Another Police fortification went down, and Moss grinned. *Only five more to go!* He nodded to Pyra, and started to attack the next one. He tried not to worry about the Police charging at them: he could see the rest of his team defending them, Pyra's flaming leaves cutting down the enemy. Moss moved his roots, tearing a large sheet of metal from the next barrier.

This is so much fun! Moss grinned.

Dusty and Aqua's troops were all scattered in the battle, each entrusted to use their weapons wisely. Moss could see Dusty and Aqua's weapons taking out many Police at a time, working as a team to decimate the Police forces.

Dusty was using his hammer to knock Police away, not wanting to squish them. He was perfectly capable of it, but the battle was supposed to last. Killing the Police would only result in their troops dwindling, and there would be less people to take out. And it was definitely something the Flavours wanted to avoid. They were trying their best to be peaceful protesters.

He swung, watching in satisfaction as a Policeman went flying knocking into one of the fortifications. A minute later a ball of fire knocked the rest of the battlement down, sending the Police behind it scurrying.

Dusty felt Aqua's whip of water slash behind him, turning to see a Police in its grasp. Aqua flicked her whip, giving the Policewoman a painful jolt, then sending her flying away. She grinned at Dusty, striking another Police, a dagger dual-wielder, and sending him flying. They definitely weren't going to be knocked unconscious from it: that was part of the plan. Rough them up enough to make it seem like they were battling, but without actually giving them any injuries that would prevent them from fighting.

Snow and Aria were taking out any Police that tried to approach the Flavour defences, easily blasting them away with arrows of air or knocking them down with slivers of ice. Their fellow archers were positioned beside them, switching off whenever someone got too tired. They could go like that for ages, and they would need to: keeping the Flavour fort to themselves was essential, because it was the means of getting Imp back. Once she was done, the fort would be the first place she'd go. A signal would be shot out, and the Flavours would retreat behind the walls of rock. With the archers holding off the attacks, they would set up more walls around the wide open gate, fighting off any Police waiting outside as they headed to their own vehicles. It didn't sound like much of a plan to Aria, but she remembered that it would probably be nightfall by that time. The Black Liquorice Flavours would mask their escape.

Imp ran, heading towards the factory as her fellow Flavours charged into battle.

As the two sides tested each other, she made her way invisibly towards the small building. It was pretty far away from the entrance, and Imp had to run. She didn't want to get caught in any of the fighting, even though she was invisible. It was still possible for a sword to strike her, and the moment she started bleeding, she would be revealed. She tried to keep her feet soft on the ground, knowing that the silence of the tense moments could give her away. But she made it without incident.

Imp stopped for breath a couple feet from the door of the factory. She didn't know what kind of traps were set to protect the factory. She was sure that as soon as the Flavours busted down the door that the traps would be put on active mode. Being careful could save her life. She needed to be at one hundred percent to avoid the traps.

Time to go, Imp thought, gathering up courage. She decided that a running start would help.

She had only taken a couple of steps when the first trap activated. Giant spikes shot from the ground, spraying dirt. She jumped over the row, the spikes growing in response to the motion. For a second, Imp wondered if she was going to make it over. But she did, hitting the ground and rolling, her sword barely hindering her. She was relieved to see the spikes roll back into the ground. Imp kept running, now only a couple of feet from the entrance...

She nearly tripped on a wire, snapping it like a twig. She dodged to the side as holes revealed themselves in the tree next to the entrance, shooting off darts. She landed on her hands, pushing herself up as more darts shot her way.

Good thing I took gymnastics! Imp thought, remembering the days when she had danced around in the school gym, learning all about jumping and flexibility.

The moment she landed another trap went off, this one more dangerous than the others. She drew her sword as tiny bots flew from holes in the roof of the factory. She had run into these before...They were stinger droids, robots that delivered poison from little barbs that punctured the skin.

Imp slashed at them, watching as little parts fell, littering the ground. None of them got close enough to sting her as she ran towards the factory.

She glanced back, seeing if any Police had charged at her. They had disabled the lab's alarm system, and the door wasn't facing towards the courtyard. She needed the Police to be as oblivious as possible.

She stepped onto the concrete porch, opening the unlocked door.

I guess they didn't expect anyone to make it this far, Imp grinned, stepping into the cool building.

Lars easily dodged a lightning projectile, careful not to touch it. He had never run into an Electric Flavour's weapon before, but he had seen what Tric could do with it. There was no doubt that every Electric Flavour could do that.

Lars gave a solid kick to the Flavour, knocking him back a few steps. He slashed, opening a large cut in the Flavour's belly. He watched in satisfaction as the Flavour backed away, towards his side's fort.

Another one that I didn't have to kill, Lars thought in relief. Every Flavour he had battled had ended up with a nasty wound, but it wouldn't be fatal if they got proper treatment. Unlike the rest of the troops...They were slashing mercilessly at their opponents, hoping to maim. In Lars' mind, they were a disgrace to the Police. He had joined them because he thought the goal was to keep the peace, not to kill others instead of capturing them.

Where's Imp in all of this? Lars wondered as he blocked an attack from an icy sword. He had been watching the entire battle, and not once did he see someone get struck down by an invisible attack.

*Unless...*Lars' heart nearly stopped as he realised the true intent of the attack.

I need to tell someone! No, there's no time! She's probably already close to getting inside of the factory!

He parried the Flavour's next blow, spinning and delivering a deep slash to his leg. Then Lars ran.

He ducked and avoided attacks of all sorts: flaming, electrified, freezing...There was no end to the Flavour's arsenal. Lars blocked a blast of air with his sword, blown back a little by the blast. But he kept moving.

He broke through the fighting, finally hitting clear ground. The factory was ahead, and Lars had to dodge more and more aerial attacks. He must have been on the right track if they were so desperate to stop him. He could see where the destroyed trip wires were. Imp had gone through this area, and had managed to avoid the traps.

I need to stop her, Lars thought. He hated the Flavourless gummy, but it was their only weapon against the Flavours. He couldn't let it be destroyed.

Chapter 28

Imp snuck through the hallway, her hand welded onto her sword.

She jumped at every little sound, drawing her sword constantly. But she would always have to sheath it a second later. The sounds that put her on edge were simple beeping of computers, or rustling of papers...

This is so creepy! Imp thought, keeping to the shadows. She had seen absolutely no one, but she had expected that. They probably would have evacuated the moment the gate blew up. But it was still strange, because there were no signs of life at all. She at least expected a cup of coffee left warm on a desk, or papers on the floor...Instead, everything was put in its place, like the scientists had left at a leisurely pace.

Was there even anyone in here in the first place? Imp had to wonder. If the gate of her workplace blew up and started swarming with her enemies, she'd run. She'd definitely not worry about putting the papers of her desk in order. Of course, the Police had been set up and ready when they got there. Somehow they had gotten wind of their plans.

The hallway that she was walking through was some kind of research hallway: it was filled with individual desks and high tech computers. Imp had thought that this facility was just for producing secret Police weapons. But apparently they conducted research here also, or at least had to monitor the production of their weapons.

Imp followed the hallway, hoping that she would somehow come across a map. Saying that she was going to go inside the factory was easy enough, but having to go inside and find what she needed was a lot harder than she expected.

A sound made Imp jump, and she immediately drew her sword, wishing that the metallic slide hadn't been so loud. The sound came again, and Imp wished she could melt into the wall. Even if she was invisible.

The sound echoed through the hallway, and Imp realised that it was rhythmic...like footsteps.

They were heavy footsteps, almost like someone was stomping through the factory. Imp squished herself against the wall as the footsteps came closer, definitely walking down the same hallway as her. She kept her sword at her side, ready to slash if she needed to.

The footsteps were just around the corner when Imp made a split second decision, running across the hall and into someone's office. She didn't even close the door in fear that she had been heard. Sure enough, the footsteps paused, as if the person was listening for something.

This is too long. They must have heard me... It took all of her will to keep from running.

After a few tense moments, the footsteps started again.

The footsteps got louder, a shadow flickering at the corner of the hall. A few more steps, and she would be able to see who it was...

Imp nearly gasped as Delyn came into view.

He looked horrible. His once bright brown eyes were dulled, with black bags underneath them. His sandy hair was messy, and not in the style sense. It looked like he hadn't combed it at all. His Police uniform was stained and slit in places, showing red scratches on his arms and legs. Imp realised with horror that he had been fighting, and she was sure that the blood on his uniform wasn't his own.

He walked past her, oblivious. He was mumbling, as if he was sleep walking, even though his eyes were open and alert.

What's he doing? Imp wondered, staring at the slouching back of her old friend.

More footsteps came, and Imp automatically knew who it was. The steps were quiet and sneaky, as if someone was following Delyn.

It was Lars, as expected. He was keeping to the shadows, watching Delyn. He was completely unscarred, although there was a little blood on his sword, which he held at ready. He looked in worse shape than Delyn: his grey eyes weren't quite as bright as they had been, and there were black rings under them. His hair was only partly coiffed, almost as if he had given up half-way through combing it. He looked like he needed sleep.

When Lars had passed, Imp's curiosity got the better of her. She slipped behind Lars, keeping her sword as ready as he did his.

If anyone knows where the nightmare gummy is, they would, She thought as she followed them through the twisting hallways of the factory.

I'm surrounded!

Dusty hefted his hammer into ready position, glaring at his enemies. They had formed a tight circle around him, and he knew that the moment he swung his hammer, he would be attacked from behind. It was sneaky and underhanded of the Police, but it would guarantee a dead Flavour.

He could see it in their eyes: they were certain of victory. The way they watched his movement like a pack of hungry hyenas. How they held their weapons in ready position. It all showed that they were sure that they had won.

Well, you're in for a little surprise, Dusty thought, grinning. He reached into his pocket, producing two gummies and chewing on them. The Police surrounding him were taken aback, the more experienced ones already taking steps back.

The taste of chocolate filled his mouth, draining all moisture from it. Dusty dissolved his hammer, the rock dust gathering around his whole body. He could feel the stone starting to encase him, watching the Police charge through tiny slits for his eyes. He grinned, even though they didn't see it. He was a golem of rock.

A sword clanged against his arm, doing no damage at all. He punched the offender in the stomach, following with a solid kick. Almost immediately another soldier came forward, ready to fight.

Dusty took out at least six Police soldiers just with kicks and punches, but more were always there to take the others' places. He was surrounded by what seemed like an infinite amount of enemies.

Someone jumped on his back, limiting his movement. He saw someone latch onto his arm though he felt nothing through the sheet of rock, and he tried to throw him off. But another Police grabbed on, and he could no longer move his arm.

They're swarming me! Dusty realised as more and more Police charged, grabbing onto him.

The weight became too much and he collapsed, dog-piled under his worst enemy.

"I'm not done yet!" Dusty yelled as a warning to his assailants. They didn't react, perhaps not hearing him from outside his rocky armour.

Dusty concentrated, feeling the rock around him. With a burst of energy he sent his armour flying.

Chunks of rock detached themselves, flying off him and pushing off his enemies. He got up, watching in satisfaction as the Police were blown away by his stones. He remade his rock hammer from the chunks of rock, ready for battle again.

Pheonix struck, melting the Policewoman's dagger into hot metal.

She had only taken a few hits, which she was happy for. She expected to be seriously hurt by now, especially with her little skill against swords. But she was doing well, all things considered.

Pheonix roundhouse kicked, catching two Police off guard. They flew away, their arms singed. Another Police came at her and she raised her hand, dispatching him with a short spurt of fire.

"Watch out, Pheonix!" Tric yelled, and she turned just in time, her leg already out for her signature kick. It hit the Policewoman in the face, delivering a painful burn that scorched her eyebrows and eyelashes.

"Nice job." Tric commented, appearing beside her as he took out another officer with his lightning. The man crumpled to the ground, unconscious. Almost immediately Tric was gone, and there was a startled yell, which Pheonix took as a sign that he had just knocked someone else unconscious.

"There's so many of them!" Tric whined as he once again went to Pheonix's side. He kicked someone in the stomach, his orange-yellow scarf waving fancily. Pheonix finished the Police troop with a flaming slash.

"What's that?" Tric asked, shielding his eyes against the five o'clock sun.

From behind one of the fiery Police battlements came first the muzzle. Then came the rest of it: a gigantic cannon.

It was made of black steel, looking like it had come from the old age. But silver steel would sometimes cause a glare. The Police had apparently added some modifications to it.

The cannon was maneuvered by hand, three Police having to push it in the right direction, while two had to angle it correctly.

Why would they go through the trouble of lugging that thing around? It looks super heavy. It must have some kind of secret weapon or something that makes it worthwhile...

Pheonix and Tric watched the Police position the cannon from the corner of their eyes, fighting off the Police nearby. The cannon was slowly being aimed to the right, then was raised a few inches...

"Crap!" Pheonix swore, looking at the cannon's muzzle that was trained directly at them.

Deep in the tube of the cannon came a red glow, seeming to pulse. Pheonix swore another time, her hand reaching into her bag of gummies. She ate two, her mouth burning with cinnamon. Tric looked at her curiously, confused. He followed her gaze, paling at the sight of the cannon's aim.

The cannon fired.

Tric gulped as the blast of fire approached, burning a deadly arc in the air. An arrow of wind struck against the fire, perhaps Aria's. It was useless: the arrow had no effect, not even slowing the projectile, or blowing out the flames. They were doomed.

Tric closed his eyes as searing heat flew in front of his face. Any second now, he and Pheonix would be burnt to a crisp. Any second now...

It was a long second.

Tric opened his eyes, tentatively at first. But his eyes grew wide when he saw a sheet of flame hovering in front of him. Somehow Pheonix must have stopped the blast.

The sheet of flame retreated, sliding out of his way. Tric turned to see if Pheonix was all right. He gasped.

Giant wings of fire were sprouting from Pheonix's back, widespread as she glared at the cannon. They were at least ten feet wide, if not more. If Tric stared long enough, he could see little plumes of flame that looked like feathers. Her wings were loud, sizzling and popping in an endless cacophony. Tric could see the gawking faces of the Police, and he realised that his face probably had the same expression of amazement on it.

"Fire!" One of the Policemen yelled, and Tric watched as the cannon got ready to fire again.

Pheonix ran in front of Tric, one scarlet wing deflecting the cannon's round. She started to run towards the weapon, using her wings in a combination of hopping and running. Any Police that got in her way was swatted with her wings. Another round was shot, but she was so close to the cannon now that it didn't even make it two feet.

The Police cannoneers scattered as Pheonix struck them away with her wings. She only had to hold a burning wing to the cannon for a second. It melted into a pool of red hot metal, steaming and dangerous to the touch.

Tric was beside her in a second, staring at the pool of molten steel.

"Wow." Was all he could say, looking at the cooling metal with a look of awe on his face. He could hear Pheonix panting beside him. Obviously she wasn't used to using her Special. Most Flavours weren't.

"You alright?" Tric asked, looking at her with concern. The wings on Pheonix's back were starting to sputter and die out.

"I'll survive." Pheonix panted. She turned to see the Police standing a distance away, waiting for her defence to dwindle. It made her angry, how they were like vultures.

I'll give them a run for their money, Pheonix grinned, and Tric backed away, sensing her intent.

Her wings sputtered out, and the Police advanced. Suddenly they burst back to life, catching the Police off guard. Pheonix sent them flying, her wings now riddled with holes. But it was enough. Their clothes were smouldering they backed off, turning tail and running.

"That was fun." Pheonix murmured as she collapsed onto one knee. She was panting heavily, and her eyelids were drooping a little.

"Don't you dare go unconscious on me." Tric warned, coming to kneel beside her.

"Just catching...my breath." Pheonix raised one finger, as if she would be completely fine in a second, "Don't get impatient."

Tric sighed. "Let's get you back to the fort."

Chapter 29

Aria shot another Police, blowing him away from Tric and Pheonix.

Pheonix didn't look in too good shape, but Aria expected that. After her little display of fire wings, anyone would be tired.

Aria heard Snow's sweater rustle, and an icy chunk knocking away a Police that had gotten too close. Tric sprinted the rest of the distance, swinging himself and the semi-conscious Pheonix behind the wall.

Tric ducked out of the way as Aria peeked from behind the wall, firing off another one of her air arrows.

"I need to get back to my troops." Tric said, "Can you guys clear a path for me?"

"We'll try." Aria looked doubtfully at the Police crowd. They had paid attention when they saw Tric and Pheonix heading towards the fort: now there was no way that they would allow Tric back to his position. They knew he was in charge of the sword-wielders, and they knew that without a leader, that sector would crumble.

"There's no way." Snow grumbled, firing off another bolt. Tric tried his hand at launching electricity, catching a Police by chance, "You're not making it out of here any time quick, Tric."

Tric groaned, looking towards where his troops were. He winced as a Police arrow struck a Flavour in the shoulder, knocking him off his feet. The Flavour was wounded, heading back to his fort. Tric nearly cried out when another arrow sunk into the Flavour's back.

"Get me out there *right now!*" Tric yelled, and Aria jumped, missing her shot.

"We're trying." Snow said gently, even though his hands were a blur of motion as he fired ice sliver upon ice sliver.

Tric ground his teeth in frustration. He was totally unhinged now, no longer the happy go lucky person SOFT was used to.

"I'm taking matters into my own hands." Tric growled, already reaching towards the pockets of his jeans. Two yellow gummies shaped like lightning bolts were produced, and just as quickly swallowed.

"Careful." Snow warned, "Don't overdo it."

"Don't worry." Tric grinned, his body already starting to spark with electricity.

He stepped from behind the protective barrier of rock, punching a Police with his electrified arm. The Police nearest him charged, but suddenly stopped. Tric's arm was no longer sparking with electricity...His *whole body* was.

Like some kind of lightning demon, Tric ran, not bothering to move out of the way of the Police. One brush from his electrified body was enough to knock them unconscious. As he made his way towards his troops, he left behind a trail of unconscious Police. The Police were now trying to avoid him, but Tric was going out of his way to run into them.

He reached his battalion, taking out a Police that was getting ready to slash at a Flavour's unprotected back. The Flavour turned around, looking surprised. Tric recognized Bolt.

"Looking good, Tric!" Bolt grinned. He had a large, bleeding scar down his cheek, and his left arm was lying useless at his side.

"You're not looking so good." Tric told him, gesturing at his arm. He realized he was still covered in lightning. He extinguished it immediately, feeling only a tiny little tug of tiredness. Unlike Pheonix, he was used to using his special attack. He could handle many more Specials if he needed to.

"Watch out!" Bolt yelled, dashing behind Tric and knocking a dagger-wielder unconscious. The Police had tried to attack Tric while he was concentrating on stopping the lightning flowing from every part of his body.

"Those Police are full of dirty tricks." Bolt grumbled angrily, electrifying an arrow that came flying at them.

"Then let's take them out." Tric grinned.

Snow launched a sliver of ice at a Police who had gotten too close, not waiting to fire with his crossbow. Another Police immediately filled his comrade's place, and Snow had to duck behind the wall of rock to avoid getting hit by a massive hammer.

"They're getting too close." Snow growled as he fired off another chunk of ice, delivering a painful blow to a Police's head. All of the Police were crowding the hall, somehow hoping to overpower the Flavours that were defending it. The unfortunate thing was that it was working. The archers just couldn't keep up with the Police's attacks.

"We need to get them away from the base!" Aria complained.

Pretty observant of her, considering she's such an airhead, Snow commented in his mind.

"What do you suggest?" Snow asked, his voice barely a murmur. Aria didn't answer at first, busy with launching more of her invisible arrows into her enemy. When she did talk, Snow didn't hear her at first over his own firing.

"Pardon?" Snow asked politely.

"Let's take them out all at once. We could use our combined Specials."

Snow nodded. Their combined 'super attacks', or Specials, as they were commonly known, would be able to take out the Police in one fell swoop. But it did come with risks. The attack needed at least two gummies. It was dangerous because the doubling of the gummies was a huge intake of chaos magic, and it took up a lot of energy. But SOFT was used to their Specials, hence the lack of effect on Tric, while it was devastating to Pheonix. She was still unconscious, and under watch in case something worse happened, at the heavily protected hospital for the injured.

"Oh, alright." Snow grinned, his normal expression of boredom turned into something malicious. His voice was betraying his eagerness. It had been a while since he had last used his Special. It was exciting.

Snow and Aria switched places with other Flavours, heading closer to the middle of the wall. The edges would be defended by others while Aria and Snow recovered from their Special move.

Aria and Snow reached into their pockets at the same time, taking out two gummies each. For a second, they stared at the candy that gave them their powers; mini tornadoes for Aria, and simple snowflakes for Snow. After a quick glance at each other, they swallowed them.

The temperature was the first to be affected.

Aria could see her breath, a sure sign of Snow's doing. The wind came next, at first only a mild gust that tugged at their clothes, soon becoming a savage wind that forced the Police to cover their faces and hold onto their clothes. The Flavours knew exactly what the wind foretold: the ones close enough to the wall abandoned their posts and huddled behind it, watching with glee as the Police struggled against the wind.

When the Police finally noticed the lack of Flavours, it was too late.

Aria's eyelashes were already rimmed with frost, and she had no doubt that on the other side of the wall it would be ten times worse. Her bursts of air could be heard whistling off the rocky wall, and she concentrated on keeping it close to the wall, avoiding having it spread throughout the battlefield, where her fellow Flavours were still fighting.

A Police gave a scream, and Aria nearly laughed as a Police was sent flying, his face seen for a second, a mask frozen in terror. There was another scream, and Aria looked at Snow, a smile flashing across his face and disappearing just as quickly. Snow had his hands on the ground, delicate frost forming around his fingers. Aria knew that the ground where he touched would be freezing cold, like a sheet of ice. She assumed that that was probably what it felt like to the Police.

A snowflake fluttered over the wall, missing its target. Aria caught it on her tongue, laughing. Snow smiled again, but this time it was a smile that stayed on his face.

"They're all gone!" One of the Flavours behind the wall yelled, her head disappearing behind the barrier.

Aria and Snow walked slowly towards the edge of the wall, catching their breath. Sure enough, instead of a Police platoon, there was a blanket of fresh, fallen snow.

"That was fun." Snow murmured before he slipped back into his mask of cool indifference.

Aqua wrapped her water whip around a Police, catapulting her enemy away. She kicked another Police in the face, delivering a painful lash to the other that had tried to sneak up on her.

So far so good! Aqua grinned to herself, *Only a couple more—Hey! What's that?!*

The sunlight had glinted on something steel starting to poke out from behind a Police barricade. There was a flash that nearly blinded Aqua. When the light cleared, she gasped.

The Police were wheeling out a cannon identical to the one they had shot at Pheonix and Tric. The black muzzle glistened in the sun, the blackness inside already beginning to glow the reddish-orange of fire. Aqua had seen its shot. The way that it had exploded against Pheonix's fiery wings was nothing short of spectacular, and would probably be even more spectacular when it would actually hit its' target.

But where were they aiming? It was hard to tell where the giant cannon was pointed at. The only way would be if it was pointing directly towards someone, like in Pheonix's case.

Wait a second, Aqua's blood went cold. If she followed the angle close enough...it was aiming at Moss!

Damn! Aqua swore, running towards him. Moss had noticed the cannon's trajectory, because he went pale and hesitated, his roots faltering.

Aqua watched in horror as the cannon launched, a dazzling ball of flame flying in an arc across the sky. Without even thinking, she reached towards the pouch that contained her gummies, feeling two with her hand. She didn't even need to look to know that they were shaped like raindrops.

She swallowed them as she tried to use her whip to slow down the fire ball, but it evaporated the moment it touched its surface. Moss raised his roots in a vain attempt to prepare for impact.

Aqua swung her arm as if she was throwing something, a giant jet of water materializing out of thin air. By her will it flowed in a steady stream to the fireball, already sizzling as it approached it. In a spectacular display of water, fire and steam, the fireball disintegrated, showering Moss with sparks and drops of water.

"Are you alright?" Aqua cried, finally coming to stand beside Moss.

He looked at her with a dazed expression on his face, almost as if the steam and fire had burned his brain.

"That was cool." Moss smiled a little.

"That's an understatement." Aqua laughed her loud laugh, before turning her heels and heading back into battle.

Pyra fired off another dagger, tearing and scorching through a Police's clothes.

With her left hand, she reached into her pocket, grabbing a fistful of leaves. She threw these in the direction of two approaching Police, stopping them in a flurry of flame.

It's getting harder to hold them off! She thought desperately. She and Moss had knocked down most of the Police defences, but they kept rebuilding them from the charred remains of the destroyed ones. It was tiring work, and the Police were noticing their exhaustion. New troops were coming in regularly, and they kept replacing the tired troops that Pyra had already beaten down. But there were no replacements for the Flavours, and the most they could rest was twenty minutes before they were needed on the battlefield once again.

There was no doubt that the Police knew that they were planning this attack. There was also no doubt that they had devastating weapons hidden behind their crumbling defences. The cannon that they had fired earlier was proof of that, even though it was now a hardened pool of molten metal.

What other tricks do they have up their sleeves? Pyra wondered, glaring at the Police defences as she stopped another Police in his tracks with a fire blast, this time from a wad of paper. They were certainly large enough to hide some big weapon of mass destruction.

What we need is some kind of attack that would knock all the defences down at once, Pyra thought, a plan already forming in her mind. Once the defences were down, it would child's play to knock out Police and destroy their plans.

Pyra pressed a button on her headset, the small speaker ready for her voice.

"I think I've found a way to knock down the Police defences." Pyra spoke into the collar, waiting for a response.

"Sounds really awesome!" Came Tric's excited voice.

"I'll have the archers at the ready." Snow answered, his voice sounding even colder over the mike.

"I'll try and rally up some of the miscellaneous." Aqua's voice sounded, "Just be sure to cover us, Snow."

"Don't overdo it, Pyra." Moss warned, his voice sounding strange in the mike. Pyra laughed. He was standing right beside her, a fact that he had apparently forgotten. He gave her a sheepish smile, embarrassed. Apparently he was still dazed.

"Let's do it, then." Pyra's grin could be heard over the walkie-talkie.

She commanded another Flavour to take her spot, going to stand beside Moss as she popped two flame-shaped gummies into her mouth. The taste of cinnamon was almost unbearable, a burning that seemed to pierce her tongue.

Pyra grew a fire ball in her hand, a concentrated flame that bathed her skin in heat. She forced the flames into a sphere, and black began to form over it. It was some kind of skin, as if the flames had cooled down and formed rock, like magma. But it was burning hot, flames still thriving inside.

Pyra created three more of those balls, one for each Police defence. Moss was watching her from the corner of his eye. He had never seen Pyra's Special before, and he was confused with what she was doing.

Pyra broke away from the cover offered by Moss, trying to get in a position where she could hit all the defences at once. She ducked under a sword, weaved past a dagger, dodged an arrow...She was in constant motion.

She reached her desired spot, about halfway between the sword and projectile troops. She immediately ducked into a defensive position, throwing one of her fire leaves towards a Police that had tried to attack her. He was blown away, and Pyra was satisfied to see that no one else dared approach her.

It's now or never, Pyra grinned, readying her bombs.

"Bombs away!" Pyra yelled, standing up and menacing the Police behind the barricades with the balls of black. Some of them heeded her warning, breaking the cover of the defences. Most didn't.

"Don't say that I didn't warn you." Pyra muttered, grasping the bombs between her fingers, two in each hand. She was trained to throw this way.

With arms perfectly toned for throwing, Pyra swung her arms, letting go of the bombs. They flew in a giant arc, overshooting the barricades by mere centimetres: but that was part of the plan. The Police behind them scattered, scared by the sight of the bombs falling. Pyra waited for them to clear, not wanting death. She just wanted their weapons destroyed.

Now! Pyra thought, sensing the bombs behind the walls. A second later the hastily constructed walls of steel and wood burst into flame, great clouds of smoke rising as the wood disintegrated and the metal melted. Police nearby dove away from the flying shrapnel, deflecting it with their weapons. As the burning pieces of the defences fell to the ground, Pyra could catch glimpses of the melting weapons that had been hidden behind it.

"Nice work." Snow said, his voice buzzing in her ear.

"Too easy." Pyra answered back, heading off to destroy the weapons that didn't melt. She could hear the Flavours' footsteps behind her as they charged the defenceless Police.

Chapter 30

Imp got a horrible claustrophobic feeling as she followed Delyn and Lars through the hallways. It was like a maze: full of twists and turns and dead ends, so many that Imp's head spun, even though Delyn had no trouble navigating it.

Lars was on edge, his hand on the hilt of his sword. He kept glancing back, as if he could sense Imp behind him. Whenever Delyn looked back, he would press against the walls or into the open rooms, his breath coming out in shallow gasps. Imp was surprised that Delyn couldn't hear him. But from the way Delyn staggered through the hallway and squinted into well-lighted corridors, Imp guessed that there was something wrong with him.

Eventually the offices became fewer and fewer, being replaced by rooms full of machinery. Imp could hear some kind of huge machine in the distance, whirring and crackling like a dishwasher with coins inside. It sounded spooky, a deadly reminder of what was ahead.

As soon as Delyn leads me to the gummy, I'll destroy it. I'll destroy it before he even notices I'm here! Imp thought, massaging her sword-holding hand. It had long since gone numb; but she didn't dare sheathe it or loosen her grip. It was the only thing keeping her from freaking out as she followed her two worst enemies into a place she couldn't even walk through without getting lost.

The whirring of the machine got stronger, echoing off the walls in a maddening way. Delyn had begun to murmur to himself, and Imp couldn't make out the words over the strange crackling noises of whatever was ahead. But from the expression of Lars' face, it was nothing that she wanted to hear.

Occasionally Delyn would glance back, and Lars would withdraw into the wall's shadows, almost becoming as invisible as Imp. Imp would wait breathlessly until Lars would emerge, following him and always ready to bolt if she was noticed.

But nothing happened, and the hallways began to turn into just a straight corridor, not as well lit as before. By now the machine seemed to make the walls quake, putting Imp on edge. But Delyn and Lars persevered on, and she had no choice but to follow.

Suddenly the hallway widened again, doors lining it. One door, left open, revealed an office full of monitoring computers, piles of paper leaving a mess beside a printer. Imp didn't have time to dawdle, because now Delyn was speeding up, his leisurely walk turning into more of a jog. Lars followed after, holding his armour to his chest so it wouldn't jingle when he ran.

The hallway ended abruptly, a huge, steel and bolted door dominating the end wall. Delyn went to it without hesitation, taking a little card from his pocket. He quickly slid the card into a contraption on the side of the door—it reminded Imp of the key card machines on hotel doors—with a quick beep acknowledging the entry. Moments later the heavy door slid open, and Delyn slipped inside, followed by Lars and an invisible Imp.

Imp nearly gasped as she followed Lars into the room, the metal door sliding to a close beside her.

The walls were dominated by pipes, all of them pumping what looked like clear liquid. Propped against the far wall was a machine that looked like some kind of hospital patient; all of the pipes in the room were hooked up to it, pumping the sparkling substance into huge canisters. Tiny spouts squeezed out the liquid onto a conveyor belt, the little beads of glittering who-knows-what disappearing into the wall, shipped off to some part unknown.

This must be the production factory, Imp realised, staring at the computer screens that filled the spaces beside the machine, their screen showing data that she didn't understand, *According to our info, the batch is unstable, and they need to control things like temperature very finely for it to work. I just need to destroy those computers, then the batch will have to deal without its fine-tuned environment. It will destroy itself.*

Imp began to sneak across the room, her feet making no sound. She knew how to sneak around, even when she wasn't barefoot. She could step silently in high heels, if she were to actually wear them.

"I know you're there." Delyn suddenly said, interrupting her silent observation of the factory. Imp held her breath in shock, every muscle in her body freezing up. How had he known that she was here?

"I don't care." Lars answered, his voice dripping with anger. Imp realised that they weren't talking to her. Delyn was talking to Lars. She once again started to sneak across the room.

"I know you're jealous of me." Delyn turned towards Lars, his voice sounding like that of a little kid.

"Jealous?" Lars asked, as if he didn't understand the concept.

"Jealous because I was chosen." Delyn shrugged, his face a mocking grin, "Jealous because I'm the one who gets to use the Nightmare gummy, and not you. Jealous that you have been replaced by me."

"I don't care who uses the Nightmare gummy." Lars answered simply, and from the hardness of his jaw, Imp could tell that he was pissed.

"Then why are you here?" Delyn asked, leaning against a mean-looking computer.

"I think that Imp is trying to invade this place." Lars answered, and Imp nearly jumped. She knew that they would eventually realise why the Flavours were specifically attacking the lab, but she didn't think that they would realise it so soon. But why was only Lars here?

"Really?" Delyn raised an eyebrow, and Imp noticed how smug and superior he was acting. No wonder Lars was angry. That was his job.

Now Imp was within arm's reach of the computer, but she wanted to get closer. She needed to make sure that she got a good slash at the computer, because the moment she did, they would be on to her. There would be no second chances.

"She is here." Lars growled, "I know it. All the traps at the front had been activated, and she somehow got through them. She's in the lab."

Delyn hmphed, tapping his foot. He looked calm enough, but Imp knew from experience that Delyn's foot tapping showed agitation, "Then where are all the Police? Why'd you come by yourself?"

"There was no time to tell the others. Imp is probably making her way to this room right now."

Oh, if only he knew.

Imp came to stand beside Delyn, keeping her breathing controlled. From the way he was draping himself over the computer, Imp assumed that he knew the importance of it. She would have to slash at the computer through Delyn's arms. The side of it was barely concealed by his left arm. Apparently it wouldn't look natural if he just curled around it completely.

Here goes nothing. Imp thought, readying her sword. She could already feel the powers of her gummy begin to fade, knowing that she was becoming more visible by the second.

She drove her sword into the machine.

The machine behind Delyn began to crackle, a thin slash opening into it. Imp appeared, holding a sword into the computer. She looked triumphant.

Lars watched as Imp withdrew her sword, taking a step back. She didn't get far before Delyn had delivered a roundhouse to her stomach. Imp stumbled back, moving to a crouched position and holding her arm over her bruised abdomen.

"Too late, Delyn!" Imp grinned, even though she looked like she was in a lot of pain.

Delyn slashed angrily at her, missing. He didn't even take a step towards her. He was staying stubbornly by the machine.

No way, Lars thought as the batch of Nightmare started to turn into a sickly green-black color. The dispenser paused, halfway through delivering a murky mix of clear and black liquid.

"No, no, no, no!" Delyn cried, bending beside the computer. He desperately pressed buttons, turned knobs, but to no avail. The mix remained its murky black.

"It can be saved. It can be saved." Delyn murmured, looking at the batch in distress. Lars almost felt sorry for him. Almost.

"Secondary computer activating." A computerized voice sounded in the room, seeming to come from everywhere at once. The black mass began to move, as if stirred, the color fading back to the clear liquid.

Imp had a shocked look on her face, immediately trying to stand. She only made it halfway, immediately clutching her side and wincing in pain.

Delyn must have broken one of her ribs with his kick. How is that possible? He isn't that strong! Lars thought, confused, *From the look on Imp's face, she didn't expect it either.*

"What are you doing, just standing there?!" Delyn whirled, his face a mixture of glee and anger as the liquid inside the tanks cleared into its old self, "Get her! Don't let her get away!"

Lars hesitated, but only for a second. His already drawn sword weighed heavily in his hand. Imp turned her head towards him, seeming to assess whether he was going to attack. In the second of his hesitation, she already had a gummy in her mouth and was beginning to disappear.

Delyn charged at her, reaching Imp before Lars. How had he gotten there so fast? Lars had been closer to her. Delyn vainly slashed at the spot where Imp had disappeared, but there was no blood splatter. She was gone.

"Spread out! She's probably looking for the back-up computer!" Delyn commanded, and Lars felt rage rise inside him. How dare *Delyn* give the orders?! Lars was much more experienced than him! But he obeyed, only because that was what he would have commanded.

Lars headed towards the north of the room, trying to hear Imp's footsteps. But all he could hear was Delyn stomping around the room.

Suddenly, he felt flesh connect with his face. He stumbled back, both from the hit and from the effort to get away. Lars rubbed his cheek, holding his sword at the ready in case Imp tried to attack again. But apparently it was a hit and run, because he felt no more painful punches or kicks.

Lars looked around while running, wondering why the room was so large. He couldn't see any sign of another computer in the room. It was hard to fight an invisible enemy, especially one that was stealthy.

Lars heard a furious tapping, and turned. Delyn was at the door, typing into a small machine identical to the one outside. With a grin he slammed the cover back on top of the keyboard.

"She's not getting out of here without a key card." Delyn smiled in triumph.

Lars nodded, using Delyn's silence to try and track down Imp. But he heard no footsteps.

Suddenly, a booming sound came from the containers. A large slash had opened, breaking the glass. The silver-clear liquid came gushing out, coating the floor.

"No!" Delyn howled, falling to his knees. He put his hands to the floor, the liquid pooling around his fingers.

*Wait a second...*Lars thought, realization dawning on him.

"Delyn! Look for her footprints in the liquid!"

Delyn was still staring at the shimmering liquid, seeming to be lost in it. Lars groaned, turning away from him and scanning the floor.

There! A row of footprints was forming itself, dripping off an invisible army boot. Lars charged towards the spot, the footsteps stopping for a second, as if Imp was shocked. Then they started again, forming quickly into a running pattern.

Lars slashed with his sword when he was close enough, the metallic clang of sword on sword echoing. A moment later the pressure eased, and there was a splash. Before Lars could react, he felt a boot connect with his wrist, leaving a wet footprint behind. He dropped his sword in pain. There was more splashing as Imp ran, another kick ramming into his back. Lars fell face first in the slick gel, and he spluttered.

"Stop, Siria!" Delyn cried out, and Lars turned his head to see Delyn sticking out his arm towards a spot behind Lars. The splashing of Imp's footsteps stopped, and the room went dead silent.

"I know why you're doing this." Delyn said, his voice begging and sincere, "Your father...he was evil. But you shouldn't have turned to the Flavours. Because of them, people like your dad get off free while the Police are distracted with them."

"People like my dad..." Imp laughed bitterly, "People like my dad...no, *murderers* like my dad get away with it because the Police are pooling their resources trying to silence our right to free speech. They're trying to stop Flavours instead of stopping real crimes. Did you honestly expect me to believe something like that?"

"No." Delyn answered, his voice turning cold and hard, "That's why I need to do this."

Lars watched as Delyn took a small, clear pill out of his pocket, the similar clear liquid on the ground starting to turn black as the room temperature dropped. In a second Lars was on his feet, picking his wet sword off the ground. He recognized that gummy. The nightmare gummy.

"Don't do it, Delyn!" Imp hissed, and Lars was surprised that her voice came from right behind him, to his left a little. He hadn't thought that she was that close.

"You don't have any power over me anymore, Siria." Delyn growled, swallowing the gummy.

Chapter 31

"No!" Imp cried, and Delyn fell backwards, hitting the ground hard. She appeared, holding her sword point to his throat.

Delyn face's morphed into a devilish grin, and Imp thought that she was going to be sick. The lights of the room, already dim, began to flicker, and she wondered what was happening. How could the lights go out at a time like this?

Suddenly Imp felt like the air was being sucked out of her. She reeled back as her sword disintegrated into stinging shards. Delyn was growing taller, towering over her as his face changed. And suddenly Imp felt small, very small. Another step back brought her to a wall that she was sure wasn't there before.

Imp felt her legs go weak as she looked at Delyn. She didn't even realize she was falling until she hit the ground, her back pressed to the wall.

It wasn't Delyn anymore. It was her father.

Imp lost track of where she was. Suddenly, she was a little girl again, cowering in a corner as her father murdered her mother.

Now it was her mother that was forming, appearing out of thin air. Her black hair flowed to her shoulders, intelligent green eyes full of fear. Imp's father was standing in front of her, the hastily-grabbed kitchen knife poised in his hand. Imp's mother was begging, the quiet, melodious voice that Imp had so admired full of terror. Imp watched as her father brought the knife down, piercing her mother's chest.

"No!" Imp screamed, covering her ears. But every sound pierced through her covering hands, her mother's high-pitched screams filling in what was happening even though her eyes were closed. She began to cry, tears welling in her eyes and sobs choking her throat. She screamed, even though her throat couldn't take the stress of screaming and crying. She screamed her throat raw, till no sound came. But still her father struck with the knife, her mother's screams growing weaker. Imp risked opening her eyes, tears blurring the scene before her. Her father plunged the knife down, red splattering at the spot he hit. Her mother's last cry died in a gurgle.

Imp felt warm seeping into her socks, and she looked down. Her grey, worn socks were turning red from the pool of blood, the cotton soaking it up like a rag.

"Imp." Her father said, and she thought his voice sounded off. It sounded...younger.

"Imp." Her father said again, his voice rising.

That's my name, Imp thought, her mind completely numb, shocked at what had just happened.

Imp dared to look up, seeing that her father was looking down on her. The knife was still in his hands.

This is wrong, Imp didn't know why, but something felt off about this scene, *He's supposed to put his knife down now...Tousle my hair...Why isn't he putting his knife down?*

Imp's father crouched down, his arm on one knee.

"You shouldn't have betrayed me." Was all he said, his voice morphing into Delyn's.

This...what the hell's happening?

One second Imp had her sword point to Delyn's throat, but the next...Lars didn't even understand it. The lights had dimmed, and Imp had stumbled away from Delyn, a completely shocked look on her face. She had even dropped her sword, falling to the ground and scooting away from Delyn as he stood up.

And it was at that point that things got really screwed up.

Lars could see something forming around Delyn, a ghostly image of some man he didn't recognize. But from the look on Imp's face, it was much more than just a semi-transparent image. It must have looked real to her, from the way she went deathly pale, her breath coming in ragged gasps.

And now, standing in front of Imp, was another figure. The only real feature that Lars could make out had black hair, similar to Imp's.

Delyn threatened the figure with his sword, now coated in the same mist as his body. The figure began to beg quietly, raising her hands in supplication. But Delyn raised his sword-knife, plunging it into the figure's chest.

"No!" Imp screamed, cupping her hands over her ears and squeezing her eyes shut. She started to cry as the figure fell to the ground, Delyn stabbing at thin air. But Lars got the distinct feeling that what Imp was seeing had to seem incredibly real. She was screaming and crying, believing every minute of what she was seeing.

Is this what Imp's nightmares are about? This...how can she dream of this every time she has a nightmare, and still be able to stand up in the morning and keep walking?! Now he knew why she was so terrified of sleeping at the motel.

Delyn started to walk towards Imp, saying her name. She didn't respond, staring at the semi-transparent pool of blood that had reached her feet.

This can't be good, Lars thought. Delyn had a chilling look on his face.

Lars tried to stand, but it felt like he was chained to the floor. He struggled, hearing Delyn say Imp's name once more. But he just couldn't pick his foot off the ground.

He looked up as Delyn stabbed Imp in the eye.

She screamed once, throwing herself away from him and falling into a ball. She cupped her hand around her eye, blood streaking down her face.

With a grim expression on his face, Delyn walked towards the fallen Imp, who didn't notice him in her pain. She had one hand clapped over her left eye, the other wrapped around her head as if to ward off an attack. Delyn raised his sword again, dripping blood on the injured Imp.

"What are you doing, Delyn?!" Lars yelled, Imp's scream still ringing in his ears.

"I'm finishing this, Lars." Delyn answered, "After all, it seems that you can't."

He can't mean—

Delyn brought the sword down.

Clang!

Delyn growled, glaring at Lars. His sword was stopped inches from Imp's face, Lars' blade blocking its descent. Lars pushed Delyn's sword away, making Delyn stumble in the process. Lars stepped protectively in front of Imp, bracing his sword for another attack.

"You idiot!" Delyn yelled, his face red with anger, "She's the enemy, not me!"

"She doesn't deserve to die! Wasn't your whole point of joining the Police to capture her and get her to redeem herself? When did that change? Now you want to kill her?" Lars answered back, not even bothering to conceal the rage in his voice.

"That changed when you told me she wouldn't redeem herself!" Delyn shouted, charging at Lars. Lars deflected the first blow with his sword, delivering a heavy kick to Delyn's stomach. He pressed him, trying to get him away from Imp.

Delyn countered his sword thrusts effortlessly, and Lars had to admit that he had trained him well. Delyn lunged to the side, Lars stopping his attempt to get to Imp with a sword hilt to the face. He scrambled back, clutching at his now bleeding nose.

Suddenly, Delyn charged forward, all pretence of clutching his nose forgotten. Lars hesitated, surprised by the sudden attack. He watched helplessly as Delyn brought the sword down...

Clang!

Lars opened his eyes, shocked to see Delyn's sword stopped by another. There was a weight at his back...Delyn gasped, stepping back.

"I...I stabbed you!"

Lars felt someone rest something on his shoulder, and he turned his head. Imp looked at him calmly, her right eye level with his face. The rest of her body was slouched against him.

How did she...? No. The reason she's leaning on me is because it took all of her energy just to get to me and block Delyn's sword. But why?

"Now we're equal." Imp murmured, her voice weak, "You saved my life, I saved yours."

Her left eye was wrapped up in shoddy pink bandages, probably torn from her shirt. She looked like she was in bad shape, having to depend on her enemy for support.

But am I really her enemy now? Lars thought, looking at how trusting Imp was being by leaning on his shoulder and using him as a support, *I defended her from Delyn, who is the one on my side. What the heck am I doing?!*

Delyn growled, glaring at Imp, then Lars. "I thought she was your enemy! Now you're... as thick as thieves?!"

"Just returning the favour." Imp answered, her voice growing stronger. She propelled herself away from Lars, her sword barely brushing his shoulder as she stepped away.

Delyn immediately charged, Imp slowly turning invisible as he raised his sword.

"You can't fool me! I can sense where you are, thanks to my gummy!" Delyn yelled, his voice echoing in the room. Delyn ran towards a random spot, slashing with his sword.

There actually was a blood splatter.

Imp materialized, clutching at her left arm. There was a long, bloody gash on it. She glared as Delyn grinned triumphantly. But when he raised his sword to attack again, she blocked it easily, using the force as a way to propel herself away from him.

"Lars, help!" Delyn yelled, turning to glare at the immobile Lars. Imp took the opportunity to strike, slashing Delyn on his sword hand and ramming her elbow into his stomach. Lars charged at Imp, who immediately disappeared. When he brought his sword down, it was met by invisible steel. Delyn struck once again, his sword swinging down and hitting the floor. He continued to slash, attacking an invisible girl who seemed to easily dodge his moves.

"Why aren't you helping, Lars?!" Delyn growled, this time paying full attention to Imp. He had learned.

"I can't exactly fight an invisible enemy." Lars answered calmly, even though he had burning rage inside of him.

"Useless." Delyn murmured, barely loud enough for Lars to hear.

He's getting cocky, Lars gritted his teeth, *Someone needs to pound a lesson into him.*

As if to prove his point, a large cut suddenly opened itself on Delyn's shoulder, his gasp following. Another slash opened the fabric on his arm, a red line appearing on his bare skin. Imp appeared, holding her sword point to his throat.

"Give up." Imp said, her voice strong even though she was panting.

Delyn gritted his teeth, glaring at her.

"I need more power." Delyn whispered and Imp frowned.

"Don't even think about it." She snarled, her sword flashing. A moment later, Delyn's hand began to bleed, stopped in its attempt to reach for his next gummy.

"Lars! What are you doing?! Help!" Delyn cried, glancing at Lars from the corner of his eyes.

"Watch it." Imp turned her head, glaring at Lars with her one good eye. He had to admit that she was holding herself together pretty well, considering she was sporting serious injuries.

Delyn laughed triumphantly, and Imp looked at him, shocked. He kicked her, right on her broken rib. She cried out in pain. Lars watched Delyn reach to his pocket as Imp collapsed to her knees. He took out a Flavourless gummy, slowly and deliberately, as Imp glared, clutching her side.

"You're the one who should give up, Siria." Delyn smiled as he swallowed the gummy.

Chapter 32

Crap! Imp thought as she watched the gummy go down Delyn's throat, *I need to find that secondary computer before it's too late!*

Imp stood up, getting ready to run. She didn't get far. Quick as lightning, Delyn delivered a roundhouse kick, sending her sprawling and crushing her already-damaged stomach. Her sword slipped out of her grip while she kept sliding in the Flavourless gel, now turned black, and slamming into a wall.

In a second, Delyn was in front of her, grinning down at her triumphantly.

How is he doing that?! Imp wondered as he punched her in the face, slamming her neck sideways, *Where did all this strength come from?! How is he so fast?!*

Maybe he has something like me in him, too, Imp heard the voice echoing in her head, nearly giving her a heart-attack. It was a dangerous voice, full of anger and malice.

The voice that always spoke to her.

Impossible! Imp yelled at it, though she knew it was true. She recognized that raw strength, that same crazy abandon. She looked into Delyn's eyes, seeing the expressive brown eyes that she had always admired full of hatred. Hatred aimed at her.

"Stop looking at me!" He roared, punching her again.

I must've been created as the precursor to what he has. You know, the "Inner Demon". You've heard that name before, haven't you?

But—

No buts. Urgh. Your thoughts are all over the place! C'mon. Let's talk somewhere more peaceful.

Suddenly Delyn's face faded away, replaced by some kind of inky darkness. And standing across from Imp was her reflection.

I'm not your reflection! I still have two eyes! See?! It gestured wildly to its blue eyes, the same hatred filling them as the ones in Delyn's.

Why are you suddenly appearing now?! Imp demanded. She didn't want to talk to this... thing. She hated it. She hated the moments of pure fear, while her body moved on its accord...

The being frowned. *Watch what you're saying! I can hear you, you know!*

Answer me!

Whoah, calm down. It raised its hands in defeat, *I'll talk. Thing is, you're dying. And I don't want that to happen, because that means I die too. Sorry to disappoint you.*

What's your point? Imp answered crossly.

Just let me take control of your body. I beat up Delyn and Lars, destroy the computer, and then let you have control again. It's a win-win situation. Deal?

Imp thought about it for a second. She could really benefit from its power...

No.

What?! The being screamed in rage, the black background taking on a reddish tinge, *You—!*

The being seemed to grow and grow, towering over her as the blackness exploded into flames. Imp could feel it. The horrible weight of every negative emotion she had ever felt, circling around her like vultures waiting for their prey to die. They were slowly gaining strength, waiting to engulf her.

No! Imp screamed, feeling like she was suffocating under its weight.

Just give up, The being said in a soothing voice, standing in front of her and taking her chin gently in its hand. But that only made the horrible emotions stronger. *Your emotions are part of you, as much as you like to pretend to be the unfeeling type.*

It's true... Imp realised, seeing it nod enthusiastically, *But...they're my emotions. I need to control them!*

The manifestation flinched, as if being struck. *No! I am much more powerful than you! You can never hope...!*

That was when giant chains erupted from the floor.

The emotion-being yelled in surprise, the chains rising and wrapping around its body, much like Moss' roots. There were thousands of them, all made of glittering silver. The flames began to die down as the being struggled against the restraints. But it was useless. There was no way Imp was going to lose to it.

You—! The being spluttered in rage, *Impossible! You can't control me! I am something beyond your emotions!*

You are something beyond my emotions. You are the form I gave to them. But I still control you, whether you like it or not.

The being chuckled, the flames disappearing. *Fine, you win. Take this stupid power.*

Wait... Imp couldn't quite believe it, *You're just going to...*

What does it look like? The being rolled its eyes, *You've got me completely under your control. Something I never would have expected from someone like you.*

What do you mean?! Imp demanded, willing the chains to tighten.

Whoah, calm down! The manifestation said, *That's a compliment, not an insult. I just never expected...someone like you, who can never forgive herself over a tiny little thing, or who holds a grudge forever yet is so forgiving.*

/—

Don't interrupt! It snarled, *Oh great, you ruined the moment. Now I forgot what I was going to say,* it sighed.

It was silent, neither one saying a word. Imp didn't even know what to say.

What are you just standing there for? The being muttered crossly, *Go! The power's yours. Honestly, that Delyn kid deserves getting the lesson punched into him.*

Imp nodded, turning her back on her trapped emotions.

"Stop judging me!" Delyn screamed, taking Imp's head in his hand and slamming it into the wall. She didn't react, watching him with her calm blue eyes...eye, now glazed over. It was almost as if she was dead...But Lars could see that she was breathing.

Why isn't she defending herself? Lars wondered, watching in sick fascination as Delyn beat up his childhood friend, *She's just... sitting there!*

It was at that moment that Imp struck back.

With surprising swiftness, she grabbed Delyn's arm, yanking him forward and using the momentum to pull herself up, slamming her elbow into his stomach. He stumbled back with a startled, airless cry. In an instant, she was invisible.

"Damn you!" Delyn yelled, clutching his stomach and gasping as he tried to fill his lungs with air.

Imp's forgotten sword disappeared off the ground, and Lars immediately raised his in defence. But apparently he wasn't her target; Delyn cried out in pain as a slash opened up on his arm, another following as his pant leg tore.

"You coward! I can see you, you know! Stop running around like a lunatic!"

"You're the coward, Delyn." Imp appeared in front of him, speaking calmly, "You can't actually see me. You're bluffing."

Delyn roared in rage, raising his sword. Imp blocked it easily, a fluid movement following as she deflected his next attack. She made it look effortless.

"Just like old times." She smirked, which only made Delyn angrier. He started pressing her harder, though she still had no trouble avoiding his onslaught.

How is she doing that?! Earlier, she was getting pounded by him! Is she...in Berserk mode? But that's impossible! She's talking calmly to him!

Delyn growled in anger, obviously not as well in control as Imp. He slashed savagely, only resulting in Imp blocking and disappearing. Delyn yelled in frustration, slashing randomly in circles.

"This is all because of the Nightmare gummy, you know." Imp whispered, and Lars jumped. Her voice had come from right behind him!

How did she sneak up on me? Lars wondered, *The ground is all wet...I should have been able to hear her splashing around...* But one look at the ground confirmed her sudden sneakiness. The gel had dried.

"The scientists are trying to ignore one of the side effects of using it." Imp continued her quiet monologue, "A lust for power. They think that it isn't a big deal, even though it is. Delyn's only been using it for about half an hour, and he already thinks he can take over the government."

"How do you know that?" Lars answered as quietly as she spoke.

"You would be surprised how many Police officers dream of reading minds. I only had to be there for half an hour to be able to read theirs."

Lars shuddered. She must have been reading Delyn's mind the whole time. He could only wonder what he was thinking...

"It'll wear off, won't it?" Lars continued.

"No." Imp said, a little sadly, "It's actually changing him. Even when the effects wear off, he'll still have the idea in his head that he can kill anybody. This weapon that the government created...If it is allowed to be mass-produced, given to every Police officer...it would create mass chaos. But the government is so desperate to stop the Flavours, they don't care."

"You're crazy. You don't know this! I'm sure—"

"I hate to repeat myself." Imp interrupted, her voice angry, "But they *just don't care*. It doesn't matter if the weapon could start a war worse than this one. So long as the Flavours are exterminated, they think that they can handle it."

"I refuse to believe you!" Lars yelled, turning and slashing. But nothing happened, and Lars assumed that Imp was gone.

Damn. She's fast! Lars thought, craning his head and trying to see where Imp had gone, even though he knew it would be impossible.

"Who were you talking to?" Delyn growled, and all of a sudden he was standing in front of Lars, looking him square in the face.

"I was talking to Imp." Lars answered simply and coldly, trying to show no weakness. The way Delyn was looking at him...was frightening, to say the least.

"Traitor!" Delyn yelled, slamming his sword into the ground. Lars jumped, surprised by the sudden hatred that seemed to be roiling off Delyn. It was as frightening as Imp's Berserk Mode, but ten times worse when he was so close, the trademark eyes of pure anger staring him down. And suddenly, Lars was afraid.

"I'm not a traitor." Lars answered calmly, gritting his teeth, "If anything you are the traitor, with your talk of taking over the government."

"You—! You shouldn't know that!" Delyn growled, sounding more animal than human, "You can't know that!"

Suddenly Delyn stumbled back a step, clutching his head with one hand.

Did Imp...?

But Lars couldn't see any blood. What was Delyn doing?

"No...He can't know that! He can't spread those kinds of rumours! My plans...they..." Delyn suddenly looked straight at Lars, sliding into a battle position, "You're expendable!"

That was when Lars struck.

Delyn blinked in confusion as Lars slashed, his sword sinking into Delyn's sword hand. Delyn cried out in agony, drawing back from Lars.

"You...you!" Delyn yelled, dropping his sword and clutching at his bleeding hand. He started to pant, and Lars felt his stomach churn. He hadn't thought that he had hurt him *that bad*, yet Delyn was nearly hyperventilating.

Why is he acting like this? Where did this extreme weakness to pain come from? Lars wondered, watching Delyn hold his hand like he was mortally wounded. He could see the cut, a thin line that was only seeping blood, nothing worse.

"Don't you see?" Imp was whispering into Lars' ear again, poisoning him with her crazy opinions, "He won't stop. It doesn't matter how many people he hurts, how many people he kills. He'll still go after blood, so long as he keeps being moved by the Nightmare gummy and by his pain, he'll keep blindly charging ahead until he either destroys himself or everything around him."

Lars closed his eyes, no longer wanting to see Delyn's madness. He could still hear his yells, the waves of sound penetrating him through the darkness he saw.

"How do we stop him?" Lars asked quietly, finally giving in to her.

"I have a plan." Imp answered, her voice soft and deadly in his ear.

Chapter 33

Imp watched as Lars charged at Delyn, his sword flashing as he brought it down towards the unarmed monster. Delyn looked up just in time, dodging as Lars' sword carved a groove where he had been standing a moment before. Delyn reached for his sword, an enraged look in his eyes. Imp knew that Lars wouldn't last long in a sword-fight against Delyn. She needed to work fast.

Imp moved her hand into her pocket, ignoring the pain of her broken rib. That was one thing that she was good at: ignoring pain. She had had lots of practice at the lab.

She found the plastic bag of gummies in her pocket, feeling for two of them. She picked them out of her pocket, looking at the pink-white gummies in her hand. They were formless, unlike the others' gummies, plain splotches in her hand.

Imp swallowed nervously, bringing up the gummies to her mouth.

I'm sorry, Delyn.

Lars groaned as he blocked Delyn's side slash.

He was tiring quickly. They had only been fighting for five minutes, but it seemed to last forever to Lars. He already had countless scratches on his arms, legs, stomach...everywhere on his body. All of them were close calls, when he hadn't been fast enough to block Delyn's sword completely. At first he had easily blocked Delyn's attacks. But now he was having more and more trouble, gaining more and more wounds as the battle dragged on.

Where's Imp? Lars wondered furiously, *Can't she see that I'm having trouble? She said that she would only take a couple of seconds!*

Lars growled as Delyn brought his sword down, too close to his face for comfort. He twisted his body, trying to kick at Delyn's side...A mistake.

Delyn took advantage of Lars' position, moving his sword out of the block and slashing at Lars' outstretched leg. Lars tried to pull away, but he was too slow; Delyn's sword cut him deeply, almost directly to the bone.

Lars cried out in pain and shock, falling to the ground. He tried to stand up, but couldn't. His wounded right leg wasn't able to support his weight.

I'm done for! Lars thought, closing his eyes against the pain and holding one hand to his leg. He felt Delyn towering over him. A moment later he felt Delyn kick him, gritting his teeth against the pain.

I can't believe it... Lars' feverish mind thought, the words tumbling themselves in his head confusedly, *Imp is still holding it together after breaking some of her ribs, getting stabbed in the eye and getting punched. But it took only one slash for me to go down...Pathetic!*

Delyn stepped onto Lars' injured leg, making him yell out. Pure pain was flowing from it, his fingers trembling as they soaked in blood. Delyn started laughing, a sound that more resembled some kind of hacking cough than laughter.

I can't go down like this! I can't!

That was when Lars swept Delyn's feet off the floor with his good leg.

Imp watched in horror as Delyn slashed Lars' leg.

I need to finish this now! Imp thought, even though she knew that it was impossible. She needed to get in front of Delyn, to get her hands on his forehead. But she couldn't do that without trampling over Lars, which was the last thing he needed. She needed Lars to do something, *anything* that would make Delyn stumble backwards so she could get in front of him.

That was when Lars kicked out at Delyn's legs, making him fall backwards.

Now! Imp charged towards Delyn, feeling the power of the chaos magic inside the gummies rushing with her. Her blood was pounding, the barely controllable power ready to be released.

She didn't bother hiding her footsteps as she ran, knowing that she wouldn't make it in time if she did.

She was just about to reach Delyn, her hand already outstretched...When he regained his balance, turning around to face her. He looked shocked and scared, knowing that he was open.

Perfect! Imp grinned to herself, her fingertips ready to touch his forehead. That was when she noticed Delyn's eyes focused right on her.

How is he—

Delyn raised his arm, grabbing her throat and throwing her sideways into a wall.

He was going to choke her.

Lars stood up shakily, not believing what he had just seen.

Delyn had suddenly reached out with his hand, grasping something and pushing into the wall to his right.

It could only mean one thing.

Imp appeared, her hands grasping at Delyn's wrist. She was trying to breathe, but she couldn't.

"Imp!" Lars yelled, trying to get to his feet.

"Traitor!" Delyn growled, glaring at Lars and pushing Imp harder against the wall. She winced.

I can't just lie here! Lars thought, trying to get his muscles to move. He managed to get four steps before he crashed to the ground. He tried to get up, straining to move his leg. But he couldn't move it. He couldn't move at all...He looked at Imp, seeing that her arm was raised, pointing at him.

She...she must have used her Special! But why on me?!

Delyn started to laugh. "Isn't that sweet? Protecting that little traitor." He leaned close to Imp's face, looking her straight in the eye, "It isn't helping, Siria. Once I'm done, I'm moving on to him."

Imp chuckled suddenly, a smile appearing on her face. "You're an idiot. You walked right into that one."

Before Delyn could react, she reached up, placing her hand solidly on his forehead. He tried to draw back, but he couldn't; Imp's power had already taken hold.

The power to turn your dream against you, Lars shivered as Delyn desperately grasped at Imp's arm, unable to break her hold.

"Stop it!" He screamed, "Stop it, stop it, stop it!"

But Imp didn't stop, closing her eyes as Delyn began to shiver and twitch, releasing his grip on her neck. She didn't even react to it, concentrating solely on what she was doing.

Lars watched as Delyn collapsed to his knees, Imp's hand never losing its grip on his forehead. Delyn stopped screaming, the only sign of life his slowing breathing.

Imp opened her eye finally, but Lars couldn't tell what she was feeling. Her face was an emotionless mask.

Delyn looked at Imp, sending a shudder down her spine.

It was him again. The real Delyn.

Imp could feel his power flowing into her, a merging of Nightmare gummy energy and Delyn's lifeforce. It was strong, something that was filling her body with strength. She could barely feel the pain anymore.

"I'm sorry." Delyn whispered, and Imp could only hear him thanks to her heightened senses, her hearing improved greatly thanks to Delyn and her hate-manifestation's powers.

"I'm sorry too." Imp told him, controlling herself not to cry. Not in front of Lars.

Delyn closed his eyes, his body giving one last shudder. Then he collapsed, falling limply to the ground.

*His greatest dream was power...*Imp thought, feeling as if all her strength was sucked from her body. But it was only an emotional feeling, because she knew that she was filled with Delyn's strength, *And I took it away from him.*

Lars watched as Imp collapsed to her knees beside Delyn. She was breathing heavily, staring down at his corpse.

Lars felt the pressure ease up, and he managed to stand. He limped towards her, but she didn't even react. She just kept staring at Delyn, as if she couldn't quite believe what had happened.

Say something! Lars urged himself, but he just couldn't. There was something so unreal about looking at his dead partner, with his worst-enemy-turned-friend mourning him.

Suddenly Imp winced, clutching her heart. Her breathing became a bit more ragged, as if she was having trouble getting air through her mouth.

"Are you alright?" Lars asked, reaching out towards her.

She shuddered suddenly, something that made her gasp in pain. Lars paused, not sure if he should touch her if she was in that much pain. She gripped her shoulder tighter, as if she was trying to stop the pain that was probably flowing from her heart.

"Are you alright?!" Lars asked again, this time trying to demand an answer.

"Don't worry." Imp said slowly, her answer long and filled with gasps, "It's just...the power. It's too much...for one person. Once...Once my gummy wears off, I'll be...fine."

Lars could tell that she was lying.

She couldn't possibly be alright. She looked like she was about to pass out. She had eaten two gummies; he knew enough about Flavours' "Specials" to know that they caused incredible strain on the user. It would take a long time for that to run out. Imp looked like she wouldn't last that long.

As if to prove his point, Imp groaned, bending over and steadying herself with her free arm.

"You're lying to me." Lars gritted his teeth, "You're not going to be alright."

Imp chuckled. "No fooling you."

Lars felt something twist in his stomach. How could she possibly say something like that with nothing more than a chuckle? Didn't she just realize that she was admitting that she was going to die?

Imp swivelled her head and looked at Delyn. She laid herself on the ground, placing her head on his chest. Lars watched her hand grasp Delyn's, her pain obvious in the way she gripped it.

"It's not the same when his heart isn't beating." She murmured, closing her eye.

Lars watched her for a second. But then he was filled with dread as he made a terrible realisation.

She wasn't breathing.

Epilogue

Lars shuffled his feet nervously, wincing as his leg protested.

He hated suits. Absolutely hated them.

Something about the black and white, the way it hung off the shoulders. It was something with the way it just gave off dignity, the way it was too clean. It frustrated him.

He jumped as Tric sighed beside him, the only sound in the all-silent crowd. Almost instinctively he reached for his sword, which of course wasn't buckled to his back.

Tric turned, seeing the movement, but stopped himself before he reached into his pocket. He laughed.

"I'm so jumpy, too." For once, his speech wasn't lightning-fast, slowed by tension, "Imagine. All these Police around me, and none of them trying to catch me. I don't like it. No offence, of course."

Lars nodded in agreement. The same went for him, except it was the other way around. So many Flavours around him, but none were attacking.

A thin, grief-ridden woman walked up to the stage. Lars recognized Mrs. Ately, someone who had become infamous lately for her rigorous quest for peace between the Flavours and the Police. She had been the one to organize the joint funeral, extending invitations to both the Police and the Flavours. Now they were all stuffed together in one of Otta's parks, tense but willing to stay as their members were finally put to peace.

She's Delyn's mother, Lars thought, shuddering at the memory of the battle in the lab, *And she's practically Imp's mother, too.*

Mrs. Ately tapped at the microphone, and the crowd went silent. She began to speak.

"Both sides of this war lost many members during what is now being called the Battle of the Otta Lab." Mrs. Ately began, pausing at the end of the sentence, "The goal was to destroy a weapon that was being implemented for use against the Flavours. The Police came, of course, to try and stop the attacking Flavours."

Mrs. Ately continued by listing the fatalities. Lars closed his eyes as she listed the names, letting his mind drift. He didn't want to hear them. He already knew that there would be minimal Police deaths, and a lot of Flavour deaths. He didn't need to listen to know that.

Mrs. Ately finished her list. "Now there will be separate ceremonies for the burial of the Flavours and Police. A temporary peace treaty has been signed by the government and the Flavour Council, meaning no fighting for the rest of the day."

There was a spattering of applause as Mrs. Ately stepped off the stage. The gathered group began to separate, heading off in separate directions. But Lars just stood there. He hated funerals.

"Hey." A female voice said, poking Lars in the back.

"What is it?" Lars asked, turning and coming face to face with Pheonix. The rest of SOFT were sitting under an oak tree, Moss absent-mindedly picking at the grass while the rest talked. He noticed that some of them were missing, but he wasn't sure which ones.

"You want to see her, don't you?" She took a slip of paper from her pocket, waving it enticingly under his nose. Lars frowned.

"As a matter of fact, I don't."

"C'mon." Pheonix whined, undeterred, "I'm pretty sure she wants to see you too!"

Lars opened his mouth to answer 'How could she?', but Pheonix shoved the paper into his hand and walked away.

Dammit, Lars thought. Obviously she knew him well. She knew he wouldn't be able to resist.

With a sigh, he looked at the address scribbled on the paper.

Lars' heart quickened as he reached his destination.

This is definitely not what I expected, He wasn't disappointed in the least. Instead, he let himself feel a ray of hope.

He was standing at a hospital.

It was clearly a Flavour hospital. It was easy to tell from the sign warning Police that it was a Flavour zone.

Lars walked to the entrance, expecting to be stopped in his tracks by Law magic. But he wasn't. He reached the door, placing his hand on the handle, without as much as a tiny spark.

Of course, Lars thought, Because of the peace treaty, *there's no need for the protection today.*

He opened the door without a hitch.

The receptionist looked up in shock, reaching for a button on her desk.

"Wait!" Lars yelled, raising his hands in what he hoped was a calming gesture, "I'm just here to see Imp."

"It's true." Said a chilling voice. Snow was sitting in one of the waiting chairs, watching him, "I saw Pheonix giving him the address of this place."

"Alright." The receptionist slowly withdrew her hand from the button, "She's in room 180. Down the right hallway. And Snow, your sister's in room 181."

Snow stood up, and Lars shivered a little as he realized how tall the Flavour was. He towered over him.

"I might as well check up on Imp, too." Snow left, letting Lars trail behind him.

It was silent as they walked down the hallway. Lars looked at the number of each door. 160, 161, 162...It was going to be a long walk.

"You have a sister?" Lars asked, hoping to strike up a conversation. He didn't like quiet hospitals. It went too well with the whole notion of death and hospitals.

"Aria." Snow answered shortly, "She's my little sister."

"What happened to her?" Lars asked tentatively. He was surprised when Snow actually answered.

"Arrow."

"Nothing serious, I hope?"

"Pierced her arm." Snow said a little chillingly, and Lars took it as the end of the conversation. That left him to ponder whether Aria's wound was actually serious or not. 'Pierced her arm' wasn't much of an explanation.

177, 178, 179.

Within a few steps, Lars was standing outside door 180.

He was no longer certain of what he was doing. What if Imp actually didn't want to see him? What if she wasn't even alive, and instead he was greeted by a dead body? He wouldn't know how to react.

"Are you going in?" Snow raised an eyebrow, stepping past him and pushing the door open. Lars summoned up his courage and followed him.

The room was empty.

"Is...this some kind of practical joke?" Lars asked, at a loss for words. It was cruel.

"No." Snow answered, and when Lars looked, he seemed as surprised as Lars was, "She must have left."

So that meant that she was alive, at least.

"I'm sure you can find her if you try." Snow told him, leaving. Lars followed him into the hallway, slightly panicked.

"You're not going to help look?" Snow probably knew Imp better than Lars did. His help would be essential.

"No." Snow told him, bluntly, "I care about Imp, but Aria takes priority."

Lars gritted his teeth, but he could see where Snow was coming from. It was his sister after all.

"Fine." Lars said, turning his back on him and leaving the hospital.

He knew where Imp was.

"Have you seen Imp?"

The guards looked at him quizzically. Of course they thought he was crazy. What would a Flavour be doing in a Police cemetery?

But Lars knew that that was exactly where Imp would be.

"No. We didn't see her." The guard said.

Damn.

Lars had thought that Imp was there for sure. But apparently not, "Thanks anyway."

He turned around, getting ready to walk away. The wind whistled eerily through the fence, sounding like sobs.

"Aren't you going to pay your respects?" One of the guards asked, "Your friend Delyn is buried here."

"Yes, I know." *That was the reason I came to see if Imp was here in the first place. But apparently you didn't see...Wait a second!* The realisation dawned on him, *Of course they didn't see Imp. She must have been invisible!*

Lars turned on his heel and rushed into the cemetery, on the lookout for Delyn's grave. He was surprised to find a bench sitting in front of it. There was a little plaque mentioning that it was donated by Mrs. Ately.

But there was no sign of Imp.

"Imp." Lars called out, "I know you're here."

He jumped as she appeared on the bench, calming regarding him with her single blue eye. It was rimmed in red.

"What do you want?" She asked, clearly not pleased that he was here. There was the slightest tremble in her voice, and Lars immediately knew that she had been crying.

"I...just came to find you." Lars said, and he realized that he had no idea what he wanted to say to her.

She didn't answer, so Lars sat down on the bench beside her. She turned her gaze to Delyn's grave.

"Why did you need to find me?" She asked quietly, still not looking at him

"I just wanted to see if you were dead or not." The moment he finished saying it he realized how stupid it sounded.

Imp chuckled, although it had a bit of a bitter tone to it. "Well, I'm alive, as you can see. Although that can't be said for all of us."

Her words were like a blow to Lars' stomach. He had to wonder...

"Do you blame me for Delyn's death?" He asked.

Imp paused. "No. I don't think it's your fault."

"But I did let him join the Police. There were times when I might have said the wrong thing, and pushed him down the path he took..."

"Obviously you feel guilty." Imp said, "I can't hate you, if that's how you feel. But what you're feeling is wrong."

"Do you feel guilty?" Lars had to ask. Imp wasn't easy to read.

"Of course I do." She answered simply.

"Then why are you telling me not to feel guilty? Shouldn't you first tell that to yourself?"

She had no answer to that. So Lars continued.

"You shouldn't feel guilty. If you hadn't done what you did, you and I would be both dead. You know that. And, to boot, he probably would have went on a rampage and killed a lot more of your friends."

"He didn't deserve to die. I could have captured him, knocked him unconscious...I could have done something! But instead...well, you know what happened." She said bitterly.

"You're just lying to yourself." Lars answered, a little frustrated, "There was nothing you could do. He had you by the throat. What were you supposed to do? Just let yourself die?"

"If that means he would still be alive, then yes."

Lars growled at her indifferent tone. "He wouldn't be. Because then I would have killed him."

Imp's grip on her knees tightened. He must have surprised her.

"Don't lie. " She sounded angry.

"I'm telling the truth. Because, unlike you, I can see the danger Delyn posed. I would have done anything to stop him. Would I still feel guilty? Of course, I wouldn't be human if I didn't feel something. But I would have accepted it and moved on."

"I can't move on."

"Then lock your regret away, somewhere it won't affect you. That way, you can move on, but never forget."

Imp stood up abruptly, much to Lars' surprise. Was she angry at him?

"Thanks." She said, completely different than what he had imagined she would say. He was so surprised he could barely mumble 'For what?

"For the talk." She answered. Then she started walking away.

Say something! Lars desperately tried to think of something. He was finding that he was often at a loss for words around Imp.

"Next time we meet…" He paused, her footsteps stopping as she listened, "I'll give you a headstart."

Imp chuckled. "If you do that, you'll never catch me."

When he turned, she was gone.

Made in the USA
Charleston, SC
22 October 2011